A MOST TERRIBLE TIMING

"If you remember anything at all, however trivial it might seem, please get in touch with Constable Jones."

He picked up his hat and in two strides was out of the drawing room and into our cramped hall, where he barked his shin on an oak settle. I followed him. There had been one question nagging away at me all morning I might as well ask it. "Chief Inspector Har—"

"It's just plain 'inspector,' Miss Redfern."

"Did anyone else see her last night after eleven o'clock . . . I mean apart from her . . . ?" I couldn't bring myself to say the word.

The deep lines from his nose to the corners of his mouth and his pouchy eyes gave him the look of a tired basset hound, but his expression was kind. "Her murderer? It's too early in our inquiry to know—we won't have the time of her death for a day or two."

The glance he cast my way, as we said good-bye, was thoughtful. I'm certainly on his list of suspects, I thought as I closed the front door.

POPPY REDFERN

—AND THE—

MIDNIGHT MURDERS

TESSA ARLEN

BERKLEY PRIME CRIME
New York

BERKLEY PRIME CRIME
Published by Berkley
An imprint of Penguin Random House LLC
penguinrandomhouse.com

Author photo owned by the author.

Library of Congress Cataloging-in-Publication Data

Names: Arlen, Tessa, author.
Title: Poppy Redfern and the midnight murders / Tessa Arlen.
Description: First Edition. | New York: Berkley Prime Crime, 2019. |
Series: A woman of World War II mystery; book 1
Identifiers: LCCN 2019022617 (print) | LCCN 2019022618 (ebook) |
ISBN 9781984805805 (paperback) | ISBN 9781984805812 (ebook)
Subjects: LCSH: Murder—Investigation—Fiction. | GSAFD: Historical fiction. |
Mystery fiction.
Classification: LCC PS3601.R5445 P67 2019 (print) | LCC PS3601.R5445 (ebook) |
DDC 813/.6—dc23
LC record available at https://lccn.loc.gov/2019022617
LC ebook record available at https://lccn.loc.gov/2019022618

First Edition: November 2019

Printed in the United States of America
1 3 5 7 9 10 8 6 4 2

Cover art by Robert Rodriguez
Book design by Alison Cnockaert

To Daphne, with love and admiration

ACKNOWLEDGMENTS

The first book of a new series involves thanks to many, but without the generosity and encouragement of my agent, Kevan Lyon, there would be no Poppy Redfern!

I am thrilled to be working with Michelle Vega at Berkley, whose enthusiasm and great insights made the editing process so much fun. Also at Berkley, thank you to Brittanie Black, Jessica Mangicaro, Stacy Edwards, and Jenn Snyder, and of course to Robert Rodriguez for the design of this stunning cover.

This book was written during a very interesting time for our family. We sold our home of nearly twenty-five years on lovely, evergreen Bainbridge Island and moved to the historic city of Santa Fe in the high desert of New Mexico. The change was made simply for the fun of a new adventure, and I think the energy, excitement, and, sometimes, the uncertainty of those fourteen months have contributed in their own inimitable way to the creation of Poppy Redfern and her world.

And with that said, my thanks go always to my children and

friends for their kindness and support, but most of all my truly heartfelt thanks go to Chris.

And lastly to my father and grandfather for their stories of World War II. I wish you were both here to enjoy my recycling of your anecdotes and memories of wartime Britain, both sad and funny alike. I am especially grateful for my father's adolescent worship of the fictional hero Biggles.

ONE

INCOMING AIR RAID. TWENTY TO THIRTY BOMBERS…COULD BE more. You have fifteen . . ." The supervisor's voice was drowned out by the warbling howl of an air-raid siren. Our response was immediate: mugs of tea were abandoned and half-smoked cigarettes plunged into ashtrays as, tightening our helmet straps, we left the fug of our Air Raid Precautions post for the cool night air outside.

I looked up; it's the first thing you do when the siren sounds. Searchlights crisscrossed the night sky. Half-ruined buildings, casualties of our last air raid four nights ago, cast skeleton shadows on streets made almost impassable with broken brick and rubble.

"If they're Dorniers we have less than fifteen minutes." Our ARP instructor looked us over and singled me out to tell me the words I had longed to hear for the two weeks of my training. "Redfern, you can take Clegg and Clave Streets solo. Humphries: Wapping High and Cinnamon, and Duckworth, you take Plumsom. Keep them calm, keep them moving, and check on as many houses as you can for the elderly and sick. Try to get them to safety in ten minutes and you might manage it in fifteen." His instructions never varied as he rapidly allotted sections of Wapping's neighborhoods to our care. Percy turned to include a group of new recruits. "The rest of you come with me."

I started to sprint toward Clegg Street, but he pulled me back by my arm. "No heroics." A frown underscored his command. "Your job is to get as *many* of them to safety as you can."

I turned into Clegg and went down its center at a brisk trot. Doors opened to the left and the right of me. Families spilled out into the narrow street between face-to-face lines of meanly built East End terraced houses that were home to the families of London's dockworkers. The gray-white glare of searchlights swung overhead, lighting up tired faces raised briefly heavenward, as we raced for the safety of Wapping's Underground station.

A gaunt young woman, her raincoat flapping open over pajamas, shouted instructions to two children. "Daisy, take Jimmy's hand, and don't let go of it." She was carrying a toddler and a couple of blankets. "Evening, Miss Redfern. You'd better check on number twenty-five, her mum-in-law took bad yesterday. She might need help."

Two doors down an elderly woman was helping an even older one out of the house. "'Course you've got to come, lovey," I heard her say. "She must come, mustn't she, Warden?"

"Yes, of course. Do you need help with her?"

"No, 's'orright, I got her. Come on, lovey, you heard what the warden said."

Ten minutes? I looked at my watch. It was more like eight and I had half the street to go. I picked up the pace.

"Bloomin' racket." An old man was shuffling along in his bedroom slippers. "Can't hear a thing except that ruddy siren." He stopped and shook his walking stick at the sky.

"No time for that, sir." I took him by the arm and walked him forward to a young woman with curlers in her hair. "Take him with you to the Underground, please."

" 'Ello there, Mr. Perkins, where's your daughter?"

"Somewhere ahead with the kiddies."

"Well, you come along with me, we'll see you safely there."

I dodged the corner into Clave Street to urge on the last of the stragglers. "Air raid in five minutes." I crossed the road to two children: one sitting on the curb with his feet in the gutter, crying, and a little girl standing white-faced with panic on the pavement. "Where is your mum?"

"She went to the pub, with my aunty." An older girl came out of the house, carrying a baby.

"I'll carry him." I picked up the little boy, who buried his face in the collar of my jacket, and I held out my hand to the girl. "Let's go and find your mummy, shall we?" She put her hand in mine. "Come on," I said to their sister, who was dithering with a key in her hand. "No time to lock up."

At the bottom of the street a crowd of people was filing down the steps into Wapping Underground station. Babies cried, children wailed, and mothers shouted out to one another as if they were meeting in the queue at the grocer's.

"Blimey, doll, you had time to get dressed?"

"Got to look nice for Jerry!"

"We only just got back from the pub!"

"Bloody Krauts, second time in four days."

"At least it isn't as bad as it was last year—felt as if I was living in the bloomin' Underground."

Now that we were near safety there was a determination among the families who inhabited the dock area of East London to pretend that our race for shelter had been a breeze. As if the danger we faced could be obliterated by their collective camaraderie: a determination not to be intimidated by a bunch of cowardly German pilots who rained down hell on us from the lordly safety of their aircraft.

The crowd had slowed to a shuffle as it made its descent to the shelter of the Underground. "You're going to have to move more quickly!" I put the little boy down next to his sister on the pavement and pushed my way to the head of the queue, knowing exactly what I would find.

"You can't make me." An elderly woman who weighed all of two hundred and fifty pounds had stopped at the top of the steps. "You know I don't go anywhere by Tube. I *always* catch the bus."

"Hullo, Mrs. White. Would you do me a favor? These little ones are scared stiff of the bombs. Would you help this little girl down into the Underground?"

I reached out to a small, skinny little scrap of a thing, clutching a grubby doll in her arms, my eyebrows raised to ask her mother's permission. She prodded her daughter forward. "Go on, Dottie, help the old lady down the steps."

The line plodded forward down into the warm, stale air eddying up from the station below. I turned to go back up the steps. "Four minutes. Keep moving. Four minutes . . ."

Clave Street was empty. Running as fast as I could, I covered the distance to the back alley that ran behind the two rows of houses. People often hid in the back alley so they could go back to bed when the all clear sounded. There was no one in sight. The sirens had stopped, but the searchlights continued their dance against the sky.

I blew three sharp blasts on my whistle. "Air raid, two minutes." My voice echoed across the broken intersection, and two figures emerged from the rubble of what had once been a corner shop and ran across the road toward the Underground.

As I followed them down, I heard the engines of the first squadron. Against everything I had learned in training, I couldn't help myself. I stopped and looked up. Silhouetted against the lit sky I saw the first planes approaching from the south: heavy black silhouettes, their wingtips almost touching in formation. They were Luftwaffe Dorniers, all right. Twenty? It looked like there were hundreds.

Ack-ack-ack. The antiaircraft guns mounted in concrete down by the docks sent bright bolts of fire up into the sky, and I heard, and then felt, the percussion of the first bombs as they hit the homes of the people who cowered under the pavement below me.

But where were our boys? Poised to race down the steps to the Underground, I looked up again. As if on cue, the cluttered skies were filled with small, fast aircraft, dropping down from above the German Dornier bombers in a shattering hail of machine-gun fire.

I heard myself cheer. It ripped out of me in a full-throated shout of approval and admiration, loud even against the racket of an air battle. Spitfires and the men who fly them are our country's heroes: their bravery and courage during London's Blitz last year had earned our absolute gratitude and respect.

I ran down the steps into the fusty protection of the Underground. My heart was racing as I pulled up short at the bottom of the steps to walk with calm authority out onto Platform One. The dull lights overhead illuminated smooth, oily train tracks as they snaked into the dark ellipse of the tunnel. On the platform Wapping's families were going about the business of bedding down for the night on gritty concrete.

I watched the garrulous efficiency of mothers, aunts, and grandmothers as they organized their children for sleep: their calm stoicism, born of months of practice, and their determined cheerfulness as they helped one another out and gave comfort to neighbors who had lost everything. "Here, Vi, I brought an extra blanket and a pillow just in case, but it's a warm night. No, love, 's'orright—don't mention it."

The earth above us shuddered and the pale lights flickered, plunging us into a dark so absolute that our silently held breath seemed to echo our fear. A heartbeat later and we were revealed to one another again. Vi moaned and ducked her head. "The West End has such nice, deep Underground stations—miles below the bombs."

"Come on, love, chin up. Nothing to be afraid of. Here, have a nip of this." What was it, I wondered, that kept them so unfailingly stalwart night after night?

At the far end of the platform, a group of girls with Veronica Lake hairstyles, wearing their fashionable all-in-one siren suits, sang along to a street musician's accordion, their eyes on a group of teenage boys whose only thought was to be a part of what was going on upstairs.

"There'll be bluebirds over the white cliffs of Dover tomorrow, just you wait and see." Their girlish voices were sweet, their faces perfectly made-up. A couple of boys darted a quick look before returning to swap cigarette trading cards featuring tanks, aircraft, and battleships. I sent the singers silent thanks for their innocent belief that the reality of night bombing could be washed away by the simple melody of a Vera Lynn song.

"Cuppa tea, ducky? Probably need one after all that galloping around." The woman from number twenty-five held out an enamel mug of milky tea that she had poured from a large green tin thermos.

"Bloody Hitler," she said without a trace of rancor. "He'll be laughing on the other side of his face when the Americans get here. When are you going home, dear? Back to your village, I mean."

"Tonight's the last night of training. I leave tomorrow morning."

"Glad you made it through, then, ducky." She pulled a blanket up over a sleeping child lying next to her on the platform. "Not everyone does."

Below London's battered streets we could feel the bombs shattering our city. I drank tea and waited for the all clear, when I would leave the sleeping families to go back up those steps to what was left of their neighborhood. Then the night would be full of different sounds: the shrill bells of ambulances and the deeper clang of fire engines. That would be when the digging would begin, and when the tally of who had really won and who had lost would be reckoned.

IT WAS REASSURING to walk down Little Buffenden's quiet, empty High Street the following evening. The soft, country-summer air was exquisitely sweet after London's thick clinker-dust atmosphere, but the simple stillness of an August evening was not mine to enjoy for long.

"You're back from your London training, then, are you?" Enid Glossop's voice, pitched to carry, reached me on the other side of the street. I didn't quite flinch, but she certainly stopped me mid-stride. "I would have thought the least they could do was have your uniform ready in time for your first patrol."

"Come on, Bess, let's get it over with—and remember not to jump up," I said to the little dog running at my side. We crossed the narrow street to stand before a tiny middle-aged woman wearing a Royal Mail–issue beret pulled down in the front, almost to her eyebrows.

"This *is* my uniform, Mrs. Glossop," I said with what I hoped was a face composed to express polite nothingness.

"That's *it*?" Disbelieving eyes swept up to my black pudding-basin helmet with *W* stenciled on it, and down again to heavy lace-up ankle boots. "What does the *W* stand for?"

"Warden. Air Raid Precautions warden."

"I see." She looked like someone who suspected she was being lied to. "I know you *say* it's a uniform, but it looks like that outfit Mr. Churchill wears when he's being photographed on bomb sites." Her mouth performed a tight imitation of a smile. Mrs. Glossop has a way about her that always manages to convey dissatisfaction.

"Yes, *he* borrowed the idea from Air Raid Precautions—siren suits are all the rage in London these days!"

"I could have sworn you were on your way to stoke the church boiler." Pursed lips and regretful eyebrows as she gave my uniform a second chance. "It's a shame they couldn't have come up with something *really* smart like the Auxiliary Territorial Service: the Bradley girls look smashing in theirs."

The last thing I needed was comparisons to the wonderful Bradley sisters, who were having the time of their lives up in London with their permanent waves and Elizabeth Arden Victory Red lipstick. While they were driving high-ranking officers in and out of the Admiralty, I was clumping about the village in my size nines as Little Buffenden's first ARP warden.

"Have you secured the blackout in your cottage, Mrs. Glossop? We must be even more careful now with our new American airfield—"

"I most certainly have, Miss Redfern—I do it before I leave the house in the morning." She turned away to lock the door of her tobacconist and sweet shop, which doubles as Little Buffenden's post office, and I mentally flipped to the third page of my ARP training manual: *"Section 2A: On Dealing with Difficult Members of the Public: Remember an ARP warden holds a legal position of authority. Speak in a firm tone and engage eye contact!"*

I am not naturally assertive, but I had learned a thing or two in my weeks of training in London. I looked directly into Mrs. Glossop's fierce little eyes and held her gaze.

"I am sure you don't want me knocking on your door when you are enjoying your evening cocoa," I said with as much severity as I am capable of, and, summoning a more convincing tone of command: "We can check your blackout right now . . ." I extended my left arm in the direction of her cottage at the bottom of the High Street as if I were directing traffic.

And, to my amazement, all she came up with was a retaliatory,

"That dog should be on a lead," as she put her shop keys into her handbag and snapped it shut before falling into step beside me. "Not one aircraft, ours or theirs, has flown over our village since the start of the war. But I'm sure *I* don't want to be the cause of our being bombed."

I remembered the smoking rubble of East End Clegg Street when I had last seen it in the early hours of this morning. "You wouldn't believe what one five-hundred-pound German bomb could do to our little village, Mrs. Glossop," I said as we walked down our High Street, renowned for its pretty Georgian shop fronts and bow windows.

Even with the neglect of wartime, it is the sort of village that looks perfect at Christmas, with a dusting of snow, and carol singers exhaling breathy clouds as they sing "Silent Night" on the church porch.

"All this"—I waved at an ancient stone horse trough and the white verandah of the Edwardian cricket pavilion on the edge of the village green—"would be gone in a flash, reduced to blackened timbers and broken brick, just because a Luftwaffe pilot saw a spark of light on his way home and ditched his last bomb." I didn't belabor the point by adding that the new American airfield would increase our chances of an air raid by eighty percent—my job is not to cause panic.

She gave me a quick sideways glance, her face disbelieving. Mrs. Glossop is the one who informs in our village, not girls with a mere two weeks of ARP training. "I am surprised that your grandmother agreed to your taking on this job: walking around the village on your own at night. That little dog will be no protection when the place is swarming with American airmen." She opened the diminutive white gate into the postage stamp of her front garden.

"I am not sure there will be enough of them to 'swarm,' Mrs. Glossop, and my uncle Ambrose still talks about his years in New York as his happiest. I think a change might wake us up a bit!" My suggestion, designed to jolly her along, was instantly shot down by a pitying look.

"Bert Pritchard says he won't serve them in the Rose and Crown. He says he had more than enough of them in the last war." I bit the inside of my cheeks to stop myself from smiling. Bert Pritchard, with his ebullient welcome and his lavish mustache, was a particularly good businessman. He would remember the day the American Army Air Force arrived in Little Buffenden as heaven-sent when he balanced his account books a month from now. I followed Mrs. Glossop up the crazy paving path between the rigid lines of vegetables growing in her victory garden.

"I feel sorry for anyone who has a daughter in this village, because from what I hear, those Americans are girl-mad. That's what Mrs. Wantage told me. Her sister's daughter is seeing a Yank, and she has become a right handful: out all hours of the night and talks back something shocking if she's asked to do the slightest thing around the house."

Mrs. Glossop pushed open her front door and looked over her shoulder. "Stay," she commanded, and Bess dropped to the ground and lay arrow straight, her long nose resting on the path well ahead of her front paws. She knew Mrs. Glossop didn't appreciate dogs, and her tabby was an old battle-scarred tom with a short fuse.

It was dark in the narrow hall, and I could see, even from where I was standing, the last rays of a subdued sunset through the uncovered front parlor window. "Blackout before electric light," I quoted from my ARP manual as she lifted her hand to the switch on the wall.

"I could have sworn I closed them before I left this morning." Mrs. Glossop darted to the window and dragged a heavy curtain across it. "There now, that's better—fits like a glove!" She gave it a final twitch to cover a chink in the corner.

I was careful not to catch her eye. "I hope you are coming to our talk in the village hall on air-raid preparedness. We are going to organize the best place for everyone to go to for shelter—"

"I was planning on an evening of bingo."

"Oh good, come half an hour early. Six o'clock, then?" I was given a reluctant but acquiescing nod and heard her sigh as she followed me back to her front door.

"It's a crying shame your grandfather had to give up his house *and* all his land for these Americans and their airfield—it's not as if your family didn't lose enough in the last one." She meant of course the death of both my parents: Clive Redfern, in the Great War, and my mother at its end, just two days after my arrival. Mine was not an unusual fate for my generation: I was the only war orphan in our village, but one of many in England. I couldn't remember my parents of course, but they were very much alive in my heart. My grandparents had made sure of that by sharing their memories of my parents as I was growing up: my father, Clive, was a quiet man with a wicked sense of humor that surprised those who did not know him, and my mother, Olivia, had been described by Granny as a warm, vibrant young woman whom she had loved as if she were her own.

"Grandad didn't give up *all* of his land, Mrs. Glossop, just enough for the airfield. And Reaches is on *loan* for the duration. Please don't forget the blackout in the rest of the house before you turn on any lights." I lifted my hand to the front-door latch.

"You heard about the Chamberses' eldest, then, about Brian?" My hand dropped from the handle and Mrs. Glossop nodded—she had me at last. But there was no pleasure in her being the first to break bad news; her deep-set eyes were sorrowful.

"They sent a telegram after you left for London—a week last Tuesday it was." She pressed her lips together for a moment before she continued. "That's both their boys lost in this bloomin' war. Mrs. Chambers went into shock when they told her. She still doesn't seem right to me."

I stood there like a stricken fool with a lump filling my throat. One summer when I was a gawky and self-conscious fourteen-year-old, at home for the holidays from school, I had a brief crush on Brian. But then everyone loved Brian Chambers; he was the kindest and brightest boy in our village, with a wholehearted zest for life. I swallowed hard so I could ask, "Where?"

"North Africa—some terrible place with an unpronounceable name—Allymain, is it?"

"El Alamein—yes, I heard the casualties were pretty bad. Poor Doreen, she must be heartbroken; they only got engaged at Easter, didn't they?"

"I am *quite* sure Doreen Newcombe will survive Brian's passing. His parents are the ones we should pity. I doubt his mother will pull through." The stuffy corridor felt oppressive. I lifted my hand to the door latch again. "*And* Mr. Edgar, as runs the Wheatsheaf, got his call-up papers a week ago—he must be all of forty. I dread to imagine . . ."

But what Mrs. Glossop dreaded to imagine would remain unheard, for all I could see of Bess as I stepped out onto the path was her round, feathery bottom. She was head-deep in Mrs. Glossop's victory garden.

"Oh my goodness." I turned to face a woman who believes a dog's place is on a chain attached to its kennel and put my hands on my hips to block her view of flying earth. "Is that the time?" I prayed that the deepening dusk would prevent those sharp eyes from seeing the havoc created in neat rows of carrots and cabbages. "I must run." But I didn't move. I stayed there at the bottom of the path to prevent her from following me to the gate.

She gave me a look of disgusted pity and closed her door, leaving me to lift Bess out of a sizable hole. I tucked her under my arm and replanted parsnips as fast as I could with one hand, thumping the earth firm around their wilting tops. Then I made off down the High Street, dusting dirt from Bess's muzzle as we went. She still had half a carrot clamped between her teeth. "How often do I have to tell you not to dig? No *dig-ging*!" I kissed her grubby nose. "Oh, for heaven's sake, you might as well have the carrot." I could feel her stump of a tail stirring in agreement.

TWO

I HAD SAID, "HULLO, YES, IT'S LOVELY TO BE BACK, AND PLEASE secure your blackout," to half of Little Buffenden before I circled back into the village at half past eleven that night. We climbed the hill to the church at its crest and down again to the foot of Reaches Lane and the lodge where we now live. Out of habit, Bess ran on up the lane in the direction of our old farmhouse. The night was warm: lilies and pinks in the vicarage garden scented the serene air, and I was more than happy to follow her as she ran low-backed and silent in the grass-filled ditch on a hunt for rabbits. We avoided the old cart track to the new airfield: acres of concrete, a petrol dump, airplane hangars, and Nissen huts now populated beech-fringed pastures where once cows had grazed. Instead we crossed the cattle grid that separated the lane from the drive, and our old stone house with its deep gables came into view, sitting high on the land and looking out over the rolling hills of the Chilterns.

The finest feature of Reaches' many simple beauties is its stone-mullioned leaded-glass windows. Out of which I was horrified to see bright light shining onto the unkempt flower beds under the window of my grandfather's old study.

I trotted up the path, lifted the forged-iron knocker, and pounded on the front door. Who on earth had left a light on? I counted to five before I banged again more energetically. Silence. Stepping back onto the path, I looked up at the darkened house. The only light was the one beaming out of the study. Mrs. Wantage must have left it on when she cleaned this morning. I trod through the weed-filled flower bed to the offending window, unbuckled the strap on my helmet, tipped it back on my head, and angled my cheek against the glass. The room was quite empty, and so was the hall beyond.

Seething at the utter carelessness of a village that had never given a serious thought to air raids since war had been declared, I continued around to the south side of the house. All its windows reflected the opaque black of a moonless sky. There was a key under the boot scraper outside the kitchen door. I could at least switch off the light, even if I didn't solve the mystery of who had left it on.

As I came through the open gate into the dense black of the kitchen courtyard, I paused to get my bearings, and in that split second thought I heard a rasping, mechanical double click.

I was halfway across the yard when the distinct aroma of a freshly lit cigarette drifted toward me on the night air. In the time it took to register that I was not alone in this hedged-in dark place, a strong hand clamped down on my shoulder and jerked me backward. My helmet went flying as a grip of iron tightened on my upper arm. Adrenaline prickled up the backs of my legs and my heart bounded up into my throat. Only one thought flashed into my mind: German paratroopers—we had been invaded!

I resisted a panicky impulse to struggle free and run for safety: after the blood, toil, and tears of the last three years, I would go down fighting—or he would. I moved sideways into him, caught hold of his belt, and slid his weight over my hip to land him heavily on the ground. There was a satisfying grunt of pain and surprise from my German paratrooper.

I had been more startled than scared when he had grabbed me in the dark, but now my legs felt as useless as wet wool. Run, I told myself, run fast! I spun on my heel, praying that I could outdistance him and sound the alarm before he came after me. I was almost through the wicket gate when I heard a string of profanity: "Goddam it . . . goddam it to hell . . ." Blasphemy gave way to cruder Anglo-Saxon epithets of the kind no one I know uses. I recognized the accent immediately, and it wasn't German.

I turned back to my attacker, and in the dull light of my blackout torch, I saw a man in American uniform getting to his feet. Now it was my turn to curse. And I chose my old school friend Lucy's brother, Ted, as the target for my "damns" and "bloody hells." On a wet spring break from school he had taught us five basic judo moves, one of which I had played out just now with exemplary dedication to his instruction.

The American straightened up, spanking dust off his uniform trousers as I walked back to him, my cheeks flame red with embarrassment, apologies stuttering from my lips. "I am so—"

"Whoa, whoa, hold it, son." He was laughing as he lifted both arms in mock surrender. "I thought for a moment our airfield was under attack. I had no idea how well trained the local Home Guard was."

"I'm just the local air-raid warden. Look, I'm most frightfully sorry . . ."

He reached out a hand and turned my torch toward my face. I heard a low whistle. "Well, I'll be damned. I can't believe I was just thrown by a girl—who taught *you* judo? Are all Englishwomen this feisty?" I took back my torch and, in its light, I watched him pick up his cap and slap it against his thigh before putting it back on his head. It took him a while to get it set the way he liked it. It's interesting how male vanity emerges in the most unlikely situations.

"Get you in action and England wouldn't need help from us to win this war." He tugged the peak of his cap a little to the right and then gave me his full attention. "What did you say you were doing here?"

Indignation washed away embarrassment. Why, for heaven's sake, hadn't he asked me what I was doing here before launching in with the heavy-handed rough stuff?

I drew myself up. "I'm assuming you *are* American Army Air Force?"

He said something about the name and number of his fighter squadron. "We call our wing the 'Midnight Raiders.'"

"Oh really? Then I would have thought you would know something about blackout. The study window of this house is leaking light, which can be seen quite easily from up there." I waved a hand at the night sky in case he didn't know where it was.

He closed the distance between us. He was tall, over six feet, but all Americans are tall, aren't they? It was difficult to see his face under the peak of his cap; the closest feature in my line of vision was his mouth, smiling widely over teeth of film-star-white evenness.

"Perhaps we had better introduce ourselves. I'm Lieutenant"—he pronounced his rank as *lew-tenant*—"Griff O'Neal."

It was at this moment that Bess decided to show up; she burst out of the shrubbery and threw herself at the lieutenant's beautifully pressed trousers. She was so pleased with him that she threw back her head and howled a long, melodic warble. The lieutenant crouched down and rumpled her ears with both hands. "Would you look at these ears? Why no tail—is he a mutt?" Bess was prancing on her short hind legs trying to cover his face in kisses.

"A what? No! *She* is a Welsh herding dog."

"She's a cutie—what's her name?"

"The blackout," was the only conversation I was prepared to have with this man.

He straightened up. "So, let's go into the house and see about that light you're so worried about." He walked ahead of me, Bess running back and forth between us barking in delight, past a car parked under the lee of the courtyard hedge: it was long and low, undoubtedly a sports model.

"Nice car," I muttered to cover how awkward I felt at being frightened into using violence by a man who had every right to be here.

"Yeah, got it as soon as I arrived; it's an Alvis 4.3 liter with a special drop-head coupe."

My grandfather still drove his old 1928 Humber Tourer and I knew nothing about it other than on cold mornings it took a lot of cranking to get it started. I found this thing's shiny newness and size even more irritating than the lieutenant's facetious attitude.

"Going to be hard to run it on petrol rationing," I said before I could stop myself. As soon as he had secured the study window, I would explain British blackout procedures to this American and leave.

"Great old house, isn't it?" he said as we crossed the paneled hall with its carved oak staircase soaring to the floors above. "Apparently, it's hundreds of years old—goes back to the civil war." He laughed. "Yours, of course, not ours."

Bess and I went ahead of him to my grandfather's study. I pointed to the blackout curtain hanging at the edge of the window. "*Every* window in *every* room in this house, Lieutenant O'Neal, has a blackout curtain. Please draw them before you switch on any lights and secure them at the edge of the sill with these grommets. Like this." I had unconsciously adopted the clipped tone of the village schoolteacher, Mrs. Ritchie. "We issue one warning. After that it is a fine of ten shillings."

"Ten bob? Blimey, that's a bit steep, ain't it?" He was laughing as he imitated what he imagined to be a cockney accent. It was so terrible I couldn't help but smile. He drew the curtain, hooking it against the frame. "I like the way you English say *leftenant* in spite of the way the French spell it." He ran his hand along the curtain's edge at the sill. "There, secured as instructed." He turned back from the window. "Let's pretend we didn't start off on the wrong foot. I introduced myself. Now it's your turn."

"I'm Poppy Redfern."

"Of course you are." He smiled at me as his gaze swept from the top of my uncovered head to my heavy boots. "Tell me, d'you get sick of everyone saying you look like Katharine Hepburn?"

"Katharine Hepburn?" It took me a moment to realize whom he meant. Wasn't she the actress always cast in Hollywood as the unfriendly but eccentric English type? "They don't, actually," I said. "We don't blurt out everything we think when we first meet someone." It was just the sort of thing a prim English snob would say, and I bit my lip to stop myself from saying more.

He obviously agreed with me, because his smile, which had been flashing away at me since we had walked into the house, disappeared. "Nice to meet you, Miss Redfern." He extended his right hand, and when I shook it he laughed with exaggerated relief and said, "Phew—so I'm forgiven, then?"

If I had been either of the Bradley sisters I would have laughed and said something about how pleased we all were that they had come to help us win the war. But I was feeling awkward, embarrassed, and thoroughly out of my depth, so I ruined it by saying, "So you are the first to arrive?" I sounded just like old Lady Bradley being patronizing at one of her snooty cocktail parties.

He drew in a breath and held it before he replied. "Yup, several squadrons are flying in tomorrow evening; ground crew will drive up here before that. I came on ahead to open up the house after visiting an old friend of my father in Wickham." He offered no other explanation, nor did he try to continue the conversation.

I turned to walk back to the kitchen. "I'll just find my helmet and then I'll be on my way." I switched on my torch and shone it under the laurel hedge and, after some poking about, found it. He stood in the open scullery doorway without offering to help. I felt miserably unsure how to end this wretched encounter, and to make matters worse, I found myself floundering into my blackout lecture. "Did you know that the glow from your cigarette can be seen quite clearly from above?"

He nodded. "And what about your flashlight?"

"My what?"

He flipped his cigarette onto the cobblestones of the courtyard and crushed it with his heel as he pointed.

"My torch? It's special issue: the beam points down."

"Miss Redfern, thank you so much for that very informative talk. I'll be sure to pass it on to the other guys when they get here." His face was solemn, but I had the strongest sense that I was being laughed at.

"If you would please," was all I could think of to say. "Good night, Lieutenant." And as I stalked off into the night with Bess trailing behind me, the tips of my ears felt hot and red. "That was a disaster," I said as we crossed the cattle grid. "How *could* I have had the gall to lecture an air force officer about the importance of blackout, for God's sake?"

THREE

"WHAT CAN BE KEEPING MRS. WANTAGE? YOUR GRANDFA-ther will be back at any moment and he doesn't like it when she hoovers his study late in the morning." At seventy, my grandmother, Alice Redfern, still has the straight back and upright carriage of a generation of nice girls raised by strict nannies. A lot of people say we look alike. We are both tall and lean, but my grandmother's once vibrant auburn hair is now completely white, and her clear gray eyes, so like mine in shape and color, are milder in expression. Perhaps that's because at Granny's age she has seen her world change so often that she has come to terms with the heartbreak of the past. Whereas my young years still have me fighting for every injustice, a ready champion for a lost cause.

I finished making our midmorning Camp coffee, if you can call what we drink these days coffee.

"I expect everyone will be running late after the party up at the airfield last night. Why didn't *you* go, dear? The party was held for the Americans to meet *everyone* in Little Buffenden."

The American I had met last week had looked heartily relieved when I had said good night. "ARP patrol," I reminded her.

"Oh yes, of course. They certainly seem to be nice boys: polite and very friendly." Mrs. Glossop had told me that Doreen Newcombe and Ivy Wantage have been out every night since they arrived: dancing or to the pictures in Wickham. Of course, she also had a lot to say about Doreen's seeing someone else so soon after Brian's death. I put it down to the war: loss, change, and impermanence are the only constants in our lives these days.

"Certainly didn't take those two pretty girls long to find boyfriends. Though, poor Audrey Wilkes was never one for the boys, was she?" She stirred milk into her coffee as she considered the merits of the unattached girls in our village and their possible chances. Granny's generation has a one-track mind when it comes to single women.

"Audrey is just more reserved than most," I said in her defense—not all of us were desperate for boyfriends, even if the gender balance in our village had tipped four to one in a day.

Her eyes sought mine over the rim of her cup, her expression encouraging.

I said nothing.

She cooled her coffee with a gentle outward breath. "I see. Perhaps you're right. It doesn't do to be too hasty."

The door opened from the scullery and my grandfather walked into the kitchen. He is tall too, over six feet. It's easy to see that Grandad was a very handsome man in his youth—it has to do with the shape of his head and his beautiful blue eyes, though sometimes they can be a bit glacial when he is annoyed. Even in his late seventies he bristles with intention as the commanding officer of the Little Buffenden and Lower Netherton Home Guard. But there was nothing purposeful about him this morning. He stood before us with his head bent, looking uncertain, as if he couldn't remember where to put the hat he was holding in his hands.

"Down, Bessie—down, girl." His voice was subdued, his lined face grim as he remembered his hat and hung it on a peg by the door.

"Is something wrong, Jasper?"

He stared at Granny for a moment and then seemed to make up his mind. "Yes, I'm afraid something quite awful has happened; a terrible thing to be sure." He glanced at me, reluctant to go on, as if I were still ten years old and must be spared the dreadful things that life has a way of dishing up. My grandparents have always been a bit on the overprotective side. "Doreen Newcombe is dead." He groped for a chair and sat down at the table, shaking his head from side to side, as if trying to rid it of an unpleasant memory.

"Drink this, Jasper; you look all in." Granny spooned almost a week's sugar ration into his coffee. "Don't say a thing until you've finished it, my dear." She used her firm voice and he obediently sipped until his cup was empty. He looked so wretched that I reached across the table and took his large hand in mine. It was cold, and I noticed how splotched with age spots the skin on its back was. I shook it, gently, to bring him back to us. "What happened to Doreen, Grandad?"

He patted my hand as if to reassure me, but his next words did far from that. "Len Smith was trimming the churchyard hedge this morning, and he found Doreen Newcombe's body underneath it— she was . . . well, she was murdered."

"Murdered?" Granny's usually gentle voice was sharp. Grandad nodded; his face seemed to have crumpled in on itself.

"I was driving back from my meeting with Davey Wilkes, and as I came up Water Lane, Len came barreling through the church-yard gate—I practically ran him down. He was shaking like a leaf and his face was a terrible color. I thought for a moment that he was going to have a seizure." He stared down at the tablecloth, his eyes troubled.

The scullery door opened again, and Mrs. Wantage came into the kitchen. The bright, flowery scarf she always wears, tied turban fashion over her pin curls, looked all wrong against her pale cheeks and reddened eyes. "Such an awful to-do down in the village. Oh . . ." She took in our stunned faces. "So, you *have* heard . . . about poor little Doreen Newcombe?"

"Major Redfern has just told us. We can't quite take it in. Did . . . ?" Granny was about to say more, but one look at her hus-band's face stopped her: there was to be no gossiping about Doreen's murder. She stood up from the table. "Jasper, such dis-turbing news, I think it would do you good to come outside for some fresh air. Come on, Bess, you can get out from underneath everyone's feet so Mrs. Wantage can get started."

"Getting some fresh air" was the phrase used in cramped quar-ters that offered less privacy than Reaches when my grandparents needed to consult in private.

The door was barely closed behind them when Mrs. Wantage said, in the sort of breathless whisper people use when something dreadful has happened, "She was strangled to death." A hideous image sprang into my mind, and like Grandad, I closed my eyes and shook my head to get rid of it.

Mrs. Wantage fumbled the strings of her apron around her waist and stacked breakfast dishes onto the wooden draining board. "She was strangled with a nylon stocking. The very ones that her new American boyfriend gave her, I should imagine—because no one from around here could get their hands on nylons." She leaned against the draining board and lifted the hem of her apron to her eyes. "Her body was just left there . . . bundled under the hedge in the churchyard—poor, poor little thing." She made a gasping sound as she struggled to bring herself under control, gave up, and let the tears flow in a lament for a young woman barely out of her teens, a girl she had known all her life.

I couldn't bear to see her standing there with her head down, tears splashing onto the breakfast dishes. I got up and put my arm around her heaving shoulders. She leaned against me and rested her head on my shoulder. I could feel her hairpins digging into my skin through her head scarf as she wept. "The doctor had to come for Len, he was that shook up by finding her." She lifted her pinny to dash her tears away. "Len said that she had been there all night. Her clothes were soaked with dew. It doesn't bear thinking about." She pulled a hanky from her apron pocket and blew her nose. To my horror she said, "I think she may have been interfered—"

I lifted my hand to block the dark images her words conjured. "Please, Mrs. Wantage . . . please, don't think about that. It will only distress you."

"You're quite right, Miss Redfern. We must remember Doreen as she was, not how she ended up." I patted her shoulder until the tears stopped.

"My hubby told our Ivy that that's the very last time she goes up to the base—or sees that American sergeant." She nodded in agreement with Mr. Wantage's decision. "I'm sorry, Miss Redfern, I didn't mean to upset you." She put her handkerchief back in her pocket and folded her arms under her bosom. "But after all these years, for as long as I can remember, there has never been a murder in Little Buffenden, nor Lower Netherton neither. Not until those Americans came here. Because it is as clear as morning that Doreen was killed by that new boyfriend of hers, that Sergeant Sandwhatsis." She lifted her hand, palm out, in defense. "And it's not just me, by the way. I'm the last to pass judgment. *Everyone* is saying that it was Doreen's new American boyfriend what done it." Her tone became uncertain. "And we all thought they were such nice boys."

"What did Constable Jones say?"

Mrs. Wantage almost laughed. "Constable Jones? He doesn't know his backside from his elbow, that one—begging your pardon for the expression. All he's good for is cautioning people about black-market petrol and diddling their ration books. At least Harold Jones has the sense to know when he is completely out of his depth. First thing he did was to telephone through to Wickham CID. How long does it take to drive from Wickham, do you think?"

"About thirty minutes, maybe less." I wasn't wondering about how long it would take the Wickham police to arrive and crouch down underneath the churchyard's thick laurel hedge to examine the murdered body of Doreen Newcombe. I was doing mental arithmetic. And I was also wondering about Lieutenant Griff O'Neal, who grabbed first and asked questions later.

POLICE INSPECTOR HARGREAVES of Wickham's Criminal Investigation Department loomed over me as I sat on the edge of my chair. The furniture, brought with us when we had moved from Reaches, was far too large for the lodge's front parlor, and so was the inspector.

"Thank you for waiting for me, Miss Redfern. I am sorry to be so late getting to you." He had the careful manners of a considerate man. "Now then, you were walking your ARP patrol last night." A glance down at his notebook. "Do you know what time it was when you met up with Miss Newcombe, Miss Wantage, and Sergeant . . ." He hesitated over the last name and mispronounced it. "Perrin?"

"I can't give you the exact time, but I can come close. It would have been between ten twenty and ten forty; something like that."

"And where was that?"

"Outside the village on the road to Lower Netherton where it junctions with the new road to the main entrance to the airfield." As I had waited for Detective Hargreaves I had replayed the last time I had spoken to Doreen. I was surprised to realize that when someone you know has been murdered, it colors everything about the last time you saw them, and so I had tried my best to remember our meeting as accurately as I could.

"Hiya, Poppy," Ivy Wantage had sung out as I walked down the lane toward them. It had taken her less than five days to pick up the slang used by the young men up at the base. Ivy is a happy, outgoing girl, but the village is all she knows, and I had realized just how naïve and impressionable she was. "You should have come to the party up at the base with us! It was ever so much fun, wasn't it, Doreen?"

Doreen had not answered her friend. She stood apart from Ivy, who was arm in arm with an American in uniform. A three-quarter moon shone through the trees on the edge of the lane, and Doreen's hair had gleamed white-gold in its light, her carefully lipsticked mouth dark against pale cheeks. She had looked like a doll I had once seen, and desperately wanted to own, in the window of Whiteleys toy shop in London: untouched, perfectly dressed, and self-contained in its glossy white box.

"Poppy, this is Sergeant Joseph Perrone. He's a flight mechanic with the American Air Force. Miss Redfern is our Air Raid Precautions warden for the village, Joe; that's why she couldn't come to the party." Ivy had completed her introductions and then said, with pride, "Miss Redfern did her air-raid training in London." Roundly pretty and taller than her best friend, Ivy snuggled closer into the crook of the sergeant's arm.

The doll came to life: Doreen laughed and shivered her shoulders in pretend fear of night bombings. But Sergeant Perrone automatically extended his right hand. "Pleased to meet you, Miss Redfern. I can't imagine what it would be like to be in London right now." His tone had been respectful. "Is it still as bad as the newsreels say?"

I had nodded. "Yes, I am afraid it is, but nothing quite as bad as the Blitz last year." And to make up for my ungracious manner when I had met Lieutenant O'Neal: "We are so glad you are all here . . . you know . . . to help us win this war. I'm sorry I couldn't come to the party."

"You weren't the only one. Bud is still in the sick bay." Doreen's laugh was dismissive. "That's what comes of being daft enough to eat Woolton pie in Wickham." She waved an unconcerned white hand with darkly lacquered fingernails at the absent Sergeant Bud Sandusky, who had monopolized all her time since he had arrived, and cast a glance under her lashes at Perrone. "I told you boys that stuff was poison. It could have been cat meat." She had deftly turned the conversation back to an evening that I had not taken part in.

"Certainly wasn't chicken potpie," Sergeant Perrone had agreed. "Now, which one of you young ladies do I drop first?"

"Me," said Doreen. "And then you can walk Ivy all the way down the lane to her house." A flirtatious laugh as she gave her consent to their continuing on alone.

I related our conversation to Inspector Hargreaves as accurately as I could. Doreen was always so sure of herself, I thought as I waited for him to write down my account in his notebook. Even when she was six it was Doreen who decided what games to play and who should sit next to her in Sunday school. The image of popular and pretty Doreen lying dead in the churchyard flew into my mind again. I had seen dead people being dug out of the rubble of bombed-out buildings and had hoped their end had been quick, but I couldn't begin to imagine what it would be like to have your life choked out of you.

"Did everything seem as usual with the two young ladies and the American?" Mr. Hargreaves's voice cut in on my thoughts. "No arguments or that sort of thing?"

It was the way he said, "American," as if he were describing a savage from a barely civilized country. After Mrs. Wantage's observations about how the village was already quite sure that Doreen had been killed by her "American" boyfriend, I found the way he said it distasteful. I was not going to endorse a change in attitude toward the base. "No, they were enjoying each other's company. I don't know about 'as usual' because it was the first time I had met Sergeant Perrone, but he struck me as a gentleman: thoughtful, polite, and considerate. We said good night and I continued down the lane. I heard the click of the door latch and Doreen's voice called out something like: 'Good night, you two—don't do anything I wouldn't do.' They all seemed to be having a pretty nice time of it."

Inspector Hargreaves cleared his throat. "And you saw Miss Newcombe go into her house?"

"No, their front door is screened from the road by a hedge. I heard her lift the door latch—she called out good night to us and then I heard the door shut."

"Door shut." He repeated as he wrote. "And you think that Miss Wantage and the sergeant followed you down Smithy Lane?"

"I know they did. I walked on ahead and had already turned right onto Streams Lane when they reached the smithy—where the Wantages live." He looked up from his notes, his eyebrows raised. "I looked back," I said. "I could see them quite clearly against the white plaster walls of the house." I did not say that they had been locked in each other's arms.

"And the rest of your patrol, how long did it take you to reach the churchyard?"

No need for hesitation now. "Forty minutes, no stops, and we were walking at a fast pace." I nodded down at Bess, who was sitting upright at our feet, her long ears pricked forward as she considered the policeman.

"You didn't check your watch, or the church clock as you walked past the graveyard?"

"The church clock hasn't kept time for years. But I was home a little after midnight; I checked my watch then." He flipped his notebook shut and tucked it and his pencil into the inside breast pocket of his rumpled suit jacket.

"You didn't see Miss Newcombe in the churchyard as you

walked up the hill?" And just like that, the tenor of our interview changed.

"See Miss Newcombe?" The thought was an unwelcome one. "No, I didn't."

"And, as you *say*, you saw or heard nothing unusual? Not as you were walking up Water Lane toward the churchyard?"

"I would have said if I had." I looked directly into his face.

"Miss Newcombe was a friend of yours?"

"Not really. I knew her, though; she grew up in the village. I didn't go to school here . . ." I stopped, at a loss to explain how isolating my girlhood had been.

"Haldean, wasn't it?" He said the name of my pretentious girls' boarding school—a place where I had spent ten miserable years, which had successfully separated me from the other children of my age in the village. His expression made what he was thinking quite clear: a Haldean girl would not run around with a baker's daughter.

Part of me wanted to say that it wasn't the difference in background that had made my grandparents send me away to school quite as much as their belief that growing up without brothers or sisters would make me an even more shy child than I already was. They had hoped that the company of other girls of my age and background would bring me out more. But I am a natural loner, so if anything, Haldean simply made me more of one.

"Doreen and Ivy are at least two years younger than I am." I sounded stiff, defensive even, and flushed with embarrassment.

"If you remember anything at all, however trivial it might seem, please get in touch with Constable Jones."

He picked up his hat and in two strides was out of the drawing room and into our cramped hall, where he barked his shin on an oak settle. I followed him. There had been one question nagging away at me all morning—I might as well ask it. "Chief Inspector Har—"

"It's just plain 'inspector,' Miss Redfern."

"Did anyone else see her last night after eleven o'clock . . . I mean apart from her . . . ?" I couldn't bring myself to say the word.

The deep lines from his nose to the corners of his mouth and his pouchy eyes gave him the look of a tired basset hound, but his expression was kind. "Her murderer? It's too early in our inquiry to know—we won't have the time of her death for a day or two."

The glance he cast my way, as we said good-bye, was thoughtful. I'm certainly on his list of suspects, I thought as I closed the front door.

AFTER A VERY late lunch—tinned sardines on toast, with gooseberries and custard to follow—I did the washing up and then walked up through Granny's vegetable garden at the back of the lodge to the old orchard. I opened the gate and Bess scampered through and made for our favorite tree. I dropped two threadbare cushions and a string bag with books and pencils on the grass. Then I picked a couple of ripe apples from a branch overhead and we settled ourselves under its shade.

"Now, Bess, not on my stomach, please—goodness, your breath is fishy." Bess had finished off the remains of my lunch and was ready for her apple. "Who on earth would want to kill Doreen?" It was a question I had been asking myself all day, and no answer had come to me. "I suppose there are plenty of people who could have killed her—but who on earth would *want* to kill a very pretty, rather spoiled, and, to be frank, awfully silly girl like Doreen?" A flicker of guilt—she didn't deserve to be judged unkindly, but then she wasn't a particularly kind girl either.

Doreen had always concentrated on what made her happy before she had considered others. It was the inevitable flaw of being pretty and popular. I finished my apple and gave the core to Bess, who had watched every bite as I had nibbled it down to a treat.

Then we settled down and I reached for an old school exercise book. It fell open to two closely written paragraphs of a novel I have been working on for months about a newspaper reporter who works in London during the Blitz.

"I wonder what Ilona would make of murder in a backwater like Little Buffenden if she had to report on it," I asked Bess. I couldn't imagine that someone as assertive as Ilona would have politely provided answers to unimaginative questions from a dull provincial policeman without throwing in an opinion or two of her own. She would have had Hargreaves gratefully thanking her for her observations as he wrote them down word for word. As a newspaper reporter who is used to handling tricky situations, Ilona is supremely confident in dealing with the police. She also lives a sophisticated life of enviable independence in an elegant service flat in Piccadilly. In short, Ilona Linthwaite is the sort of woman I long to be, and the heroine of my novel.

Ilona, in some form or another, has been with me for years: my imaginary playmate when I was very young—she was always the one who dared me to be naughty! My confidante throughout my years at Haldean. During the classes I disliked the most—algebra, geometry, and math—I would sit silently at my desk, with a "listening" face, as Ilona and I escaped into a world of fantasy adventures.

Now, no longer content with merely imagining "What if . . . ?" I had decided to write a novel, and who better to be its protagonist than my alter ego?

I flipped to the back of my exercise book and wrote down a timetable of my patrol through the village. And then I jotted down the highlights of my last conversation with Mrs. Wantage.

"What time did Ivy get home from the dance at the base last night?" I had asked her.

"When her dad told her to be home." Mrs. Wantage's daughter was not the one lying murdered under a laurel hedge in the churchyard. "That Joe Perrone walked her home and she was in by eleven."

I counted on my fingers. Doreen had been safely home at ten to eleven. So, what was she doing out again after she had said good night to her friends?

My fingertips did more addition. Doreen must have left the safety of her house, and then she went to, or was taken to, the churchyard. That meant she went up Smithy Lane to the edge of the green and then on up the High Street to the church—a twenty-minute stroll, less if she was walking fast. My next thought brought me upright from the grass, toppling a sleeping Bess. I had walked past the churchyard at about twenty to twelve. Was Doreen already dead or—the thought appalled me—about to die, as Bess and I sauntered past just feet away?

Pull yourself together! I told myself. If Doreen was fighting for her life we would certainly have heard something—Bess most certainly would. Doreen must have been killed after that; it must have been around midnight, when I was safely back at the lodge.

FOUR

JUST A MOMENT, DARLING, BEFORE YOU RUN OFF TO CHANGE. Your grandfather and I have something we want to talk to you about." Granny opened her mending basket and searched for gray wool to darn Grandad's already much-mended socks. I hovered in the drawing room doorway. I knew exactly what was coming next.

"I know how important it is for you to keep yourself usefully occupied and to do your bit for the war effort, but it would be madness for you to continue patrolling the village at night after this terrible thing has happened." She glanced at my grandfather as he put his newspaper to one side. "I will have a word with the vicar and he will find someone else to do the job. A big strapping lad; that's who they should have had in the first place." Her voice was quiet with conviction, her customary vagueness gone. "I am sorry, my darling, it is all most unfortunate, but there it is."

"There are no big strapping lads in the village, Granny. They are all off at the war." I cast a hopeful look at Grandad. It was he who had so wholeheartedly supported my ARP training, but Granny held her own quiet authority, especially where I was concerned. I made myself wait respectfully. The last thing I wanted was to be gated in the lodge night after night.

My grandfather took a sip from his glass of port and settled himself more comfortably in his chair. "Both your grandmother and I are not prepared to let you patrol the village at night, my dear." He put down his glass on the table next to his chair and shot us each a look that was both triumphant and playful. "Alone, that is."

Optimism flared briefly, but Granny's pale brows were arched almost to her hairline, and she sighed as she ran her darning needle through the heel of her husband's sock. "I am *quite* sure she should resign from ARP night duty until this awful business has been cleared up at the American airfield, Jasper."

"I don't think we should jump to the conclusion that Doreen Newcombe was killed by her American friend, Alice. That is a job for Wickham CID." Grandad's voice was loud in its emphasis. He frowned, and so did Granny, and her frowns last longer. He went on with less volume. "Would you agree to her continuing if she had one of my Home Guard to escort her?"

"I can't imagine for one moment that either Mr. Edwards or Mr. Wilson would be of any use if someone waylaid them on a dark night. They are both over sixty!" Grandad cleared his throat, steepled the fingers of both hands together, and waited courteously to make sure Granny had finished her objection. "It would be utter folly," she finished.

He nodded in apparent agreement. "I wasn't referring to *Private* Edwards or *Sergeant* Wilson, my dear, but to Corporal Ritchie. He's an alert and fit young man—"

"Who couldn't join up because of his asthma," Granny pointed out. "And Sid has always been rather a timid boy—not his fault, of course."

"Nothing timid about Sid Ritchie: a year in the Home Guard has done wonders for his morale—"

"But any sudden shock might bring on an asthma attack, and what would he protect Poppy with, a cricket bat, perhaps, or maybe a popgun?"

Grandad, looking pleased with himself, was now ready to give us his news. He swirled the port in his glass; took a long, appreciative sniff; and smiled at us both before he took a sip. His smile transformed him into a younger Jasper, one who had charmed my grandmother into marrying him fifty years ago. "Why, with his Sten gun, of course! Sid and several others of the Guard have spent the last two days at Wickham GHQ being trained in the use of small arms. They got back this afternoon. The Little Buffenden and Lower Netherton Home Guard are now fully armed!"

"Sid Ritchie with a machine gun?" Granny put down her mending. "Good heavens above, but would he have the pluck to use it in . . . real life?"

Grandfather's laugh was courteous, as if she had made a joke. "What a strange question. Of course he would use it in 'real life.' Corporal Ritchie will be well equipped to escort Poppy until the CID have discovered who committed this terrible murder. That is, of course"—he cleared his throat—"if you are in complete agreement that she may continue her duty, if she has an armed escort."

My grandmother pulled a needleful of yarn through the sock and looked first at me and then at her husband. The mention of duty had its effect—the Redferns abide by duty to king and country first and foremost. "If he has a proper gun and knows how to use it . . . then I suppose . . ."

I didn't wait for any more objections to be raised, but I was careful not to look too triumphant. "Don't worry, Granny, most of my patrolling is done at dusk, and we are off duty before midnight, when everyone in the village is tucked up for the night."

"It's not the village I am worried about."

"THAT GUN LOOKS frightfully heavy, Sid." I reached out to touch the cold gleam of the gun's metal barrel.

Sid lifted his shoulder to move the weapon away. "Crikey, whatever you do, don't *touch* it, Miss Redfern. It's a submachine gun *and* it's loaded. This thing could bring down an elephant."

He looked so terribly serious standing at the bottom of the vicarage garden carrying this menacing-looking weapon on a perfect summer evening that I had to turn my head away. I've known Sid for most of my life; he is only a year or two younger than I, but I have always felt decades older. He is an earnest young man who suffers from a complete deficit of wit.

"It would be better if you briefed me on patrol, Miss Redfern, because I promised Mum I would be home by eleven pip emma."

"Pip emma?" Since he joined my grandad's Home Guard, Sid's vocabulary has been larded with military jargon.

"Royal Air Force for 'p.m.'; 'a.m.' would be 'ack emma.'" Sid imitated what I supposed he fondly imagined were the flat, clipped tones of the fictional fighter pilot and hero of *The Boy's Own Paper*: Squadron Leader James Bigglesworth, known affectionately to his fans as Biggles, who performs acts of heroic derring-do in his Spit-fire fighter plane, or "Spit," as Biggles devotees call it.

"Right then, Corporal Ritchie, here is your brief: we patrol the entire village and surrounding area twice: once as a reminder about blackout and then again when everyone leaves the pub at closing time—they get a bit careless after a pint or two."

I had only half his attention. "Would you put the dog on your other side, Miss Redfern?" He blew his nose. "I'm allergic to dogs and cats—they give me asthma."

"Enough of this Miss Redfern business. It's Poppy, all right? And you can tell her yourself. Just say 'down' very firmly and she'll leave you alone. That's the way," I added, as Bess lost interest in someone who bleated like a sheep and ran on ahead. "Where was I? Right, we usually reach the Wheatsheaf by ten o'clock, and then continue to end our patrol at the Rose and Crown by eleven. Another once around the village and then up Water Lane to the church. That's it—nothing to it, really."

"Unless there's a raid." He tightened both hands on his gun, and I had to bite my cheeks and look away to keep from laughing.

We were halfway down the High Street with the village green on our right. I could see the Rose and Crown on its far side: there were several elderly men sitting outside the pub on wooden benches, their backs against stone walls still warm from the day's sun.

"The Rose and the 'Sheaf will be chockablock tonight because of what happened to Doreen—they can't stop talking about it; it's disgusting how they gossip." Sid's usually mild expression was wrinkled with disapproval. I couldn't have agreed with him more: all talk, all day, throughout the village and its surrounding farms, had been of Doreen's violent death.

"Cripes." Sid blushed with embarrassment. "And here's Mr. Newcombe. You've got to hand it to him, Poppy, he's all about duty."

Ordinarily our baker reminds me of a robin. He has bright, shiny eyes and often puts his head to one side when he's listening to you, but the man who was cycling toward us had none of the sprightliness of a cheery bird. His face was haggard and he seemed to slump forward over the handlebars of his bike as he neared us.

Mr. Newcombe would have been baking his first batch of bread on the night when Doreen was killed, I thought as he drew level with us. I lifted my hand in greeting. "Good evening, Mr. Newcombe. I am so sorry . . . about Doreen."

"Thank you, lass." The baker stopped and stood astride his bike. He couldn't bring himself to look at us; he gazed up the village street to the haven of his bakery. "I am not sure it has quite . . . well, you know, sunk in . . . yet. The house is empty and quiet, but Mrs. Newcombe told me we must carry on, as if she was still with us. She's right, of course . . . and the village has to eat . . ." He put his right foot on the pedal.

"Mum said she would pop round and look in on Mrs. Newcombe, with her condolences," Sid said, staring at his boots, so he wouldn't have to see the pain on Mr. Newcombe's face.

"Thank you, Sid, that's kind of her. Beryl will appreciate it. Best be getting on." He pushed down with his right foot and cycled on.

"Whoever killed Doreen was off his rocker," Sid said as the baker disappeared inside his shop. "She was such a gentle, pretty girl. Why would someone want to do something like that to her?" He adjusted the strap of his gun. It looked completely out of place hanging off his round shoulders.

Sid is quite good-looking: he has a well-shaped head, a nice straight nose, and lots of dark brown hair slicked down carefully with Brylcreem. He would be almost handsome if he didn't look quite so . . . well, I have to say it: daft. His large brown eyes are by far his most attractive feature, and now they were swimming with tears. "I wouldn't mind getting my hands on that Yank; I can tell you that for nothing. Doreen was a wonderful girl, she was . . . the sweetest in the world." His voice broke and he dashed tears from his eyes with the sleeve of his jacket. I reached out and patted him on the shoulder as he struggled to pull himself together.

It was well-known in the village that Sid had been soft on Doreen, but to everyone's disappointment she had treated him with all the dismissive affection of a sister to a brother and had become engaged to the now-dead Brian Chambers. Granny had hit the nail on the head, of course: "Ivy would make a much more suitable girlfriend for someone as unassuming and gentle as Sid, because she is outgoing and not quite as self-interested as Doreen. I am sure the two of them will get together in time: Sid is what we used to call a late developer—just like dear Mr. Churchill."

We had reached the village pond at the bottom of the green, and the late summer sun blazed its last rays across its surface, turning the water to mirror gold. A few straggling ducks were swimming to their nests in the reeds, creating bright orange Vs behind them. It was a tranquil scene; the air was quiet and still and it didn't feel like there was a war on. It didn't feel like someone in our village could be a murderer, either. I waited by the pond's bank, staring steadfastly at the ducks to give Sid a moment to recover.

After a few moments, he squared his shoulders. "All right . . . sorry about that, it won't happen again. Now, back to business. Where do we go next?"

"Quite a bit of walking involved in this job, I'm afraid, Sid. In fact, that's all it is, really," I reminded him as we crossed the end of the street and turned left down Smithy Lane. Sid is not much of an outdoors type. He had been sickly as a boy: earaches, colds, and bronchitis had blighted his childhood in winter. In summer he stayed inside to avoid hay fever and stuck stamps in his album while we swam in the river and picnicked at the top of Marston Downs. He had failed his army physical because he had flat feet, couldn't possibly join the RAF because he was color-blind, and had been turned down by the navy because of his asthma.

We walked past the Newcombes' house and went on to the smithy at the bottom of the lane. Sid was more relaxed now that we had passed all the Newcombe family landmarks. "I'm building battleships at the moment—from kits. Finished three of them already; the detail on them is wizard."

"I thought all battleships were the same."

Sid snorted as if girls could hardly be expected to know the difference. "Oh no, there are many different classes: dreadnoughts, frigates, aircraft carriers. I'm going to build a model of HMS *Ark Royal*. Dreadnoughts are top-hole; they . . ." He launched into the Royal Navy's inventory, and somewhere around an avid description of minesweepers I had a conversation in my head with my fictional heroine, Ilona, about men who love war.

I was grateful when we reached the lane that led up to the Wilkeses' farm. "Oh dear," I said, not feeling in the slightest put out. "Mrs. Wilkes hasn't drawn her scullery blackout. We'd better remind her." It was the tiniest crack of light, but I needed a respite from Sid's passion for the armed forces. I also wanted to see how Audrey Wilkes was taking the death of one of her friends.

We walked up the lane and I knocked on Mrs. Wilkes's kitchen door.

"Good evening, Miss Redfern . . . Oh dear, have I forgotten? I am so sorry; we have been at sixes and sevens all day." Mrs. Wilkes ushered us into her kitchen and adjusted the blackout. "I just can't get little Doreen Newcombe out of my mind. Such a wicked thing to happen. What is wrong with the world? Nothing has been the same since this dreadful war. Both Audrey and I have been that upset." Mrs. Wilkes is a tall, broad-shouldered woman, and her daughter takes after her. Both Audrey and her mother dwarf Mr. Wilkes, who is a short, upright, wiry individual with gray hair and a neatly clipped beard.

Audrey looked up from a magazine she was leafing through at the kitchen table and nodded. Her face wore its usual shut-down, brooding expression. Something about her silence made me want to find out what was going on behind that blank facade. After all, one of her childhood friends had been brutally killed, and you don't find out important information by being polite all the time. Ilona never lets that sort of thing get in the way of her reporting.

"I was talking to Mrs. Martin the other night, and she told me how helpful you had been in making the church crypt comfy in case we have an air raid." No answer. I was determined not to be shut up, so I blundered on. "It was a good idea to run an electric cord down into the crypt, so we can make hot milk for the children." Audrey shrugged her shoulders and turned another page of her magazine. It was an old one, prewar, featuring Hollywood's favorite matinée idol and heartthrob: "Errol Flynn *is* Captain Blood," the headline read over a picture of Flynn with shoulder-length curls and a doublet unbuttoned to his waist.

Audrey examined the photograph for quite some time before she said, "I thought the kiddies might like a cuppa something hot; it can get cold down there." Her tone was expressionless, but her deep-set eyes were watchful. At the sound of her voice, Bess, who had been sitting quietly at my feet, went and stood by the door.

"Terrible thing to have happened to your friend, Audrey. I'm so sorry, you must feel miserable."

She continued to study her magazine, and without lifting her head she said, quite casually, "You wouldn't catch *me* running around with a Yank, but Doreen was always a flirt."

It was such an implacable announcement, devoid of any compassion. I heard sensitive Sid's sharp intake of breath as Mrs. Wilkes rushed in. "Doreen was always so full of life."

Audrey reached out a hand without lifting her eyes from the page and picked up an apple, and Mrs. Wantage's words came back to me: "I'm worried sick about Ivy. She's been crying all day and hasn't eaten a thing." I heard Audrey's savage first bite as Sid and I said our good nights and followed a jubilant Bess down the drive and up the lane toward the second of the village's watering holes.

"She's always been that way," Sid said.

"What way?" I was Ilona again—on the hunt for information.

"Grumpy . . ." He stopped and groped for the right word. "No, she's more like . . . surly: never cracks a smile, that one. I think she resented Doreen—resented her popularity and how much people were drawn to her. She wasn't very popular at school; they used to call her Big Aud. But she's not a bad sort—really."

"Children can be very cruel," I said, remembering my boarding school and the bullies who reigned over us.

He chuckled in the dark. "No one teased Audrey much. She was fearsome if she lost her temper. She threw Brian Chambers off the climbing frame when she was only eight. He must have been at least eleven at the time. He landed on his arm and broke it."

My mind went back to Audrey hunched over the kitchen table. I saw again her broad-palmed hands, her strong fingers turning the pages of her Hollywood magazine. Doreen was such a tiny little thing, with delicate wrists and ankles and a long, slender neck. I shivered, lost in dark thoughts, as we trudged onward into the night.

Sid resumed his paean to machines of destruction, this time to the great British Lancaster bomber. "The Lanc is primarily a night bomber, Poppy, but is also used for daylight precision bombing and can carry the twenty-two-thousand-pound Grand Slam earth-quake bombs. The largest payload—"

"Here's the Wheatsheaf, and it's easily another half an hour to closing time!" I cried, not wanting to hear any more about ma-chines of death and destruction. "We can take a break and have a shandy if you like."

The moon had gone behind a cloud and Sid was a dark shape in the road next to me, but I saw his head whip round. "My mum made me promise not to touch a drop until I turned twenty-one."

"You can have just plain lemonade, then. Come on, Sid, my treat."

But he shook his head. "And that means that I don't go into a pub until I am twenty-one either."

IT SEEMED LIKE hours had creaked by as we plodded back into the village. Sid was dragging his feet as we tramped over the wooden footbridge past Streams Farm, and as we turned into Water Lane, I noticed that he was limping.

"I think I've got a blister," he said as we walked past the house that had been rented to a retired solicitor from London, and then the one that belongs to our local doctor and his wife, to the smallest of the three redbrick Victorian villas, where Sid lived with his mother.

"No need to come any further, Sid," I said, desperate to be rid of his sighs and complaints and to return to my thoughts about Audrey and her friendship with Doreen. "The church is just a bit up the hill, and then it's only a few yards past the vicarage to Reaches Lane."

"Yes, but that was where Doreen was found—in the churchyard. That place gives me the willies, anyway." I could see he was torn between getting his boots off and his duty.

"But I am not going *into* the churchyard, Sid. You go on in; it's well past eleven." He stood, unsure, by the side of the road, his hand already on the garden gate, his right shoulder slumped forward with the weight of his gun. I was walking away from him toward the churchyard with Bess racing alongside me. "I'll see you tomorrow night, then, Poppy," he called after me.

Saint Bartholomew's Church and its surrounding graveyard sit up on a rise, buttressed at their steeper side—the side I was approaching from—by a flint stone wall. It is not a steep gradient, but whether it was the deep dark, or just the knowledge of what had happened here in the middle of last night, I was out of breath as I came level with a grove of ancient yew trees on the edge of the churchyard. Their heavy boughs blocked the pale light of the stars and I couldn't see a foot in front of me as I stumbled on the cobbles of the lane, wishing I hadn't been quite so quick to say good night to Sid.

The absolute silence under the trees felt almost threatening, and the hair on the nape of my neck lifted as I peered into heavy shadows for Bess. "Here, girl—here, Bessie," I called—to no avail.

And then the still night air was shattered by a scream. It echoed across to me from the meadow below the lane: a harsh, plaintive cry that sent shivers up and down my already crawling spine. I must have been terribly on edge, because of course I knew that it was only the call of a vixen on the hunt, but the almost human sound had added to my worst imaginings. The palms of my hands were clammy as I picked up the pace, humming aloud to keep up my spirits. As I came level with the churchyard's tall hedge I heard another sound: a movement in the undergrowth and then the brittle snap of a tree branch. Heart pounding, I switched on my torch, pointing the low beam to a break in the hedge.

Silly girl, I told myself, it's nothing to be afraid of: just field mice or rabbits scared by the vixen. But rabbits don't break branches, and mice are too light to disturb the undergrowth that audibly. I was so demoralized that I didn't dare turn my back on the hedge, not even to run down to the vicarage and pay the Reverend Fothergill a call. I wondered whether he or his housekeeper would hear me if I shouted for help.

Rooted to the spot, I peered into the hedge. The shadow underneath it was unfathomable, as if a deep cavern had opened into the earth. I had never felt this nervous alone at night before. All my earlier curiosity about who could have reason to kill Doreen Newcombe evaporated as the beam of my torch danced up and down in my trembling hand.

I drew a long breath to calm my nerves. My heartbeat slowed, and I was just beginning to laugh at my earlier fears when I heard the unmistakable sound of someone, or something, moving toward me through the undergrowth.

I groped for my whistle on its lanyard, raised it to lips so dry I had to hold it between my teeth. My torch beam swept the bank again, and in its feeble light I saw, quite clearly, a hand lifted to shield a pair of eyes. I took in a breath to whistle for help. It was at this moment that Bess erupted from the hedgerow on the other side of the lane, barking hysterically, as she threw herself forward. I let the whistle drop from my mouth, because it was Ivy Wantage warding off affection from Bess joyfully leaping around her like a little porpoise.

"Can you turn that off, please? For heaven's sake, Poppy, you're blinding us." And out from under the shelter of the trees came Joe Perrone and Ivy. My laugh was almost hysterical.

"Ivy?" I said. "What on earth are you doing here at this time of night?" And why would you want to be in this terrible place where your best friend was killed? was my second thought.

"What was that terrible cry?" the sergeant asked. "Made my blood run cold—especially as we were standing in the middle of a cemetery."

I was grateful they couldn't see how scared I had been. "It was a vixen—she was probably hunting."

"A vixen?"

"A female fox."

"It was like something out of a ghost story!" He laughed, and Ivy smiled, but her face was wan and tired, and I could see dark smudges under her eyes.

"Ivy, does your mum know where you are?"

Joe put a protective arm around her shoulders. "She's really upset, and she wanted to bring flowers." He shrugged his right shoulder behind him toward the laurel hedge where Doreen had been found not twenty-four hours ago. "Anyway, she is quite safe with me. But you're right; her mom might be worried if she found she wasn't at home."

He jumped down from the bank and turned to help Ivy down. Standing together in the lane, we made an awkward trio.

"I am so terribly sorry about Doreen, Ivy, but what made you come here of all places?"

"I just wanted to . . ." She paused and hung her head in misery. "Wanted to . . . bring her . . ." She gave up and started to cry, dashing the tears out of her eyes with the back of her hand.

I put my arm around her shoulders, and she sagged against me, weeping incoherently about Doreen. "She feels awfully cold, Sergeant. We should get her home. Come on, Ivy, let's get you moving." I chaffed her cold hands, and then something made me say, "I'll walk along with you." I had no intention of leaving Ivy alone with a man she had known for only seven days.

FIVE

"NOT A SINGLE YANK IN SIGHT, FOR ONCE." SID SPOKE FOR the rest of the village as we tramped down the High Street the following evening. "Why didn't they have them all confined to base right from the start instead of waiting until this morning? Then perhaps this terrible thing would never have happened."

We crossed the green in the direction of the Rose and Crown. "There were nearly always four or five of them lounging around the pub at opening time. I wouldn't mind *that*," he said, making a huge concession to men who drink beer, "but they were so loud. Why did they have to shout out to their friends the way they did?"

I had rather liked the banter that flew back and forth between American airmen with their pints of beer, calling out to their pals sauntering down the High Street to join them, hands in pockets, caps tilted: warriors returning victorious from battle. Their teasing was always good-natured, in that slightly mocking way of men who work and live together. Yet at the same time it was clear that their sociable ribbing was a front that preserved distance over genuine emotion. When a full squadron took off in a roar of petrol fumes and smoke in immaculate formation, it rarely came home complete. We had seen the ragged numbers returning across the horizon of our village and knew that there were faces we were just getting to know and voices we had begun to recognize in our pub that we would no longer hear again. Little Buffenden had learned not to ask after familiar faces now missing. In the short weeks that they had been with us, the village had accepted our Friendly Invasion.

"I am sorry not to see them on the green. I think they brought hope to our lives when they first came," I said to Sid. "Not just in helping us to win the war, but in helping us to believe that our fear, our deprivations, would be a thing of the past, that we can believe that the end is within reach." I didn't say that their youthful exuberance, their swagger, and their laughing banter made our village community a brighter and happier place. I knew where Sid stood on our Yank invasion.

"It would be an affront to our grief if they were still lounging about the place as if nothing had happened. It is right and proper for them to be kept on base." Sid's bunions were playing up, and army-issue boots didn't help. He had also pulled a muscle in his shoulder, so I carried his Sten gun when no one could see us, out on the country lanes.

"They have been flying missions all week: night and day," he complained. "We can hear them taking off even down in our little dip in the road. I expect they are going to Germany to revenge the Luftwaffe's raid on Ipswich and Canterbury, if it was Ipswich and Canterbury they were aiming for," he scoffed. Like all patriotic Englishmen, he made a point to be sneery about anything German.

"Why on earth would the Luftwaffe bomb Ipswich and Canterbury? I thought they concentrated on our industrial towns."

"Because they are *old* towns. It's all part of these . . ." He hesitated over his pronunciation. "These Bed-something raids."

I hadn't a clue what he was talking about and decided that I must make an effort to listen to the evening news more often. If I relied on Sid for what was happening in the war, I would end up sounding as half-baked as he did.

All I had thought about for the past two days was who could possibly have a reason to kill Doreen. Unlike everyone else in the village, I couldn't quite bring myself to suspect Joe Perrone simply because he was an American. But I had been reluctant to let him take Ivy home alone when I had bumped into them both outside the churchyard. I thought about this for a moment. Had I gone with them to see Ivy home because I felt naturally protective toward her, and she was so distressed, or was it because her friend's brutally murdered body had been found under a hedge the night before and we were all at risk now? My sense of Joe Perrone was that he was what we call a "nice" boy; at least that had been my impression.

But more important than that, I found it hard to shake the image of Audrey's sullen anger toward the dead Doreen as she leafed through her magazine with those strong hands. So it was difficult to concentrate on my companion's account of the latest German air raids.

Sid was still struggling with a name that was eluding him. "It's on the tip of my tongue. I don't know how to pronounce it, because they say it so fast on the radio. But ever since we bombed their precious Lubeck, the Germans have been hitting back, choosing cities like Bath and York, you know—places of historic interest."

Light dawned at last. "Baedeker?" I suggested. "After the guide-book?"

He stopped, and I heard him chuckle in the dark. "Bi-decka, yes. That's what it was. I knew you would know because you're so clever." There was admiration in his voice. Sid really is the nicest boy, and is quite bright really, but he's easily influenced, and it is his lack of curiosity that holds him back. Not his fault: village life usually makes for a narrow point of view.

"I think it's wrong to bomb towns at all, especially at night." I could see women herding their children and the elderly along Clave Street toward the Underground and remembered a six-year-old girl rooted to the pavement outside her house, trembling with terror. "It's wicked to bomb civilians and cowardly to do it at night."

He looked quite stunned for a moment. He obviously thought I was being unpatriotic. For people like Sid, the only good German is a dead German. It was time to move away from tender subjects.

"Have you finished *The Three Musketeers*?" I asked him. "I was wondering what you thought of it." Granny had donated a lot of my old books to the village library and Sid had told me on our first patrol that he had borrowed two by Alexandre Dumas. I hoped Dumas would at least get him off the topic of battleships, or, even worse, rip-roaring, jolly old Biggles. His response, though enthusiastic, was predictable. "They were wizard!" he said in the strangulated vowels he imagines his hero Spitfire pilots use.

"Which did you prefer, *The Count of Monte Cristo* or *The Three Musketeers*?"

"*The Count of Monte Cristo* was really good, but I liked *The Three Musketeers* best—because of Milady." I sensed from the sound of his voice in the darkening lane that he was smiling. "You just can't keep up with her—she's all over the place."

I liked his description of the slippery Milady.

"You see, with men," he went on to explain, "you know where you are. They usually declare what side they're on and fight for that side, but not Milady. It's frightening how wicked she is—beautiful and wicked."

We had arrived at the intersection on Smithy Lane where the new road led up to the airfield. It was usually busy with ground crew waiting for the bus to Wickham to catch a movie, as Americans called the pictures, or to go dancing at the Palais de Danse. "Not a Yank in sight," said Sid with approval. "That's why it's so nice and quiet. Pity they don't keep them on the base all the time." I couldn't help but laugh, because sometimes Sid sounds just like a peevish middle-aged man who shakes his copy of the *Telegraph* in outrage at the antics of today's youth, and not a young man of twenty.

"Grandad told me that airmen have one of the most dangerous jobs in the war."

I should have known better than to talk about airmen to a Biggles fan. "Major Redfern was talking about the Royal Air Force, I expect. Our chaps take all the most dangerous missions, which is why their casualties are so high."

I didn't want a lecture on British versus American bravery. "Do you think the village will make trouble for them because of Doreen's death?" I wondered. Sid is not a gossip, but his mother is very thick with Mrs. Glossop, so he has probably heard all the rumors that fly around Little Buffenden, and it is easier to sound him out than to interrogate our postmistress, who takes over every conversation.

I heard his snort of disgust. "I don't know about trouble. But the gilt's off the gingerbread for the American Air Force, so they had better behave themselves in our village." His voice was throaty with the emotion he felt at the loss of his friend.

"But what do *you* think?"

"I don't know," he wailed. "It's all so horrible, I can't bear to think about it. I can't sleep at night for worry."

"What does the village say?"

"Who cares what they are all saying? The old gossips. Most of them think it was either Doreen's new boyfriend, even though he was in the sick bay, or that other one, Ivy's boyfriend, Joe Perrone. The rest of them think it was some tramp. Do you remember that awful business over in Wooten Hayfield? Of course you do. It was about five or six years ago. Those girls who disappeared? Come off it, Poppy, you can't have forgotten. The papers were full of it."

I did remember. It had been the talk of the county all one summer. "Weren't their bodies found months later?"

"Six months later, when they were bringing in the harvest. Just thinking about it gives me the willies. Anyway, they got the chap that did it. He was a tramp—a vicious character who had been in prison for all sorts of violent crimes—but there haven't been tramps around here for ages. It has to be someone from the base."

"Did you go up to the party at the airfield the night when Doreen was killed?" I asked. It would be interesting to hear what Sid thought about Ivy and Doreen and their American boyfriends.

"No, I was away doing my small-arms and machine-gun training at Wickham GHQ." He stopped and adjusted the strap on his Sten gun. "And even if I hadn't had training, I wouldn't have wanted to go." I couldn't see his face in the dark, but his tone was lofty. "Americans are so loud they make my ears hurt. And some of them have such strong accents I can't understand a word they are saying. There were two in the post office the day after they arrived. I was in there getting Mum some cough drops. They wanted 'candy,' whatever that is. Mrs. Glossop understood what they meant; she told them that she couldn't sell them any sweets unless they had a ration book. One of them told her that they send candy over from America for them. Can you imagine?"

"Imagine what?"

"It is kind of sissy, isn't it? Grown men having sweets shipped over for them, as if they can't survive without their chewing gum. Anyway, they wanted to buy English candy and send it back to their brothers and sisters in the US. That's what they call America. Mrs. Glossop gave them pretty short shrift, I can tell you. Suggested that they might want to hand out some of their 'candy' bars to the village children."

"What did they say?"

He shook his head. "I don't know because I left. But Mum said they turned up at the school with three huge boxes of chocolate bars and asked her if she would distribute them."

"That was generous. I bet the kids were delighted."

He shrugged one shoulder. "Mum said she handed them out before the children went home. There were enough for two each!" He stuck his fingers in the air to emphasize the shocking fact. "*Two* bars of chocolate are the equivalent of a six-week sweet ration, and they gave boxes of them away—just like that." He paused and giggled. "Mum brought one home for me. And you know what? It didn't taste like our chocolate at all. I can't imagine what they make it with."

LITTLE BUFFENDEN DID its best, for the Newcombe family's sake, to settle down to normal after the shock of Doreen's death. And still the Americans were confined to base, and apart from the racket of squadrons of Fortress bombers and Mustang fighter planes taking off every evening, it was almost as if the Friendly Invasion, as the popular press called the arrival of our allies, had never occurred.

But it was impossible for me to resume my life as if nothing had happened. My quiet night patrols were now full of Sid's passion for war and his lectures on British superiority. "Really, when you think of it, Poppy, there isn't a country in the world that shouldn't go down on its knees and thank God for the British Empire." Most of Sid's opinions were barely-thought-through adolescent twaddle, but responding to them required a certain kind of stamina, so it was hard for me to ignore him and concentrate on finding answers to the questions batting around in my head.

Who in our village could possibly have a reason to murder Doreen? And even if they had a reason, was anyone among us capable of strangling a healthy young woman? We are a village of women, children, and middle-aged to elderly men. Little Buffenden's younger fathers, husbands, brothers, and sons had long joined up to fight in the war, leaving very few men who would be physically able to commit the crime, which left me with a list of women and the same unanswered questions.

I returned to my list of possible male suspects. Sid Ritchie, unable to join up because of ill health, is what we might call an able-bodied young man, physically capable of murder, but he had been in training at Wickham GHQ.

Our vicar, Cedric Fothergill, is probably in his mid-forties, and certainly fit enough to overpower a young woman, but it seemed sacrilegious to think of him as a suspect for murder.

Mr. Wantage, who used to be our village blacksmith, is, at fifty, so crippled with arthritis that he would be incapable of wringing a chicken's neck. Then there is our butcher, Mr. Angus, and the publican of the Rose and Crown, Bert Pritchard, both of whom have led lives of blameless innocence except for a little mild flirtation with other men's wives; and of course, there is our baker, Mr. Newcombe, who was hardly likely to have murdered his daughter.

Mr. Wilkes, who owns Streams Farm; his cowman, Percy; and our verger, Len, who found Doreen, are all far too mild-mannered to even think of violent death, let alone commit it. And, finally, there is my grandfather, who is physically capable of strangling half a dozen Germans if they happened to invade England but is incapable of being violent to a woman.

Rounding off a list of men who were either too mild mannered or too geriatric was our newcomer to the village, the retired Mr. Ponsonby, a deeply reserved man whose only interest was in birds, and Dr. Oliver, who, at sixty-eight, was hardly a specimen of athletic manhood.

"Of course, we will win this war, even if the Americans hadn't come to help us. You know why? Because we have Mr. Churchill." Sid's voice interrupted my list making. I had to stop myself from harrumphing in disgust because most people with an iota of brainpower know that Winston Churchill had crawled on his knees, for years, to the American president Mr. Roosevelt and begged him to come to our aid. It was all such rubbish that I didn't have the heart to start in on a list of how many women would like to do away with Doreen.

SIX

NEARLY FORGOT." GRANNY LOOKED UP FROM HER KNITTING.
"I volunteered you for the children's clothes exchange in the village hall."

"Not again, Granny, surely?"

"There are a thousand and one things to do in this village to help out, dear. We all have to pitch in."

Most wartime duties are monotonous and dreary, but the clothes exchange is the most draining of our many chores. "I did the summer one. Do I have to do the winter one too?"

"Yes, and you know perfectly well why. First, you are impartial, since you don't have children, and if there's a falling-out, no one is better at smoothing over difficulties than you."

"Only because I don't have children."

"It's the same difference, darling. And second, poor Mrs. Martin is relying on your help because she has just about had enough of Mrs. Ritchie—she's obsessing about the jumble sale again. And if you need a third reason . . ."

"No, Granny, of course I'll do it."

"There is an awful lot of our mending to do. Perhaps you would rather help me with that?"

"I'll go and help Mrs. Martin—anything but darning. At least the clothes exchange is over and done with; darning just goes on forever."

She smiled her thanks to me and threaded her needle. "Who would have thought that a change in season could cause us all so much tension? Mrs. Newcombe says her boy has shot up like a weed, and none of his winter clothes fit. Even with clothing coupons, the things available are shoddy and expensive."

Out of necessity Little Buffenden has become one huge family, where hand-me-downs make the rounds of the entire village. And the ructions this causes among mothers trying to keep their children warmly clothed border on desperation.

I sighed. "The only problem is that Mrs. Angus takes more than she donates, and it upsets Mrs. Pritchard, and there is not much love lost between them anyway." I finished my tea and resigned myself to a peacekeeping mission that no one else wanted to take on.

"WOULD YOU LOOK at this?" Mrs. Angus, the butcher's wife, held up two worn sweaters. She is a skinny little woman with absolutely no sense of humor. There is an air of "the boss" about her, and it is said that she keeps her silent husband completely in check. "This one is full of the moth—and someone looks like they were pulled through a hedge backward in this. I think I'll just unravel and knit them up again. Only thing you can do with them, really." She glared at us as if we were moths hungry for wool and dumped four sweaters into her bag.

Mrs. Pritchard's round, handsome face was puckered in a frown of concentration. She pushed her curly dark hair out of her eyes and bent over a large cardboard box filled with children's winter shoes, each one tied to its mate by the laces. "Eight, eight," she said as she looked at sizes. "Stop running around, Nigel, and come over here. I want you to try these on. I think it *says* eight, but the print is all worn away." She peered into the shoe as she said to Mrs. Martin, "He shoots up every summer. Nothing fits."

The hall became silent, and I looked up from sorting wool socks into pairs to see Mrs. Newcombe come in through the door carrying a heavy suitcase. "Oh no, Beryl, there's no need to give away Doreen's . . ." Mrs. Pritchard bit back her words as she saw her friend's face.

I hadn't seen Mrs. Newcombe since Doreen's death. She had always been a well-set-up woman, but she seemed to have shrunk in size since her daughter's brutal murder. Her pale blue eyes were almost apologetic as she stood in the doorway as if waiting to be invited in.

"No point in keeping them all hanging in her wardrobe where they are no good to anyone." Mrs. Newcombe's eyes were red-rimmed with exhaustion, her face pinched with grief. "It's wrong to hang on to good clothes when there are so many girls going without these days. Look, this would do for your Yvonne, wouldn't it?" she said to Mrs. Pritchard. "She's taller than Doreen was." She held out a winter coat in almost-new condition. "Might need to let down the hem a bit . . . but it should fit her nicely."

There were exclamations of commiseration and comfort as mothers gathered around the forlorn figure of a woman who would never see her daughter married with a family of her own, would never enjoy her grandchildren. Mrs. Angus, who is always fully aware of what is going on around her, whispered to me, "I don't think this is a good idea, Poppy. How will she feel when she sees one of the schoolgirls in the village wearing one of Doreen's dresses? I know I couldn't stand it."

Mrs. Martin, her spectacles halfway down her nose, a sheaf of lists in her hand, joined us. "She's right, Poppy. I can understand why Mrs. Newcombe is doing this, because she is a generous soul. But . . . can you imagine how she'll feel when she sees someone walking ahead of her up the High Street in Doreen's favorite coat?"

Mrs. Newcombe lifted the suitcase up onto an empty table, sliding her hands across the latches to open it. The women stood in a silent group, as far away from her as they could get, careful not to catch anyone's eye. Mrs. Pritchard, who had been presented with Doreen's red coat, looked down at her shoes, blinking away tears and shaking her head.

I walked over to Mrs. Newcombe as she raised the lid of a perfectly packed suitcase. "Thank you for bringing these over, Mrs. Newcombe. It is very generous and thoughtful of you. But something just occurred to me. Would you be prepared to give us permission to ask the vicar to run these over to Harrowdean? They have a lot more girls of Doreen's age than we have in the village staying at the hostel there. You know, the munitions factory girls? What do you think?"

She hesitated as she looked down at the suitcase, laying a hand on a layer of tissue paper. "Oh, I hadn't thought of that."

"They all have to be up ever so early to go to work, those girls. And with the colder weather coming, they could probably do with some nice warm clothes."

She nodded, gazing down at the half-open case. "Yes, yes, you are right." She smiled down at the top layer of clothes, her hand stroking the smooth fabric of a rich royal blue worsted skirt that shouted "prewar." "Doreen did so love her clothes. Her father said she had far too many of them. I just wanted to make sure young Yvonne had her red winter coat." She turned and nodded to Mrs. Pritchard. "That shade would look lovely on your Yvonne." She closed the lid of the case. "Thank you, Miss Redfern, it *is* a good idea. Will you see to it?"

"I would be pleased to." I followed her to the door, opened it, and stood aside to let her pass.

"If you would just return the suitcase when you have delivered the clothes, I would appreciate it," she said, and walked off down the street.

THEY SAY THAT the garments of the dead reveal a lot about who they were. I carried the suitcase into the village hall's storage room and started to sort through Doreen's clothes. They were of good quality, and because she had had a lot of them, they didn't have the drab, overworn look that most of our clothes did these days. It is a good thing Doreen was an only child. We only children are always given so much, I thought as I sorted winter clothes from summer frocks. A baker couldn't possibly afford to clothe a large family to this standard. I put aside Doreen's summer frocks and concentrated on repacking the suitcase with cashmere sweaters, beautifully cut skirts, dresses, and suits. Then I started to put away her summer clothes, for the exchange in May, in the large chest of drawers we use for storage.

I folded the last frock. It was a lovely rose-and-cream georgette silk with a flared skirt. As I carefully shook out the skirt, a folded piece of paper dropped out of its pocket.

I picked it up. It was folded in four and the words "To My Doreen" encircled in a lopsided heart were printed in ink on the outside quarter. The last thing in the world I wanted to do was read a love letter to Doreen Newcombe. It was, most probably, from Brian Chambers, who had asked her to marry him on his last home leave and had died weeks later at El Alamein. I turned the folded paper over. On the other hand, this letter might be from someone else, written recently—perhaps days before Doreen had been murdered.

I don't know how long I stood there, holding the folded paper, trying to decide whether I should read it or not.

"It's pandemonium out there." I jumped as Mrs. Ritchie, the village schoolmistress, and Mrs. Angus put their heads around the door. "It seems that all their boys"—Mrs. Ritchie jerked her head toward the raised voices behind her in the hall—"need size eights and there are only size tens, nines, and sixes. Mrs. Martin asked if you would go through the box of shoes set aside for summer and see if there are any winter ones mixed in. I'll give you a hand if you like." She came into the room and I thrust Doreen's letter back into the pocket of the dress and laid it on top of the others in the drawer.

"Of course we can have a look, but I think they are mostly canvas shoes." I closed the drawer and helped her tug out an old lidless trunk from behind Mrs. Martin's desk.

"We've already been through that trunk; there's nothing in there for winter." Mrs. Angus looked tired and dispirited. Doreen's mother arriving with her daughter's clothes had reduced Little Buffenden's already keyed-up mothers to a collective hopelessness.

The rest of the afternoon passed without any of the usual arguments that desperate mothers on the lookout for clothes for their children were often reduced to.

"I am utterly relieved to report that after three years of war, the mothers of Little Buffenden can now manage to attend a clothes swap without any serious fallings-out," I said to Granny as I sank down into the sofa and kicked off my shoes.

"And I am sure it was because you were there to help smooth things along, my dear. Thank you."

"Or perhaps they were all on their best behavior because Mrs. Newcombe donated Doreen's entire wardrobe to the clothes swap. It was heartrending to see her, Granny. She is so completely devastated."

Granny's head bent over her knitting as she counted stitches. "Yes, there is nothing more terrible than the loss of a child."

MRS. NEWCOMBE'S FACE as she had walked away from the village hall, and a love letter to a dead girl, made me a preoccupied companion as Sid and I turned into Streams Lane that night. On our last loop of the night's patrol I was still lost in my thoughts. I couldn't decide whether to retrieve the letter from the village hall storage room and hand it over to Inspector Hargreaves, or just leave it in the pocket of Doreen's dress, where it might be read by its next wearer. I made intermittent *mm-hm* noises throughout Sid's lecture on ground artillery as I argued with myself.

We were almost to the wooden bridge in the lane when Bess, who had run on ahead, started to bark: loud and staccato—her alarm bark.

"Strewth." Sid put his hands over his ears. "What a bloomin' racket—it goes right through your head. Can't you get her to be quiet?"

I hurried forward to the edge of the deep stream that bisected the farm's cow pastures. Leaning out over the bridge, I shone my torch down into the water—trying to train its beam in the direction of her frantic barking. I couldn't see Bess, but her yelps were coming from underneath the wooden bridge, which amplified them like a loud-hailer. It was futile to call out to her, but I did anyway. "Come, Bess," I shrieked over a further volley. "Come, Bessie, good girl." I whistled, but it only served to increase her volume, making me even more anxious. Something was not right. "She won't come." I turned in panic to Sid. "I think she's stuck—maybe she's caught up in the weeds. You have to help me, come on."

"No flippin' fear of me going down there. That water must be freezing. I don't want to catch pneumonia, thank you very much." I pushed him out of my way and scrambled down the side of the steep bank to land booted feet in the water. It was extraordinarily cold. Crouched low, I trained the beam of my torch under the bridge, cursing its ineffectual light.

The water was swirling around my legs, fast and strong. I still couldn't see Bess, no matter where I shone my torch. Panic almost submerged reason: she weighed only twenty pounds; she could be caught in the swift current and swept downstream. "Bess," I called into the darkness, wading forward, water up to my knees. "Bessie, come on, girl." For the life of me I couldn't see her, but her shrill barks bounced off the bank and the wooden roof of the bridge overhead in short, sharp bursts.

I shook my worse-than-useless torch in exasperation. What a

ridiculous thing it was! And then its feeble beam picked out the outline of my little dog's head, her long ears pricked forward. She appeared to be standing on a large boulder yelling at something with such intensity that her forepaws came up off the boulder with each effort.

Bending under the low beams of the bridge, I sloshed toward her, the leather soles of my boots slipping on the round stones of the stream bed. As I got closer I could see that her ruff was up from the base of her neck, down her spine, to her tailless rump, which was wagging in furious agitation.

"Bessie, how on earth did you manage to get up there?" The water was frothing around the base of her boulder and was well over my knees. I slipped on the slick stones of the stream bed and went down on one knee, making me gasp with shock: the water was like ice. I reached out an arm toward her, but she completely ignored me.

"Why on earth do I bother?" I shouted at her in frustration. "You are the most obstinate and annoying dog." I righted myself and took two more wading steps, and then I saw why she was so upset.

In the light of my torch, not three feet away, a bloated white face, its head pillowed on the pebble bed of the stream, turned to gaze up at me. Long dark hair streamed like ribbons in the current. How I managed to keep walking forward I simply don't know. I took two more steps until I was half crouched over the submerged body of Ivy Wantage.

Bess scrambled around on her boulder until she was as close to me as she could get. "It's all right, Bess, good girl. You found her, didn't you?" The little dog squirmed up into my arms and covered my face in kisses. She was soaking wet. "Good girl, clever girl. Well done." I dropped my face into her ruff to block the sight of Ivy's drowned face. "Oh, Bessie, oh, Bessie." I was shivering all over. Holding her in my arms, I started to back up.

Above us on the bridge I heard Sid's booted feet pacing up and down. "Sid," I called. "Sid, come down here, quickly."

"No fear, Miss Redfern." I've noticed that Sid always becomes more Biggles when he doesn't want to do something. "I can't bally well get wet at this time of night—I'll get bronchitis. Wait a mo'; can't you just pick her up and bring her back?"

Pick her up? My shock at finding Ivy was so great that for a moment I imagined that Sid was suggesting I carry her heavy, waterlogged body up onto the stream bank.

"Sid, it's Ivy. I've found Ivy!"

"Ivy? What the heck is she doing down there at this time of night? It can't be her. She went over to Lower Netherton to see her auntie yesterday evening."

"Is he really this dim?" I said to Bess. I could feel my self-control beginning to snap—my voice was almost strident. "Ivy's *dead*, Sid. She is *lying* under the bridge in the stream *drowned*, and she is *dead*." Nothing would make me shine a light on her poor face again.

"Who?" he wailed, and, God forgive me, I cursed in a way my grandmother would have been mortified to hear.

"How many bloody people do you think are under this damned bridge with me? I'm talking about Ivy Wantage, for Pete's sake. She is down here drowned in the stream."

Silence, and then: "Well, you had better get out of there."

However dense he was determined to be, his advice to get out from under the bridge was sound. Tucking Bess under my arm, I turned and waded forward. Seconds later I was being helped up the bank by Sid. His face was ashen in the light of my torch.

"Is it really Ivy?"

I was drained, utterly exhausted. All I could do was nod. "Good girl, Bessie, good dog," I kept saying. A warm tongue licked my hand. The familiar comforting gesture helped me to gather my wits.

"Sid, run up to the farm and tell Mrs. Wilkes to phone Constable Jones. Tell her that Ivy Wantage is lying under the footbridge. Tell her that Ivy is dead."

He started to panic. "Oh no! She can't be. You are sure she is . . . dead?" He raised both hands and shook them in distress.

"I am quite sure, Sid. Now, go . . . *run*. I have to stay here with Ivy."

"I can't leave you here, Poppy. Major Redfern would have my guts for garters."

"For heaven's sake, Sid, just go!" And off he went. I could hear him half running, half walking along the footpath to the lane. As his footsteps disappeared into the night, I noticed that he had slowed to a walk.

IT SEEMED TO me, as we sat on the bank of the stream, that Bess and I kept vigil forever. Cold, lonely minutes ticked silently by as the moon came out from behind the clouds and shone down on us. What had Sid told me the RAF call a full moon? A bomber's moon. I almost laughed. "All we need right now is an air raid, Bess." I was on the edge of hysteria.

How long had Ivy been under the bridge? Perhaps she had never reached her aunt's house; maybe she had been here since last night. And why hadn't her aunt reported her missing when she didn't arrive in Lower Netherton? I remembered that Mrs. Wantage's sister was a silent woman not given to much chat; possibly she had assumed that Ivy had decided not to visit after all—she probably didn't even have a telephone in her cottage.

Bess stiffened in my arms and her ruff came up as she growled, pricking her ears forward to listen. Mr. Wilkes's voice broke the silence, then I heard the higher pitch of his wife's, and it sounded as if their cowman, Percy, was with them too. Constable Jones's West Country burr lifted above the others—he always put *R*s in where they didn't belong. "Yurr two come along ur me. No, Sid, norrt you. Yurr stay here with Mrs. Wilkes." Their voices fell silent. And in my shivering shock I heard another voice, cool, calm, and supremely collected: *Blimey, dahling, you Little Buffenden people are in a pickle now. Looks like you have some sort of lunatic loose in the village.*

I got up and stood swaying on cramped wet feet. Ilona was dead right. Another thought came to me. It didn't matter who had written to Doreen and encircled her name with a heart. If it was Brian, he was long past caring about this world. I had no right to conceal the letter; I must take it directly to Inspector Hargreaves.

SEVEN

Mrs. WANTAGE DID NOT COME THE NEXT MORNING TO make beds and run the vacuum cleaner around our house complaining about dog hair. The lodge was miserably still and silent as I made my way downstairs at half past ten that morning to make my report to Detective Hargreaves.

"I think my granddaughter is still suffering from shock, Detective, so I hope you can make your questions brief. I can't imagine why this couldn't wait until tomorrow." Granny's gentle voice still managed to make her point.

"Granny, I'm fine. Really I am."

"You are very far from fine, my dear. And the inspector has agreed to keep this meeting brief, haven't you, Inspector?" Hargreaves nodded his heavy head. His doleful hound face wore a concerned expression as he flipped open his notebook.

"Just briefly, in your own words, Miss Redfern, tell me what happened last night."

"Whose words would she be likely to use, I wonder." Granny had not been this acerbic for years: violent murders in a small community do more than lengthen the gossiping queue at the local shops.

I took a sip of the hot tea she placed in my hands; it was sickly sweet, but I made myself drink it. Then I related the events of the previous evening, being careful to keep my account concise and clear, the same facts that I had given to Constable Jones last night.

When Hargreaves had finished writing, I asked, "How was she killed, Inspector?"

"She was strangled . . . same way as Miss Newcombe."

"With what?" It was out before I could stop myself. Granny made a moue of disapproval.

"With a tie—looks like an American Air Force tie, or something closely like it."

Something closely like it? It was either an American Air Force tie or it wasn't. The Americans were apparently far better kitted out than our Royal Air Force, or any of us, for that matter. An American Air Force tie would have been the first thing investigating police would have noticed.

"Do you know how long she had been there . . . under the bridge, when I found her?"

"Too soon to say with any accuracy, but judging by her appearance, a day, maybe two."

Her body just left there under the footbridge in the middle of the stream. I ducked my head so Granny wouldn't see my tears and call the interview to a halt.

"What on earth was the girl doing out at night, alone? I heard she was supposed to be visiting Mrs. Wantage's sister in Lower Netherton." Granny was incredulous.

I kept my head down so I would not have to meet their eyes. As far as I knew, when Ivy went out at night, she was not alone; she went out to meet Joe Perrone.

Inspector Hargreaves must have caught my expression. "Anything you would like to say, Miss Redfern?"

I cleared my throat. "On the night after Doreen was killed, as I came up Church Hill on the last part of my patrol, I saw Ivy. She was with Joe Perrone."

"Were you on your own, and what time was this?"

"I am not quite sure of the time, but it was a bit before midnight. I had just said good night to my Home Guard escort, Sid Ritchie." Granny's sharp exhalation was audible. "I was just a few yards from our house," I explained to her.

"And did you speak to Miss Wantage and Sergeant Perrone?"

"Yes, briefly. Ivy had brought flowers to put in the place where she thought Doreen had died. She was very distressed and so I walked her home. The sergeant came with us, at least as far as Smithy Lane where it Ts into the road to the gate guard for the base." Granny drew in a breath; there would be more to come on this later.

I waited for Hargreaves to write all this down, and then I told him about the letter that had fallen out of Doreen's dress pocket. He didn't say a word but jammed his hat on his head and opened the front door, motioning me to join him before Granny had time to object. I tried not to catch her eye as we disappeared through the front door, but I knew she would be waiting for me when I got back.

We drove over to the village hall, and I unlocked the storage room door.

"Why do you have a key to the storage room?" he asked.

"It's my grandmother's key. She organizes the clothes exchange and the jumble sale with Mrs. Martin and Mrs. Ritchie."

"Who else has a key?"

"You will have to ask Mrs. Martin."

I pulled open the drawer, lifted out the top frock, and slipped my hand inside the pocket of its skirt. There was nothing there. In my surprise I looked down into the drawer at the neatly arranged skirts and dresses.

"It's not here," I said.

He thumbed his hat back on his head and looked at me as if assessing how much the shock of my finding a murdered body had addled my wits.

"You're sure you put it back in the pocket of *this* dress?"

"Yes, I was interrupted, and I pushed it back in the right-side pocket of this skirt, until I decided whether I should bother you about it."

"Why wouldn't you bother me?"

"Because it might have been a letter from her fiancé. He was killed in North Africa a few weeks back." I felt his eyes on me and looked up. He was watching me, and his expression was no longer kindly. I struggled on. "I-I-I thought that it was private business and then . . . I thought it might have something to do with her murder." I felt hot and incredibly stupid—it was so wrong of me to have concealed evidence.

"Did you read it?"

"No."

"What made you change your mind?"

"Finding Ivy . . ."

"You finally understood, quite rightly, that this situation wasn't yours to judge. Who interrupted you when you were standing here with the letter? Names, please."

"Mrs. Ritchie, the local schoolmistress—she always helps Mrs. Martin for the exchange and the jumble sales—and Mrs. Angus . . ." I didn't add "the butcher's wife," because it sounded so melodramatic.

"I would be grateful if you would not try to do my job for me, Miss Redfern."

We left the village hall and I trudged wearily back up the hill to my lecture on "being sensible and not taking silly risks" from Granny.

THE VILLAGE WAS humming like a hive of bees when I joined the queue outside Mr. Angus's shop to pick up our meat ration. Not the hypnotic sound of a working drone but the agitated buzz of bees in danger from a wasp's nest that had built itself overnight on the edge of their community and was threatening their existence.

"I knew those Americans coming here would do us no good."

"They say that Ivy's boyfriend, that Sergeant what's his name, had no alibi . . ."

"Constable Jones says she had been under that bridge since the night before."

"It's just like Jack the Ripper—he went in for mass murder, didn't he?"

Their anger and fear zipped up and down the High Street, in and out of the bakery and the newsagents like an electric current. Faces were tight, and arms folded. Little Buffenden was under attack.

"Constable Jones says Joe Perrone broke curfew on the base."

"I told you that American sergeant was the one who killed them."

"He must be an agile one, then; that fence around the airfield has got to be all of fifteen feet high and it's got barbed wire on top."

"How did he get out of flying missions?"

"He's not flight crew—he's a mechanic."

"That's right. Once they all take off on a raid, he can probably do whatever he likes."

"Well, it's a good thing they arrested him, then. Pity it took them so long."

IT IS A testament to my powers of persuasion that I set out on my ARP patrol that evening at all. Grandad met Sid at the back door when he arrived and gave him a few sharp words about my being left alone for any part of my patrol.

"What is the point, young man, of your escorting her in the first place, if you say good night and leave her to walk up past that churchyard alone? I should charge you with dereliction of duty. Except that Poppy tells me that leaving you at your house was her idea." I had expected Sid to pout, but he stood to attention and took Grandad's criticism with dignity, as any real fighting man would. He even snapped off some respectful "yes, sirs." And we were released after a few more minutes of caution and advice.

Is the entire village in either the Rose and Crown or the Wheat-sheaf? I thought later that night as Bess and I walked across the green toward the Rose with Sid marching alongside. The Rose and Crown, always the more popular of the two pubs with the locals, was packed. The farmers' wives who ran their farms with the help of the Land Girls sometimes pop into the Wheatsheaf and have a glass of sherry or a shandy in the lounge, as it is the more genteel of our two drinking establishments, but it is the Rose and Crown that is the heartbeat of Little Buffenden.

The door to the pub was wide open, the blackout curtain pushed to one side—I could have read a book out on the green by the light coming through the door. I pushed my way into the pub's smoke-filled interior. With the arrest of Joe Perrone, the lockdown on base had been lifted but no American voices could be heard in the pub. I elbowed my way through a crowd standing in the middle of the room.

"The good news is that they have him locked up—Emergency Powers Defence Act: police can detain anyone for however long they like on suspicion alone." Gladys Pritchard, in a bright cherry-red sweater, pulled a pint of best bitter and put it up on the counter for Mr. Angus. The butcher raised his tankard in his thick red hand and took a reflective sip before he continued. "He's not in Wickham jail, though, is he, Gladys? They've got him locked up on the base. Rightfully, he should be tried in our court since he committed a crime on British soil. They shouldn't be allowed to deal with it their way."

It's always a bit surprising when our butcher makes a public pronouncement of some length. He has a high-pitched wheezy kind of voice like an old squeeze-box, and he rarely says more than two or three words together. Angus took a long swallow of beer and looked around the bar for agreement. "He has to have a fair trial like any one else." And then, obviously feeling he had monopolized the conversation, he buried his nose in the rest of his pint.

"The vicar says that he will be dealt with just as fairly by an

American court-martial, but I don't believe that." Mrs. Pritchard, who had advised me to find myself a boyfriend on the base, put two frothing tankards down in front of Mr. Wilkes and Percy the cowman, who had helped Constable Jones pull Ivy out from under the bridge.

"Here, Percy," she said. "This one's on the house. Must have been a shock for you having to pull young Ivy out of that stream."

"It was a terrible thing." Percy's Adam's apple rose and fell as he sank half his pint in one long swallow. "Terrible, it were. She been strangled with . . . her boyfriend's tie." He glanced around, proud that he had vital information to share. "I don't hold with violence to women."

His observations were met with a chorus of approval. Percy was not a popular figure in our village—his past was a little too murky for that—but he was certainly voicing popular thought.

"That's right, Percy, never been anything like that happen here before."

Percy looked proudly around the bar again and added, "Not before . . ." He jerked his thumb toward the airfield.

"That's right, Percy, that's right."

Mr. Wilkes gave his cowman a nudge and Percy subsided into his beer. "No need to jump to conclusions." Mr. Wilkes was a peaceable man, and certainly not one to rush to judgment. "There has to be a full investigation."

A derisive snort from Bert Pritchard. "I always suspected that the arrival of those Yanks would bring disaster. I said so right from the start, didn't I, my love?"

"You certainly did, Bert." His wife wiped the counter down and set up two more pints of best bitter.

"War Office should send 'em all packing. What's wrong with our boys—why aren't they up at the airfield? Why do we have to have Americans?" Mr. Angus is hardly an enlightened soul, but then that's village life for you.

I pushed my way up to the long wooden counter of the bar. "Mrs. Pritchard— Please excuse me, Percy. Mrs. Pritchard, every time someone comes through the door they forget to close the blackout curtain. I know everyone is upset, but I will have to close the pub if this continues." Five or six heads turned apologetically to look at the door. I had pulled the heavy curtain closed across it when I had come in, but several people, on their way to the 'Sheaf, had left it wide open.

"I KNEW THOSE airmen were a bad lot," said Sid, who had been waiting outside for me. The pub was closed now, and the villagers were straggling home, and by the looks of things, some of them would be the worse for wear tomorrow.

"Good night, Mr. Angus. Please remember your blackout when you get home!" I called to our portly butcher as he wandered across the road on unsteady feet toward his cottage. He waved his hand in reassurance and fumbled in his pocket for his latchkey.

"No respect, none of them—the way they jaw on about what happened." Sid looked exhausted with grief. His Home Guard battle dress hung on him, and his gun seemed to weigh him down so heavily that his shoulders were slumped forward. "I grew up with them; Doreen and Ivy were like my sisters." His eyes filled with tears again, and I mustered the last remains of my patience. I had listened to and consoled Sid all evening. By the sound of his voice, he was crying again, and it took all of my patience not to be brusque with him.

I saw Ivy lying in the stream, her hair drifting around her head like pondweed. There was still a nightmarish quality to the memory of her face under the water. But like all nightmares, the image was fading, and I was left with a feeling of being not quite in the world of my village. I felt separate and distant from it—an observer only.

It was different for Sid; he was far closer to Doreen and Ivy, not just in age but in the enclosed way of village life. They were all connected, all part of a whole. Sometimes this sort of closeness is a burden: it is hard to lead a private life in Little Buffenden—everyone knows everyone else's business—but when times are bad, it is also a haven. In the past week the village had become a sanctuary of support for the Newcombe and now the Wantage family—all petty feuds forgotten, all differences forgiven. The American base had gone from being an exotic place in our narrow world—generously offering American candy, cigarettes, and a night out of dancing in Wickham—to being an alien, destructive force. Feelings were running high: outsiders must be shut out and kept out.

"They are holding a double funeral on Friday for Doreen and Ivy. Are you coming to it?" Sid blew his nose in an attempt to be coherent.

"Of course we are, Sid," I said as gently as I could. "Grandad is reading the lesson in church, and Granny is doing the flowers. I just wish there was more we could do."

He reached out a hand and put it on my forearm. "You *are* doing it, Miss Redfern—your family always have." A little shake of my arm. "Not like those stuck-up Bradleys. I just wish they would go away, don't you?"

"The Bradleys?"

"What?"

I summoned all my fortitude. "You mean the Americans, don't you, Sid? *If* Sergeant Perrone is guilty, and please remember he has not been tried yet, that doesn't mean the Americans wish us harm." I had found the lynch-mob attitude of the village almost as disturbing as the murders. "They are here to help us fight the war. Perhaps after a while, when all this is behind us, everyone will see it differently."

There was a long pause, and then he said, slowly, in a voice determined to be reasonable, "Yes. I understand what you are saying, and I hope you are right, I really do."

And on he went with his eulogy to two girls he had grown up with. But I wasn't listening. The upper-class drawl that I imagine for Ilona came into my head again. *Seems a bit obvious to me. I mean, if you are going to kill a girl, why on earth would you use your own tie?* Her voice was so real, so clear in its offhand observation, that I nodded in agreement. On the two occasions that I had met him, Joe Perrone hadn't struck me as being stupid. If anything he had appeared to be a man of above-average intelligence. Ilona was right: if Joe Perrone was the murderer, why had he used his own tie to strangle Ivy?

EIGHT

GRANDAD SHOOK HIS NEWSPAPER AT ME. "YOU WANT TO hoover in here again? You've only just turned the wretched thing off."

"I forgot to dust."

"God knows, I am not an unreasonable man, but for pity's sake, give the dusting a miss for once, would you please? I have to go to the village hall to brief the men on hand-grenade procedure in twenty minutes." His voice threatened like far-off thunder. I dusted carefully around him. Grandad's voice had barked across three fields in his hunting days, but I have never been bitten once, no matter how much he growls and bristles.

"Now that Ivy and Doreen's funeral service has been held, perhaps the village can start to return to everyday life," I observed as I dusted the Dresden shepherd and his pouting shepherdess. "German china," Mrs. Wantage would have said, and sniffed in disgust as she flapped her duster at them.

"Mm," and a shake of the *Times* was his only reply.

"Mr. Angus turned his old sow, Mable, into pork sausages and

I am going to make toad-in-the-hole for dinner tonight," I said as I moved behind his chair to attend to a more acceptable Royal Worcester ewer.

The sweetest smile that ever crossed a tiger's face beamed up at me. "Well done, my dear. There's nothing like a substantial dinner to lift morale."

My toad-in-the-hole has a leathery quality and is as heavy as lead, but Grandad says he thinks it's more substantial that way. He put down his newspaper. "All well in the village last night?"

"Oh yes, they are really very good about blackout these days. No complaints." In some strange way the murder of two Little Buffenden girls had made the inhabitants of our village consciously patriotic. They were determined to do their bit for the war effort as if their overdue diligence would somehow atone for Doreen and Ivy: no one cheated on their food rations or petrol coupons and not a single light could be seen after dusk.

"You will miss young Sid when you return to patrolling alone."

Oh no, I won't, I thought. Finally, I would be able to enjoy the solace of my patrols.

"Have they definitely charged Sergeant Perrone?" I asked.

He nodded, his face grave. "Yes, they have. The sergeant is facing a charge of first-degree murder." Before he returned to his paper, he said, "Are you sure you don't want Sid's company for a few more patrols?"

"Crikey," I said, imitating the voice Sid used for Biggles. "A little bit of Sid goes a jolly long way, you know. Things are either good or bad; black or white; English or American." And in Sid's Biggles voice again: "It's a piece of cake patrolling on my own."

He laughed at my imitation. "You have to admit that the boy has come a long way since he joined the Home Guard. He's much more . . . I don't know if I can use the word 'assertive,' but he has certainly come out of himself more. Being cooped up in that house with his mother fussing over his health is no way for a young man to live. He needs to get to know some of these American chaps— have a pint or two with them at the pub, branch out a bit."

I was about to explain how much Sid disdained the Americans and that a pint at the pub was his idea of consorting with the devil, when there was a light knock on our front door, sending Bess, who had been curled up in her basket, into a tizzy. "No one we know uses the front," Grandad said as if this was a reason not to answer.

We trooped into the hall and threw open the door, and there, standing on the doorstep, head bent to avoid the overgrown honey-suckle climbing over the porch, was Lieutenant O'Neal. I had seen him a couple of times in the village since our first meeting, enjoying a pint outside the Rose and Crown with his fellow officers. He had seen me too and had given me a salute—a rather ironic gesture that I had no choice but to acknowledge with an airy wave.

Grandad's response to seeing him on our porch was far more enthusiastic than mine, and Bess was almost beside herself. "Come on in, my boy, that's the way." Grandad adores real fighting men and had been hobnobbing with the American Air Force command-ing officer ever since our Yank invasion. The simple prejudices of those who believe one bad apple means the entire barrel is rotten are not for the Redfern family.

Lieutenant O'Neal stepped over the threshold into our humble front hall and took off his hat, passing the flat of his hand over per-fectly combed hair. He displayed the sort of grooming we had all enjoyed before the war, when an abundance of coal had produced copious amounts of hot water. But it was not his immaculately starched shirt and his faultlessly pressed uniform that we were happy to see. It was the genuinely pleased-to-see-you expression on his closely shaved face that made us welcome him so warmly.

O'Neal's pristine appearance made me realize how much of a fright I must look wrapped up in a faded pinny three sizes too big for me, with my hair in pigtails and tied around with a frayed old scarf.

"It's Lieutenant O'Neal, isn't it? We met when you first came to the pub, didn't we? You must have been flying a lot; we hear those planes take off every evening." Grandad ushered the lieutenant into our drawing room. As Mrs. Glossop had prophesied, Bert Pritchard had refused to serve the Americans in his pub when they had first arrived, until my grandfather waded in on their behalf, and the Rose and Crown had been full of American airmen until they were confined to base after Doreen's death.

The lieutenant was holding a large bunch of roses, which I recognized came from my grandmother's beloved garden at Reaches; their fragrance filled the hall, the blooms still glistening with dew. "Oh, how lovely, Granny will be delighted!" I said as he filled my arms with them.

"They are for you both, Miss Redfern, a sort of roundabout present from your grandmother's garden."

Glad to get away to do something about my eccentric appearance, I said something about a vase. I trotted down the hall to the kitchen, where I put the roses in a sink full of water and pulled off my pinny and scarf.

Granny was pottering around in her victory garden. "We have a visitor from the base, Granny. He brought us some of your roses."

As I waited for the kettle to boil, I unplaited my hair and quickly combed it through with my fingers. I could hear Granny taking off her gardening boots in the scullery, and feeling a bit dithery, I laid the tray, made tea for her and coffee for us, and arranged the roses. Then I carried the lot back into the living room.

"Tea or coffee, Lieutenant?" I said as I set down the tray. "Thank you, again, for the roses. Look how lovely they are."

"You know you should really come up to your house and pick them whenever you want," Lieutenant O'Neal said as Granny arrived and buried her nose in the silken petals.

"Madame Hardy, Celsiana, and look how well the Blush roses are doing so late in the year. It's the heat; they love the heat." She smiled at O'Neal. "Thank you, Lieutenant. Someone at the base must be watering the beds."

As I dispensed tea and coffee, Lieutenant O'Neal said rather tentatively, "I am here with an invitation. Our commanding officer, Colonel Duchovny, asks for the pleasure of the Redfern family's company for dinner. And since none of us are flying tonight, would it be too late to ask for this evening—say seven o'clock for cocktails?"

And the three of us immediately accepted.

MY GRANDMOTHER LOOKED around her drawing room at Reaches and nodded at the flying officers gathered in a respectful and attentive group as they were introduced by their commanding officer. After a roll call of names and a sea of alert faces, two corporals circulated with trays of cocktails. I took what I recognized as a martini glass and glanced around what had once been our drawing room and was now the officers' mess for the base.

Without the Aubusson rug, the gray damask curtains, and our family paintings and furniture, the room looked nothing like our drawing room. The dismal collection of Ministry of Works utility chairs and sofas scattered through the room looked shabby and third-rate against the Wedgwood blue of the walls.

I took an experimental sip from my glass. Whatever it was, it tasted extraordinary, in a shuddery sort of way, like one of the vicar's housekeeper's herbal tonics. Lieutenant O'Neal appeared at my elbow holding a crystal bowl of nuts. "Good evening, Lieutenant," I said as I took a bolder sip from my glass.

Large, serious eyes sought mine. "Would it be too much to ask you to call me Griff?"

"Griff, is that your full name?"

He sighed. "In fact, it's Griffith, but Griff is what I prefer." He offered the bowl as I took another sip of my drink. "That's gin you're knocking back. Better take a handful of peanuts; otherwise you'll be flat on your face by the time we eat. Our commanding officer is a two-cocktails-before-dinner man, just like your Winston Churchill."

The roasted nuts were salty and sheer heaven. I could have eaten the entire bowl. "If this is all you give us this evening, it will be more than enough," I said, and he laughed.

"It's easy to forget what austere lives you have been leading here, when we have everything we need in the States. No shortage of anything," he said, and I believed him.

A tall man in dress uniform came in through the drawing room door and made his way over to us. Griff made introductions. "Miss Redfern, this is Lieutenant Colonel Franklin. I guess he is the American Army Air Force equivalent to a wing commander in your

Royal Air Force. He spent quite a bit of time in your country before the war."

Franklin had a deep voice with an extraordinarily slow way of talking that seemed to breathe palm trees and soft trade winds. "I'm from Florida, Miss Redfern. We take life at a gentlemanly pace in the South, unlike these upstart Californians." He winked at Griff. "My mother was a York: connected way back to one of your big aristocratic families over here." I nodded, wondering if he meant the Plantagenet royal house of York. I wasn't quite sure what I was supposed to say to this information, and since we Redferns don't know any old aristocratic families, I simply smiled and nodded as he launched into his ancient ancestry. Mercifully, he was interrupted by Colonel Duchovny with my grandmother in tow. "I was just telling your grandmother, Miss Redfern, that I feel as if I know you all through this beautiful old house. I understand Reaches has been the family home of the Redferns for . . . I'm not exaggerating if I say centuries, am I?" he asked Granny.

"Three centuries, Colonel, through both good times and bad. The colonel is fascinated by the history of the house, Poppy."

Granny is far better informed on the ancient lineages of families that died out centuries ago, and I was only too pleased to introduce her to the genealogist Franklin, and escape to say hullo to our vicar, Cedric Fothergill. He is also my boss, I suppose, since it is he who runs the ARP in our district.

I think Mr. Fothergill is probably one of the most irreverent of reverends when you catch him in his private moments. He was having a moment now with a large glass of scotch and soda. Village rumor has it that our vicar was quite a tearaway in his youth. He had wanted to be an actor in Stratford-upon-Avon with the Royal Shakespeare Theatre and had even auditioned and been accepted as a junior member. But his father put his foot down: there were to be no actors in Sir Wendell Fothergill's family, so Mr. Fothergill did what was expected of him: he read theology at Oxford and became a vicar, which is what the third sons of baronets are supposed to do. Before the war he was the director, producer, and wardrobe master of the Little Buffenden and Lower Netherton Players, whose notable hits, *Lady Windermere's Fan* and *Lord Arthur Savile's Crime*, were due to both his directing and his acting skills.

I have never seen Mr. Fothergill without his clerical collar, but I can easily imagine him dressed in a black velvet doublet with a starched Elizabethan ruff at his neck and a black pearl earring in one ear, standing center stage as Duke Orsino, and he does a very credible Rosalind if you half close your eyes.

"You look very festive, Poppy," he said, lifting his beaky nose out of his scotch and soda. "That shade of blue suits you."

"It's very old," I said, which was crafty of me, since he is also a connoisseur of women's fashion between the wars.

"That is what makes it so beautiful. Prewar fashions are far more elegant than the skimpy little things I see women in today. The cut of that dress is superb—it's perfect for you." And almost immediately I felt myself become more graceful: a tall, willowy redhead elegantly dressed for dinner in London's West End circa 1930 and not an overgrown schoolgirl whose nighttime wardrobe usually includes heavy boots and an ARP helmet. His thoughtfulness is why I am very fond of our eccentric vicar.

More officers drifted over and formed a group around us. None of them, I noticed, as they referred to their few weeks on English soil, mentioned the murdered girls. They were far more interested in telling us about our beer.

"Two things I fell for immediately were your beer and . . . fish and chips," a pilot officer said, and his navigator chimed in, "And your movies. I am in love with Margaret Lockwood. I could listen to her all night."

"Not like James Mason." The pilot looked like he was all of eighteen years old. "I can't understand a word he says."

"That's because you're from Alabama." Another officer joined us. "We can't understand you either." Uproarious laughter—they were all so relaxed with one another, in a rather competitive way.

More cocktails were served, and the talk became louder and the laughter came a little more often, and just as I was beginning to really enjoy myself, I looked up and saw Fenella Bradley standing in the doorway of the drawing room.

Fenella has a perfect porcelain-white complexion and almost blue-black hair. With a voluptuous bosom, tiny waist, and rounded hips, she generally creates a stir wherever she goes, which she thoroughly enjoys. She stood quite still in the open door as Colonel Duchovny put down his glass and started toward her, and when all heads had turned in her direction, she walked slowly into the room and stood in its center.

"Colonel Duchovny." She smiled. Her lipstick, a deep, dramatic red, emphasized the curve of her sensuous mouth. "So sweet of you to invite me to dinner. My sister, Betty, is still in London—duty calls." She rolled her mascaraed blue eyes. She was in uniform and looked positively dashing. I noticed that Griff O'Neal's eyes were nearly popping out of his head, but he managed to stop himself from leaping toward her—just about.

Fenella saw me and inclined her head. "Poppee! Mummy told me that you are now Little Buffenden's air-raid warden—what fun!" She laughed and shrugged her shoulders. She certainly didn't make being an ARP warden sound like fun; she made it sound dull, which I suppose it really is.

Her eyes went to Griff O'Neal, standing next to me, and I knew she would lure him away to be fascinated. "Lieutenant O'Neal, we met the other night in the Rose and Crown. Nice to see you again," she murmured with a sideways glance through long lashes, as if they had enjoyed more than half a bitter. "How long have you known Poppy? We grew up together, always been great friends, haven't we, Pops?" She didn't make it sound like being my friend was much fun either.

"Poppy and I met my first evening here," Griff said. "It was dark, and it was late: we sort of bumped into each other." He smiled at me as if our meeting had been the most fascinating experience of his arrival. "It was quite an introduction." I was grateful that he stayed by my side and was not enticed away by Fenella's compelling brand of sex appeal. After a thoughtful glance at me, she drifted off to talk to a tall captain, who blushed with delight that she had chosen him, and I decided that I rather liked Griff O'Neal.

"Why didn't you tell me the other night that your grandfather owned this house? I felt like such a fool when I found out that the Redfern family has lived here forever."

I smiled up at him. "As you said to Fenella, it was quite an intro-duction. There didn't seem to be time to give you my entire family history." I wanted to excuse my ungracious behavior, but dinner was announced, and we walked in an informal group across the hall to the dining room.

"Beautiful staircase, Mrs. Redfern, is it Jacobean?" Duchovny asked, and Granny smiled with pleasure.

"It certainly is, Colonel, and there is an interesting story attached to it. Ask Poppy to tell you all about the Gunpowder Plot of 1605 . . . She knows the history of this lovely old building, and our wicked ancestors, better than I do." I could have laughed aloud; my granny had no doubt appreciated Fenella's arrival onstage—only an Edwardian woman could applaud another's sense of dramatic entrance. But she had obviously decided that Fenella had had enough of the limelight, and she knows how much I love the story, long enjoyed by the Redferns, about an ancestor who had been executed for treason. Several heads turned in my direction with the hope that a fascinating tale was about to be told.

"Is it true that one of your ancestors was executed for treason?" Everyone leaned forward. I am often tongue-tied in mixed company, and small talk is not something I am good at, but the history of our unorthodox ancestors makes for a good story, and I had enjoyed two very ginny cocktails. I looked around the table—Fenella was at the far end in deep flirtation with her tall captain.

"Yes, it is true. His name was Everard Digby. He was a young and very political Catholic. Everard and his wife, Mary, had converted to Catholicism, which in early-sixteen-hundreds England was a very chancy thing to do, since Henry VIII's departure from the Church of Rome eighty years before. Like many Catholics of his time, Digby hoped the new monarch, King James VI of Scotland, who became our King James I of England, would be more sympathetic to English Catholics since his mother, Mary, Queen of Scots, was not only a devout Catholic but one who had plotted all her life to bring Scotland and England back to papal Rome."

"Isn't she the one that was executed by Good Queen Bess for treason?"

"The very one. Mary was rather a tempestuous character: she was always in the middle of some scheme or plot, all of which failed.

"Unfortunately, the new king of England showed little tolerance for the Catholic nobility, and the persecution of Catholics continued. A group of young aristocrats led by Robert Catesby and including Everard Digby decided to assassinate the king and rid themselves of the strongly Protestant House of Lords at the same time. Their plan was that they would put King James's nine-year-old daughter, Princess Elizabeth, on the throne as the new Catholic head of state and rule as her protectors. They put barrels of gunpowder in the cellars under the Houses of Parliament to blow up the king and the House of Lords when Parliament reopened. Unfortunately for them, gunpowder in those days was particularly unreliable. The plot failed, and Everard Digby and his coconspirators were all herded up and executed."

"Off with their heads!" Tall, even for an American, Captain Peterson was a giant of a man. He threw back his big blond head and laughed at his joke.

"They were not quite so lenient in those days. I am afraid they were hanged, disemboweled, and then their bodies quartered and nailed up at the four gates to London as a warning—the penalty for high treason."

"You mean they really did that?" Disbelief and laughter echoed around the table.

"Yes, they really did that."

"And is it still? The penalty for treason," Griff asked, and I shook my head.

"No, of course not. We are not quite *that* savage!"

"I heard your grandmother say they took up the floorboards and the staircase to this house," Peterson said, leaning forward to look across me as he winked at Griff. "Why was that?"

"In those days if you were executed for treason, your family were also punished. Everything you owned was forfeit to the Crown. Apparently, Digby, at his trial, pled guilty and asked for forgiveness. 'I request that all my property might be preserved for my wife and children . . . I also request that I be beheaded instead of hanged.' Well, they were lenient with Mary Digby, but not with poor Everard."

"What happened to her, to Mary?"

"The local Protestants in the area couldn't bear to think that Mary would get off so easily. They took out the staircase and lifted the boards throughout the ground floor. It must have been awfully difficult to sleep on the joists, because they took all her furniture too—every stick of it. Years afterward a new staircase, the one you see today, was built."

"That's a really good story—do you believe it?" Peterson asked.

"Yes, of course I do. It is historical fact."

"That's quite a cautionary tale," Griff chimed in. "We must remember not to upset the locals—can you imagine eating dinner on just the joists?"

The table was beautifully laid with good-quality china; silver and crystal shone in the candlelight, and the generous dinner that was put before us was delicious.

"Must be difficult for your grandmother to see strangers living in her house." Griff's voice was pitched for only me to hear, and I was touched by his sensitivity.

"My grandmother might not look it, but she is quite a tough old bird. But it's her garden she misses the most."

In the center of the long, well-polished table were three arrangements of Granny's favorite Old Blush roses. She had smiled at them when she came into the dining room, as if she had been greeted by old friends, and I heard Duchovny say, "You know, if you would like to come up to the house and enjoy your garden, Mrs. Redfern, we would be delighted to have you here."

Granny's smile deepened. "How very kind of you, Colonel. I would love to. But I would have to bring the verger with me; it is as much his garden as mine."

"The verger?" It was quite clear that Colonel Duchovny had no idea what she meant.

"Our sacristan," explained Cedric Fothergill, who had been enjoying a perfect beef consommé as he listened to the talk around him. "The Anglican Church appoints a member of the parish who is responsible for the order and upkeep of the church buildings. Kind of like a butler but with gravedigging responsibilities!" There was a ripple of laughter around the table. "Our verger's name is Leonard Smith and he's also Mrs. Redfern's right-hand man, or was her right-hand man, in her garden before . . . well, before you lot arrived."

"Your vicar is quite a character. He's nothing like how I imagined a vicar in an English country parish would look." Griff was thoroughly enjoying himself. He sipped his wine and gazed across the table at Mr. Fothergill.

"How *does* a vicar in a country parish look?"

"Short, balding, fat, and jovial was what I had in mind. Why isn't his wife here—they can marry in the English church, can't they?"

"Yes, but Mr. Fothergill chose not to marry. His house is kept for him by Mrs. Martin. She is the parish's pillar of strength: caring and kind, but with boundless energy and frighteningly efficient."

"So, why hasn't he married her?"

I laughed at the idea of Cedric Fothergill marrying the rotund and matronly Mrs. Martin. "She's at least sixty. But there *is* a rumor." I lowered my voice. "Apparently, Mr. Fothergill fell in love, about ten years ago, with a dean's daughter. She was young, pretty, and loved the theater (one of our vicar's passions), but when Mrs. Martin said she did not think she could possibly share her vicarage with another woman, Mr. Fothergill hesitated for a little too long and the vicar's daughter did rather better for herself and married a bishop. I have no idea if this is true or not."

"Jilted!"

"I don't know about that. He just chose not to lose Mrs. Martin." I didn't add that Cedric Fothergill possibly prefers a life of untroubled comfort over the ups and downs of passionate love.

Talk around the table, led by my grandfather, had returned to the topic of our ancient Gothic church and its charming old Georgian vicarage.

"Colonel Duchovny and I were wondering if we might arrange for some of his officers to come to Sunday service at Saint Bartholomew's. Cedric, what do you think? It might go some way to mending the relationship between the village and our American friends." My grandfather and Colonel Duchovny had had their heads together after Ivy and Doreen's funeral, and I realized that this dinner had been cooked up as an opportunity to discuss how best to heal the rift in our Anglo-American alliance.

"I think it is a splendid idea." Mr. Fothergill spoke around a large mouthful of succulent beef. "We could do Sunday lunch afterward."

What on earth is he thinking? I asked myself. Who is going to cook this Sunday lunch and what on earth are we to eat? I couldn't see how we could measure up to the kind of hospitality we were being offered this evening—except perhaps for the gin.

Grandad put down his glass and looked at his wife for her support. "We could certainly ask two or three of you over for luncheon after Matins. My dear, do you think we might fit that many in our dining room, with the Rev of course, and perhaps"—he glanced at Fenella—"you and your parents might like to join us."

Fenella looked up from an intense conversation with the very southern Lieutenant Colonel Franklin. I didn't think she looked too enthusiastic. Sunday lunches after morning service were hardly what she and her family were used to. The Bradleys have always kept their relationship with the village formal, preferring the sophisticated company of more elite families in the county. I suppressed a giggle at the thought of Fenella and her snobbish mother eating lunch with us—they might have graced us with a visit to Reaches, but they would hardly be enthralled with lunch at the lodge. But the idea was taken up with enthusiasm by Cedric Fothergill and my grandmother.

"Perhaps it's too soon for us to try and mend bridges. I don't think I would be very forgiving if my daughter had been murdered by a Yank. I can't imagine any of us will ever be welcomed in the village again," Griff O'Neal said in an undertone to me.

"I think"—I chose my words carefully because things were going so swimmingly, I really didn't want to ruin it—"that given time, things will improve, but it would be a good idea not to flood the village with men from the base for a week or so. At the best of times Little Buffenden is insular, and it was hard for most of the villagers to accept even the idea of an airfield here, let alone an American one. But I like the idea of Sunday lunch after church. I just can't imagine who would do the cooking!" It would certainly not be something we could ask of Mrs. Wantage. "I am more of a toast-and-jam sort of cook, and Granny is even less talented." I didn't mention how disappointed these Americans, with their flown-in beef, would be to eat shepherd's pie with minced gristly mutton.

"I'm a great cook," he said as he finished his wine with a flourish. There was not a shred of modesty in his announcement, and I laughed. "I love to cook. Back home in California I was taught by our Mexican cook—tamales, pozole . . . you name it. It just went on from there!"

"What about an English Sunday lunch? Ever made roast beef and Yorkshire pudding?" Then I heard myself. "Not that our ration books could stretch to that sort of fare. We haven't eaten beef for months—years even."

"Roast beef? Sure I can, and what's more, the United States will be providing the beef. But what the heck is this Yorkshire pudding? Sounds like something our lieutenant colonel would approve of."

Even I could manage to make Yorkshire pud. "It's a Sunday lunch tradition: the perfect accompaniment to a roast," I said.

"Good, then let's get this idea rolling: I'll see you on Sunday morning. We can make lunch together."

I was so pleased that I blushed—a thing I hadn't done since I was sixteen.

NINE

"I AM QUITE SURE I DON'T WANT TO SPEAK OUT OF TURN." MRS. Glossop pressed her lips together and I bit the inside of my cheek to stop from smiling, because Mrs. G. specialized in the inappropriate. "I have the utmost respect for Mrs. Redfern, and the Reverend Fothergill. But . . . I think it's a huge mistake to start encouraging these Americans to be part of our village, so soon after what has happened here. And on a Sunday, too."

I wasn't too sure what Sunday had to do with it, but I was brought up to be respectful to my elders, and this morning Mrs. Glossop was looking particularly peevish. I waited politely for what was to come. "The people in this village have been pushed to the end of their endurance, Miss Redfern. It would be wrong to start behaving as if nothing happened. Don't they have their own padre up at the base? Surely, there is no need for them to come to our place of worship . . . where the offended parties might have to see them."

I could see that if Mrs. Glossop had her way, we would live in a state of silent enmity with our allies for the rest of the war. "A man has been arrested for both murders, Mrs. Glossop. He happens to be an American, which is unfortunate. But the rest of the men up at the base are innocent. And some of them are Episcopalian, which I believe is their version of our Anglican Church, so I think the Christian thing to do would be to welcome them into our community." I could almost hear Mr. Fothergill tittering at my lumping our low-key Anglican attitude to religion in with the many complicated sects, factions, and offshoots that America apparently tolerated—if Captain Peterson was to be believed.

Her mouth was as tight as a button mushroom as she put down the aerogramme letter forms I had ordered on the top of the counter. "That'll be one and sixpence for the aeros and another two and six for the postal order. Four shillings altogether, if you would be so kind."

I counted out coins and her hand came down to stop them from spinning on the smooth wood of the counter with such finality that I knew she was far more annoyed about Grandad's Sunday-lunch-after-church idea than I had first thought. But I didn't want her to lead the village in a witch hunt against the Americans either. "Sergeant Perrone has been detained on suspicion of murder, but he has not yet been tried and found guilty. None of us can be sure that he killed Doreen and Ivy. I hope he gets a fair trial," I said in what I felt to be a conciliatory and reasonable tone. She didn't care for it.

"He's being *court-martialed*—not tried in an English court, which he should be after killing two English girls."

"Either way, he is innocent until proved guilty . . ."

A sharp intake of breath from Mrs. G. and I looked up to find her watching me intently. "You don't believe he did it, do you?"

There was no point in denying it. "I don't see how he can have done *both* murders. After Doreen's death all the Americans were confined to the base. You have to hand it to them; their security is amazing. Have you seen the perimeter fence that encloses the entire base?" She stared at me, her face like stone, so I explained. "He would have had to climb a ten-foot woven wire fence crowned by four or five strands of barbed wire."

Fierce little eyes bored into mine. "Who, then? You are not going to suggest it was one of *us*?"

Why not? I wanted to say. Why were *we* so above reproach?

Her stare was so intimidating that my voice almost shook as I answered her. "I am not suggesting anything, Mrs. Glossop. I am only supporting my grandparents' decision to try and heal a rift by including the young men up at the base in our village community. That is of course if they want to be part of it. After all, they have come to help us win this war, haven't they?"

I heard the breath hiss out of her like an old bicycle tire with a puncture, and her face became thoughtful as she folded her arms underneath her nonexistent bosom. "All right, then," she said as she tucked her chin down into her neck and pondered the alternatives. "So, if you're so keen on finding a culprit off base ... what about that Mr. Ponsonby? Him who has retired, so he says, from London. Lives on Water Lane in the little house below the doctor and Mrs. Ritchie."

I knew where Mr. Ponsonby lived. And I am quite sure my jaw must have dropped, because it had never occurred to me to cast around for a culprit who had not come from a family born and bred in Little Buffenden. But that's Mrs. Glossop for you, and she represents the majority in our village. You are an outsider if your family doesn't go back at least four or five generations. Newcomers are politely greeted and then, equally politely, excluded.

I was about to say, What rubbish!, when I remembered that Mrs. Glossop's voice is listened to in this village and that it carries weight. But what was far more intriguing to me was that she evidently had information, and if I was respectful and patient, she would share it.

"Mr. Ponsonby?" I saw his pink, shiny bald head with its neatly clipped fringe of iron gray hair and his tidy, almost obsessively neat appearance. Always on the periphery of village life, Mr. Ponsonby, since he had joined our stiflingly close community, had wandered around its edges like a timid heron—cautiously wading through our ditches and fishing about on the edge of the village pond. A self-proclaimed naturalist, he acknowledged the bustle of village life with a diffident "Hullo" followed by polite excuses to hurry homeward. I had met him once or twice just after he had moved here. I know how wretched it feels to be awkward, and there was a hesitancy to Mr. Ponsonby's reserve that made me protective. I strongly objected to him being drummed up as a suspect by Mrs. Glossop simply because he was—like the Americans—an "outsider."

"He spends a lot of his time out at night." She had him pinned as the sort of man who lurks in the dark—awaiting his chance to kill young virgins.

"But that's because he's a naturalist and a *bird-watcher*. I saw him just the other night with his field glasses around his neck and one of those little canvas folding stools under his arm."

"Bird-watching at night—with field glasses? For crying out loud—I have never heard anything so barmy in all my life!" She heaped scorn on me, her eyes screwed up in disgust, as if I were witless.

I swallowed and braved further contempt. "I believe he specializes in owls, Mrs. Glossop. He is observing the hunting and domestic habits of a family of tawnies." The last time I had seen him, he had been almost conversational about the owl and its remarkable hunting skills.

A derisive laugh. "Field glasses at night—pull the other one."

"There are such things as night-vision binoculars and cameras. Mrs. Glossop, they've been around for years. They are quite common—expensive but easy to come by."

She breezed past this useful information with a wave of her hand. "Doesn't go to the pub, doesn't come in here for tobacco. Only person in the village who has his paper delivered. He's *that* secretive, I wouldn't be at all surprised if he's up to no good," came the inevitable response of the unenlightened.

"Or he's a reserved man who has an interest in owls."

We had reached a stalemate. Her mouth twitched, and she narrowed her eyes. "Why don't you ask Audrey Wilkes about your Mr. Ponsonby, then?" she demanded. My disbelief in Mr. Ponsonby as malevolent had goaded her on, so determined was she to win her point. "He gave her the fright of her life the other evening. She was walking down the lane and out he pops from behind a tree."

"He was probably—"

"Bird-watching? Oh *yes*, I'm sure he was. Watching young girls, more like. He followed Audrey down the lane, and every time she stopped, he did too. She said her nerves were in shreds by the time she got to the gate of the farm. And then do you know what he did?"

There was an unwholesome gleam in her eye. I wasn't too sure I wanted to hear what Mr. Ponsonby had done.

"He climbed over the stile right there by Bart's Field and ran off into the woods. Probably thought Audrey's dad might come and ask him what he was playing at."

Her dark, beady little eyes were shining with triumph, but I didn't care. All I was thinking was: what on earth was Audrey Wilkes doing out late at night in the pitch-dark and where had she been?

I decided not to respond to Mrs. Glossop's thoughts on what Mr. Ponsonby had in mind for Audrey, and she smiled as if she had more than scored her point.

SUNDAY CAME, AND I leafed through *Mrs. Beeton's Book of Household Management* and ran through her recipe for Yorkshire pudding again. It seemed so easy that I was sure I had overlooked something. The vicar and Dr. and Mrs. Oliver were coming to lunch after Matins to meet three American officers from the base.

The Olivers must have hugged themselves in delight when they were invited, because we were having roast beef! No one in our village had sunk their grateful teeth into a sirloin of beef since 1940. Batting for America were Captains Robinson and Lombardi; Lieutenant Davis, the navigator who was in love with the actress Margaret Lockwood; and of course the self-proclaimed chef extraordinaire: Griff O'Neal. We would be stretching the limits of our dining room to the bursting point. "Friendlier that way," Grandad had said when Granny worried about being tightly packed.

I took stock of my kitchen inventory: a mountain of peeled potatoes and unstrung string beans; a panful of chicken stock I had been worrying over all morning; and two apple pies sent over by Mrs. Martin, the housekeeper at the vicarage, which would sadly have to rely on Bird's custard powder made with half water, half milk—we hadn't had cream for months.

My new American friend was bringing the beef, and I sent up a fervent prayer that he really knew how to cook and it hadn't been the martinis talking.

Dressed in my best indigo georgette dress and wrapped carefully in a clean pinny, I was tasting the stock for the third time when there was a knock on the scullery door. Before I had a chance to open it, Griff O'Neal was in the kitchen. He had a bulky parcel wrapped in butcher's paper in one hand—it had to be the sirloin—and a bottle of red wine in the other, which he waved in a cheery salute. It was quite clear that Lieutenant O'Neal had not spent the morning on his knees in our beautiful old church.

Whether it was the scent of fresh meat or an unrestrained passion for the lieutenant, I have no idea, but Bess managed to make a complete fool of herself. If I owned a stopwatch I could have timed her noisy greeting as lasting well over three minutes. When she had calmed down sufficiently, Griff waved away a cloud of dog hair and said, "Mmm—smells delicious in here. That must be your chicken giblet stock."

"Yes, it was quite easy." I tapped *Mrs. Beeton* to acknowledge her instructions. "I had no idea you could make stock from just simmering giblets and vegetables. We usually use Bisto." I pointed to the packet of gravy mix I had on standby in case the stock turned out to be awful and watched him shudder as he sniffed the contents of the package.

"And does *Mrs. Beeton* tell you how to make Yorkshire pudding?" He was clearly intrigued, and I knew that he would probably find our favorite Sunday dish disappointing.

"It's just a batter of flour, milk, and dried egg. Cooked in the fat from the beef in a hot oven."

"What did you say?"

I repeated the ingredients.

"Dried egg? Are you kidding? That stuff is disgusting."

"Welcome to England."

"You don't have real eggs?"

"Yes, but we use them for special occasions." We had exactly four eggs in the pantry; Granny had traded a pot of honey from our hives with Mrs. Pritchard for half a dozen eggs the day before yesterday.

He snorted. "When I am about to roast six pounds of prime rib, swiped from our mess unit, it is a special occasion, believe me. Get out your eggs. I'll replace 'em."

As he bustled about our rather primitive kitchen, Bess and I watched—she in case he dropped something edible, and I in sheer awe of how at home he was with a knife in his hand. He was deft and skillful as he chopped carrots, celery, onion, and parsley to a heap of little pieces all the same size. He looked up to answer my silent question. "Mirepoix," he explained. "The base for the wine reduction—sautéed in . . . any butter?" I handed him a plate of bright yellow margarine and his top lip lifted in a sneer. "Oh Lord, I'll just have to forgive you," was all he said as he flipped a spoonful into a pan and added the vegetables to sauté. When he was satisfied with their condition, he opened the wine he had brought with him, poured a splash into two glasses, and then emptied the rest into his pan and put it back on the stove top. "Let it come to a boil"—his voice was reverent—"and then immediately turn the flame low to . . . the gentlest simmer." He put a lid on the pan and cocked it to half cover. "We'll just let it stay that way for an hour . . . and then we'll turn up the heat and reduce it down to the essence of deliciousness." He lifted his wineglass, took a sip, and turned to me. "The secret is this: we'll add your reduced stock to my reduced wine, and then . . ." He laughed as he stirred, as if this was just a madcap game and there weren't at least six people trying to concentrate on their prayers during morning service because their mouths were watering in anticipation. "And . . . reduce the whole thing all over again!" Another sip of wine. "And it will be"—he held his glass as a toast to his efforts, his face quite serious—"exquisite."

"What do you mean by reduce?" I had to know; all this chopping and dicing had made me feel a bit breathless.

"It means quite simply we *boil* it down. You have no idea how heavenly a slow-cooked wine-and-vegetable stock and meat stock taste when they are reduced together. Trust me, it's sensational."

Before I could sip the wine in my glass, he raised his. "To the roast beef of Old England!"

I raised mine in salute. "To the roast beef of Old England cooked by a Yank!" I responded, and we drank.

"This is quite good." I was surprised he was using reasonably good claret just for gravy. You can laugh about the way we English cook all you like, but we certainly know something about wine.

"Never make a wine reduction with an inferior wine—it would be a complete waste of time," was the only explanation I was given for his profligate use of excellent claret before he turned his attention to our oven and decided that it would do.

A short, hardworking silence as he concentrated on seasoning the beef—but not so short that he didn't have time to explain his passion for cooking as we allowed heat and a combination of perfect ingredients to do their magic. And explain he did. I was used to the natural reserve and minimal chitchat of Englishmen—not that you would ever find an Englishman in a kitchen to begin with. But Griff had no such inhibitions. With very little prompting from me, he told me about his childhood in California—I think it is somewhere on the other side of their vast country; at any rate he referred to the ocean a lot.

"My grandfather was the one who planted our citrus groves. He had come to the area prospecting for silver in the late 1890s. He knew nothing about farming when he first started because he was a city boy from San Francisco." He laughed. "What a character he must have been in his youth: a real Mick on the Make. When I knew him he was just a doddering old chap who drank whiskey for breakfast. He learned about growing orange trees as he went along. You see, everything was there: good dirt, plenty of water, and sun all year round. My pop was the one who really made everything profitable after the Great War. So, now we have tripled our acreage and we just specialize in oranges."

"Just oranges?" I didn't want to sound too easily impressed.

"Yep. Have you ever had freshly squeezed juice from an orange picked right off the tree?"

I couldn't imagine anything more decadent. "No, never. Ours comes in a tin, and that was before the war."

"You don't mean a can, do you?" He waved away canned and tinned juice with a shrug of his shoulders. "You haven't lived if you haven't woken up in the morning to a glass of freshly squeezed juice," he said, and I realized that he was right. I hadn't lived. I had spent nearly all my life in Little Buffenden when I was not seques-tered in a dreary girls' boarding school interminably preoccupied by keeping out of the way of popular girls like Fenella Bradley, my inability to embroider or play field hockey, and the correct way to eat fish. Apart from my two weeks in London for ARP training, when my sophisticated uncle Ambrose had taken me to a nightclub, I was, essentially, as green as a cucumber.

As Griff diced, simmered, and basted, our talk turned to the village, and then, as if it was quite natural, to the murder of the two girls.

"Assuming, of course, that whoever killed Doreen must have killed Ivy too, I just can't see how Joe Perrone could have killed Ivy. After Doreen's body was discovered, the next morning no passes were issued to anyone—we were confined to base; no one could possibly leave. But on the night of Doreen's death, since there were no missions that night, there were something like a hundred and forty-two men, all of whom were at leisure to leave the base or attend our party before the gates were locked at midnight, which is normal curfew time."

"What happens if someone is off base after midnight?"

"They are considered AWOL."

"AWOL?"

"Absent without leave. It's a serious offense. Days in the lockup, court-martials, and, now we are at war, imprisonment." A pause for consideration. "Didn't your Royal Navy hang men for being absent from their post?"

"I have no idea."

"Anyway, getting off our base after curfew can't be done. There are two entrances, the one that leads from the airfield to your old house, which is now the officers' mess, and the main entrance outside of the village, which Ts on Smithy Lane; both are heavily guarded." He sipped wine and thought for a moment. "The entire airfield is surrounded by a perimeter fence: ten feet high with barbed wire that only a fool would try to climb, and it's patrolled by guards, night and day, with dogs. Getting off base without a pass is impossible. And Joe didn't have one after we were all confined to base. I should know."

I looked away, not sure how much to confide in this man, however much I liked him. But information about the base and its security since Doreen's death helped clarify my thinking about the time I bumped into Joe and Ivy in the churchyard. I knew Joe Perrone had not broken curfew on that night. After we walked Ivy home, he had apologetically left me at Smithy Lane because he had minutes to go to midnight, when he would break curfew. The next morning the base locked down and no one could leave. It seemed to me that anyone in Little Buffenden and on the air force base could have killed Doreen, but the Americans had a collective alibi for the time of Ivy's death. "I only met Sergeant Perrone twice, and he didn't strike me as a man who killed girls," was my only response.

"D'you know something? *We* are in a perfect spot to find out more—you know everyone in the village, and I know most of the guys on the base." He looked up from basting the beef; the smell was sensational. My mouth watered, and Bess made a wistful moaning sound deep in her throat.

I wasn't at all sure how to respond to his open invitation to "find out more." "Help me with the table?" I asked, and he followed me through into our dining room.

He polished a crystal glass, held it up to the light, and polished some more. "Flowers?" he asked as we finished setting the crystal and silver.

I led the way out into Granny's vegetable garden. "Our gardens are very practical these days. I'm afraid we don't have space for flowers." I looked at rows of vegetables where I had picked green beans for lunch just hours ago.

"I should have brought roses. What are those?" Griff pointed to wild willow herb growing in the ditch. "Those purple things are nice." And then with a complete change of tack: "It must have been terrible to find your friend under the bridge like that."

"It was." I knew I would never forget her face, ever. At night I slept with the windows closed, the blackout curtain pulled tightly shut, and the light on. Wasteful, I know, but it was terrifying to wake up from seeing Ivy's drowned face to a pitch-black room.

"Were you alone?"

"No, Sid Ritchie was with me." Loyalty prevented me from saying that he had been worse than useless. "I was thinking . . ." I was embarrassed to go on because this was none of my business, but part of me was intrigued by his straightforward curiosity. "It seems rather unfair to look to the base for a killer when there was such tight security. Sergeant Perrone was arrested, or detained for questioning as they call it, almost immediately after Ivy was murdered. I can't imagine that the police spent much time on their inquiry."

He was watching me closely. "That's exactly what I thought too! Of course, no one in Little Buffenden wants to believe that someone they know killed two innocent young girls, loved by everyone, and with their lives before them."

"But they weren't loved by everyone," I said, rather rashly, thinking of Audrey Wilkes and her bitter dislike of Doreen. "Or at least I don't think Doreen was."

"You don't say." He was instantly alert. "You mean Doreen was

actively *disliked*? Now, don't you think *that's* interesting? Who *dis-*
liked her?"

I found myself telling him about my conversation with Audrey
Wilkes the night after Doreen was killed, and he hung on to my
every word.

"You should check into this Audrey," he said as we walked back
into the kitchen to find a vase for his wildflowers. "Go and talk to
her some more. There's information to be had there."

And right on cue I heard Ilona say, *Well now, sweetie, it looks as
if my help is going to be redundant now that you have this gorgeous
chap to chew things over with.*

TEN

———

LL OF US COMFORTABLY FULL OF A LUNCH THAT HAD AL-
most made our Little Buffenden guests feel that there was
no such thing as war, talk around our dining table turned to America. Captains Robinson and Lombardi were from Boston and Man-
hattan, respectively, and Lieutenant Davis from a place called
Philly. Dr. and Mrs. Oliver were seasoned travelers but had never
been west to America and were curious about where they were all
from.

As Grandad got up to pour the last of the wine, Mrs. Oliver
turned to Griff. "My husband tells me you are from California,
Lieutenant O'Neal. Is that where you learned to fly?"

"Yes, my father taught me."

"He was in aviation?"

"Sort of. He was a barnstormer in the 1920s. He belonged to an
outfit that traveled to little towns around the country and did flying
demonstrations. He was quite a daredevil. He owned an old World
War I Curtiss biplane and he would do some pretty wild things:
spins, dives, loop-the-loops, barrel rolls, and flying through barns."

Mrs. Oliver looked a bit puzzled. "They would open the big double doors at each end of a large barn, and then the pilots would fly their planes right through them." I could tell he was enjoying himself.

"Good heavens, how terribly dangerous!" Mrs. Oliver was enthralled.

"Yes, so dangerous that in the end the government put all sorts of restrictions on flying aircraft. My dad was offered a job as a US mail carrier, but he turned it down because he missed California. He flew his Curtiss back home and settled down to grow oranges on his father's farm. But he kept his plane, and when we were kids, he taught me and my brother to fly."

"How old were you when you first flew?"

"Before my older brother did." Griff laughed.

"And why was that?"

"Because I was tall for my age, taller than he was, and I could reach the controls."

AFTER OUR GUESTS had made their way home, I spent the rest of the afternoon writing a thrilling description of Ilona being hunted through the darkened streets of London, in the blackout. I was so involved with the world I had created that I almost forgot my planned visit to the Wilkes farm.

I tore myself away from Ilona's heart-pounding fear as she dodged through the backstreets of Soho, went downstairs, and pumped my bike's tires, Bess standing very close to me—her head on one side listening intently to the breathless, squeaky sound of the pump. And then we went over to the vicarage to see the vicar's housekeeper, Mrs. Martin, who was full of the village gossip about our first Sunday lunch.

"Mrs. Oliver told Mrs. Angus, who told Mrs. Glossop, who of course told everyone, that she had never met such politely mannered and charming young men!" Her eyes were shining behind her spectacles. "I told the reverend that if we wanted the village to stop being so suspicious of every American that went into the pub for a pint, you should have invited Mrs. Glossop right off the bat."

"Ah yes, Mrs. Martin, but if we had done that, you see, she would have sensed we needed her approval and would have worked hard not to give it. Granny says that we should do a couple more lunches and then invite her. She will be frantic to give her approval by then."

Mrs. Martin folded her arms underneath her motherly bosom and shook her head. "Whatever you do, Miss Redfern, do not put her back up. Mrs. Glossop is a wonderful ally but a formidable opponent!"

Then I asked her my favor, and with her agreement, I got on my bike and cycled down Water Lane and on to Wilkes Farm.

It was a beautiful afternoon: clear blue skies and a gentle breeze; the air smelled of that particularly sweet, nutty scent at the end of summer, when the wheat is ripe in the fields and the grass is dusty along the side of the roads. I had to go over the wooden footbridge to the Wilkes farm, and the hairs rose along my arms as I heard the hollow echo under my bike's wheels. "Stay with me, Bess," I called out to her. I didn't want her to go investigating again. I don't think I will ever feel the same about that pretty bridge we used to fish from when I was a girl.

It was Audrey who opened the kitchen door, when I had expected her mum.

"Hullo, Audrey," I said as brightly as I could in the face of a formidable frown. She stared at me in silence, holding the door ajar, as if I were going to try to burst my way in.

"I have just been talking with Mrs. Martin, and we need your help. Do you have a moment?" She obviously did have the time, for behind her I could see another magazine spread open on the kitchen table. She said nothing at all as she waited for me to state my business.

"Perhaps I could come in?"

She considered for a second or two. "No dogs in the house."

No fear of that, I thought—Bess was busy inspecting a hedgerow; she knew when she wasn't welcome. Having established the rules, Audrey pulled back the door just wide enough to let me squeeze through.

"I know if I take you into my confidence you will respect the need to keep this just between us," I began, avoiding the slate gray stare of incurious eyes. I swallowed and continued. "But the vicar, Mrs. Martin, and I are planning an air-raid drill for the village, and for it to be effective, it will not be announced." Her stare made me feel awkward, so I said, rather unnecessarily, "You know, as a practice."

She sighed as if I were wasting valuable time. But I was determined not to be shut down.

"Would you consider being there at the church crypt before the drill, to help Mrs. Martin with the children? Most of the families at that end of the village are mums with very young children and with no help since their husbands are away." It seemed strange to be asking this taciturn individual for help with children, but I had been assured by Mrs. Martin that Audrey was patient with toddlers. Her eyes flickered, and she raised her heavy brows a fraction as if she suspected that I was taking advantage of her good nature. "You see, we are arranging for the air-raid siren to sound, so everyone in the village will think it is an actual raid. So, the children—"

"Will be frightened," she finished for me as if my blathering was holding up her day.

"Yes, that's right . . . so would—"

"I be there ahead of time. You already said that."

"I know it's a lot to ask, but—"

"All right, then."

I managed to stop myself from overdoing the thank-yous. But I was nowhere closer to a conversation about Doreen and Ivy, which was the purpose of my visit.

"Originally, you see, it was Ivy's job to be at the crypt to help. And now, of course." She nodded, and to my amazement her face flushed and she looked distressed.

"Ivy was good with kids," she said to the kitchen table.

"Was she really? I had no idea."

"She would have made a good mum."

"Oh," was all I could say, stricken by the thought that Ivy had been denied the chance to marry and have a family of her own. "I know it will take Mrs. Wantage a long time to get over it . . . Ivy's death."

"Her murder, you mean. And she won't." It was final. And then to my surprise: "Cuppa tea?" I nodded, dumbfounded that Audrey apparently approved of Ivy Wantage. So, it was just Doreen whom she didn't like.

I watched her as she moved to the kitchen range and slid the kettle onto the hob. I'm tall for a woman, but she is at least a head taller than me, and her shoulders are as broad as a man's. If she didn't frown and glower quite so much, she would be what my grandmother would call imposing. A long, strong arm lifted up to the tea caddy. She turned and took down cups and saucers from the Welsh dresser. Every movement was unhurried and carried out in complete silence.

As I stood there wondering at her callous indifference to Doreen's death and her compassionate acknowledgment that Ivy had been denied her future life, I realized that I tended to avoid Audrey. And I knew I probably wasn't alone: it's difficult, and quite frankly off-putting, to try to engage someone who never volunteers anything other than a curt yes or no and who avoids any conversation, or if she does respond, does so with relentless contempt. Most people just give up, I suppose. But I had come here to find out, if I could, what Audrey thought about the deaths of Doreen and Ivy, and to check on Mrs. Glossop's story about her peculiar incident with Mr. Ponsonby. She had unbent enough to talk about Ivy, so I decided to persevere with our conversation and see where it led.

She put the tea things down on the kitchen table and moved her magazines off to one side. The page had been open to another article about Errol Flynn. "Did you see *Captain Blood*?" I asked her, determined to keep things light and conversational. "I thought it was wonderful."

She nodded. "He's Australian, you know," she said as she poured tea through a strainer into the cup in front of me.

"Oh really?"

"Educated in London at some posh boarding school; that's why he talks so nicely. But he was chucked out for stealing." And the taciturn and grudging Audrey took off on a detailed history of Errol Flynn's background, or rather his swashbuckling love life— for Flynn it seemed was as much of the great lover offscreen as he was on. She listed every single one of his films and affairs with costars, and her opinion of each one. I just sat there sipping my tea and nodding along, waiting to introduce the topic of Mr. Ponsonby and his odd behavior when he had followed her down the lane.

"He tried to join up." Audrey had reached that stage in his career when Flynn, now an American citizen, had become one of America's top matinée idols. "But he had a bad heart, so they wouldn't take him. He also had VD—because he had a problem, you know, with women."

She laughed at my shocked expression, and I realized that this was the sort of thing Audrey did. Every so often she would say something so crude, so without grace or consideration, simply to embarrass. She liked to shock; perhaps it was the only way she felt she could get attention.

But I wasn't going to let a little thing like that put me off. "Funny how some men have that sort of reputation," I said. "Sounds like Flynn was not the sort of man you would want your daughter dating!" I laughed, but she did not join me. "Someone told me that Mr. Ponsonby has a bit of a wandering eye too." I leaned forward, feeling like a cheap gossip.

"Someone!" she jeered. "That would be old Ma Glossop. So, that's who you've been talking to, is it?"

"Did he really follow you down the lane at night, in the dark?" I asked, eyes wide, avid for information as if I were as bad a gossip as our postmistress.

"He didn't follow me . . . he was lurking."

I shook my head as if I couldn't believe what I was hearing. Audrey didn't need any more encouragement.

"I came down Water Lane and saw him cross the road toward Bart's Field. He scurried into the hedgerow by the gate. When I walked past he hid behind a tree; it was quite pathetic, really. I stopped and waited for him to speak, but he just stayed there. So, I said, 'I know you are there, Mr. Ponsonby, there's no need to hide.'" She folded her strong arms across her chest and was scowling across the table at me as if I were Ponsonby. It was the sort of frown that made you want to rush in with an apology.

"What did he say?" I almost whispered it.

She shook her head. "Nothing, but I knew he was there, hiding. The coward."

"You weren't scared?"

"Of that little pip-squeak!" She laughed—it wasn't a pleasant sound. "He wouldn't dare try it—not with me." She was completely sure of herself, and I envied her, her self-possession.

"He came out onto the lane after a bit; he was carrying his camp stool and his notebook—he looked downright silly. He muttered something about owls and then beetled off, up the lane. I think he's touched. Everyone knows bird-watching is done during the day." She drew a breath. This was probably the longest speech I had heard her make—except for her lecture on Errol Flynn.

"What do you think he was doing?" I asked.

She thought for a moment, as if this had not occurred to her before. "When a man goes in for lurking like that, it isn't for a good reason, that's for sure. I think he is one of those awkward types."

"Do you think he might have killed Dor . . . ?"

She shook her head. "How?" Her laugh was sarcastic. "Just how would he do that? Doreen and Ivy wouldn't have let a little creep like that anywhere near them."

But they might have been taken by surprise, I thought. He might have lurked in waiting and then crept up and strangled them from behind.

"When did this happen?"

"The night after Doreen was killed."

And what were you doing out and about at night when Doreen had been brutally deprived of her life in the churchyard the night before? I wanted to ask, and she answered me as if I had spoken the words aloud. "When it's this warm at night and I can't sleep, I go for a walk. Just up the lane and back. I sometimes see you doing your patrol. It's nice to walk at night, isn't it?"

My jaw dropped open. "But aren't you scared of, you know . . . whoever killed Ivy and Doreen?"

"No, I'm not." She lifted her arm, clenched her fist, and shook it: Boadicea advancing on the Roman legions on her shaggy pony sprang to mind. "If some Yank tried it with me, I'd give him what for." Her slate gray eyes met mine and she smiled at me—and this time her smile was inclusive and almost conspiratorial.

I WHEELED MY bike down the path from the Wilkes kitchen door and mounted it in the driveway. Bess came running up and jumped around to say hullo, but I was too preoccupied with the strange conversation I had had with Audrey Wilkes to pay much attention to her. As I pedaled down the lane, I think I was more confused than ever. I had always thought that there was something impassive about Audrey, often to the point of being rude. It's hardly encouraging if you call out, "Hullo, Audrey, how is your mum doing—over her cold yet?" only to be met by a blank stare and a snort of contempt. I could understand her disinterest in village goings-on— I don't have much interest in bingo, singing in the church choir, and celebrating May Day on the green either—but you simply can't live in Little Buffenden and ignore everyone.

Up until now, I assumed Audrey wanted to be left alone, and then, to my surprise, she had opened up and had launched into a detailed account of the life of a Hollywood film star whom she had studied as if she were going to sit an entrance exam. I couldn't put this more forthcoming version of her down to something as simple as my asking her to help us out at the air-raid shelter we had made in the crypt. But perhaps it *was* as simple as that. Perhaps Audrey rarely spoke to anyone in the village because we had taught ourselves to ignore her. I felt guilty, and, worse, I felt false. Audrey was a lonely girl who had immersed herself in the glamorous lives of Hollywood's movie stars because there were no friends in hers.

I pedaled miserably up the road and made a promise to myself that, if she was inclined, I would go out of my way to spend time with her. But however sorry I felt for this solitary young woman, I couldn't get her dislike of Doreen out of my mind. Could Audrey have murdered Doreen? She was certainly physically capable of doing so, but I found it hard to believe that she would have strangled poor little Ivy.

ELEVEN

I T WAS WARM IN THE ORCHARD AS I SCRIBBLED AWAY IN MY
exercise book, putting Ilona in more danger in the backstreets of
East London. Writing about murder and violence has a strong effect on the nervous system, and when a long shadow fell across my
exercise book, I nearly jumped out of my skin. But it was just Griff
O'Neal standing over me, holding Bess in his arms. Bess usually
doesn't like being picked up, except by me, and here she was
perched up there with her head leaning casually back against Griff
O'Neal's chest as if she owned him.

"You look busy," he said. He bent down to release Bess, and
his face was so close to mine that I noticed for the first time that his
hazel eyes had flecks of blue in them. His proximity made my stomach do a little flip, and I felt my breath catch. I looked up into his
large, clear eyes fringed by long, dark lashes. If the rest of his fea-
tures weren't so masculine, his face would be almost feminine in its
beauty. As it was, he was only the most handsome man I had ever
seen in my life. I turned my head away—writing about Ilona and

her string of glamorous admirers was having a ridiculous effect on me. I got to my feet, and to my relief, he did the same.

"Let's walk Bess up the lane and back, and you can fill me in on all the wonderful things Audrey told you about her secret life. I bet you're good at getting people to confide in you: you're such a good listener."

That's probably why you like spending time with me, then, I thought, as I brushed bits of leaf and twig off my slacks. And then I caught myself—I might not have Ilona's boundless confidence, but I must make the effort to be less self-critical. Granny has told me that I have a very nice face, and I know I'm a lot brighter than most girls of my age, so there was no need for a defensive attitude. I resolved to believe that this man was dropping in to say hullo because he liked me—because he might even find me attractive!

"What were you writing—your case notes?" he asked as we walked up the lane with Bess racing ahead to retrieve sticks.

I said yes, because I had no intention of telling him about my book. He was far too curious and would immediately want to read it, and I will never have nerve enough to let anyone do that.

"So, tell me about Audrey Wilkes, any development there? What d'you think *she's* all about?"

"She has a bit of a thing for Errol Flynn."

"Are you kidding me?" He was genuinely at a loss. Well, who wouldn't be? I have seen only one of Flynn's films, and he borders on the repellent. "Did you really say 'Errol Flynn'?" He stooped to pick up another stick for Bess. "He has a tremendous following in the States. I didn't even know the British knew who he was."

"Oh yes, we do. I think he is a terrible actor—and I certainly don't find him attractive," I said.

"Well, that's good, because I think he might be batting for the other side."

I had no idea what he meant. Americans use all sorts of interesting phrases and terms, and unless they are explained, you have no idea what they are talking about half the time, so I just carried on. "I think Audrey Wilkes is rather a curious type. She has the reputation of being a loner in the village: reserved almost to the point of rudeness. And . . . it seems she can be quite aggressive when she is annoyed." And I told him all about her exchange with Mr. Ponsonby, mostly because he is sharp about people, and because I really needed to run my thoughts about Audrey by someone else—someone who wasn't from our claustrophobic little community. Someone who came from a wider world who might have a different perspective on our village loner. To my disappointment he wasn't particularly interested in Audrey and her challenge to Ponsonby to come out from behind his tree. He was much more taken with our nocturnal bird-watcher.

"Bird-watching at night?" He ignored Bess, who was begging for another stick. "Didn't you say he was a newcomer to the village? How long has he lived here?"

"'Bout a year?" I frowned. Ponsonby was one of those men who sort of melts into the scenery. "No, hold on a moment, he came here at about the time we moved out of Reaches and down to the lodge, more like six months ago."

"Okay, Bessie." He leaned back to throw a stick for her, and I saw his face tighten with the effort of getting it over the hedge into the field. "And he *says* he's a bird-watcher," he said in a thoughtful tone as he watched Bess fly through the gate.

"*Is* a bird-watcher: tawny owls—there is a family of them in the wood next to Bart's Field this year." Once again, I found myself being protective of yet another village eccentric.

"Uh-huh."

"Bird-watching is the sort of thing city people do when they retire."

"At night?"

"Owls are nocturnal."

He lost interest in Ponsonby. "And old Audrey just gave him hell?"

"In her own subdued way."

"Good for her. I like a woman with spirit. There is nothing worse than a man who hides in hedges when he should be taking off his hat and saying a polite good evening." His face expressed admiration. "You Englishwomen," he said, and then he laughed and shook his head. "You're formidable, you know that, don't you? For-mi-da-ble." I must have looked surprised. "No, really, it's true. Some fella does something you don't like, you call him out, right then and there, or you grab him by the belt and toss him over your shoulder." Bess appeared with bits of shredded stick hanging from her lips and danced around us, barking like mad. "Even your dogs don't care how little they are; they just shout at you to do what they want. Okay, okay, Bessie."

We climbed the five-bar gate and sat on the top bar. Griff pulled two apples from his pocket and handed me one, and we crunched away in amicable silence.

"I missed oranges when I first came here, had no idea they were considered exotic fruit. But these apples are incredible, crisp and full of juice." He finished his in two more bites. "Must be the Irish in me, because I feel as though I've sat on this fence with you all my life, Poppy," he said, taking care not to look at me. It was the first time I had seen this serious and rather hesitant side to him. I pushed the hair out of my eyes and took a carefree bite of apple.

"Funny how that is, sometimes," was all I dare let myself say. Because it was true. I felt so completely at ease with him, as if I had known him for years. Not that sort of longtime comfortable knowing that you have with one of your girlfriend's brothers—or a boy you grew up with, like Sid Ritchie. But however at ease I felt with Griff, there was always that delicious little current of tension underlying our meetings, as if a hundred possibilities danced on the turn of a moment.

We threw the cores for Bess. And then, laughing at her ferocious greed, we jumped down from the gate and resumed our walk down the lane. The soft light of late summer shone through the oaks, turning everything a glorious golden green, and the rich leaf-mold scent of the hot earth as it cools under their shade was, to me, far more romantic than any Hollywood film starring an Errol Flynn who had lost half the buttons to his shirt.

"You can tell you are inland here," Griff said as Bess lost interest in us and dropped down into a ditch to lap muddy water. "There is that locked-in feel to the heat of the day. If I was home right now, I would go down to the beach and swim in the ocean. The waves are so powerful that you can coast in on the surf, right to shore." I wondered what it would be like to go swimming in a great ocean with this man.

We had arrived at the end of the lane and the gate into the orchard. I was about to say good night—I had to change into my uniform for patrol—when he took me by the arm and said, very seriously, "When a man hides in a ditch or cowers behind a tree, it doesn't say much about his character, Poppy, but I am sure you know that. So how about you give Ponsonby a wide berth, okay? I haven't met Audrey, but it sounds to me like a lumberjack would envy her physique. And however good at judo you are—black belt, is it?" I told him no belt. "Belt or no belt, it would be a good idea not to mess with Ponsonby—just in case. Who else do you have on your list of suspects?"

I hesitated. "Well . . . it's a pretty obvious choice—and by the way, I haven't crossed Audrey off my list, especially since she was out and about at night after Doreen was killed—but Percy Frazer, the Wilkeses' cowman, was pretty untrustworthy with young women a few years ago. I wondered . . ." Now I felt particularly silly. "If he might have, you know, gone completely bonkers and killed Doreen and Ivy."

He raised his eyebrows. "Bonkers? Is that the same as being a flasher . . . or is it worse than that?"

"A what?"

He looked momentarily at a loss. "In the States we call them flashers." When I shook my head, he colored at having to be more specific. "They, you know, flash . . ." He made a brief gesture as if opening a coat and closing it again.

I started to laugh. "Yes, that's right. We just call them dirty old men."

TO SAY I loitered on the other side of the stile that led to Bart's Field that night and the next one, and then, with less patience, the one after that as well, is an understatement. And just when I was about to give up and accept the fact that Mr. Ponsonby had transferred his attention from nocturnal birds of prey to those who favored sunshine, worms in the lawn, and crumbs scattered on the garden path, I was rewarded. As the moon came out from behind a cloud, I saw, scrambling nimbly over the stile I had stood sentinel over for three nights, the slight figure of Mr. Ponsonby.

With his camera and binoculars swinging from his neck, he made short work of the hill that led up to the wood where his tawnies lived. When I was sure he was not aware that I was following, I dogged his steps all the way to the edge of its tree line. I waited for him to unfold his camp stool to wait for his owls, and as if on cue, a long, low *to-wit-to-woo* echoed seductively from a large beech tree on the edge of the wood. If I was a bird-watcher, I would have pulled out my pencil and my bird journal right then and there, but Ponsonby pressed on into the wood without even so much as lifting his head. And I followed.

I love long walks in the woods on a hot summer afternoon, but there is nothing inviting about a wood at night. I was only a hundred feet in when I wished I could catch up with the tweed-clad figure ahead of me and fall into step beside him for company. Closely grown trees and heavy underbrush can be gloomy places even during the day, but at night with the moonlight filtering through the upper canopy creating shadows and dark hollows, it is an eerie and foreboding place to be. The path veered sharply to the right, and the man I was following was lost to view. As I went on alone, the only sound I was conscious of, when I stopped to make sure that I didn't come up too close behind Ponsonby, was the incessant soughing that might have been the wind in the trees, or the pattering of animal feet as hunter pursued hunted through the wood's ferny undergrowth.

The path straightened, and in a patch of starlight I was grateful to see Ponsonby's shadow moving ahead of me. My breath came a little more easily and my palms had just stopped sweating when the air was split by the eerie whistle of a night raptor followed almost immediately by a stricken shriek from a rabbit that had fallen victim to its penetrating beak and strong claws, but my naturalist hurried on as if he couldn't care less.

Our journey through the wood had completely unhinged my original resolve, and I was about to lose my nerve completely, when we broke cover into the reassuring moonlit expanse of Bart's upper field. My bird-watcher started up the climb of a gentle slope toward what was now the open land of the American Air Force base. The ground was still scarred and rutted with the tracks of machines that had leveled pastures for the airfield months ago. And there, against the sky, loomed the wire fence that separated England from America.

Ponsonby hurried out of the wood with an intensity of purpose that had me almost tripping over myself to catch up, but as he approached the slope, he slowed and, bent double, crept toward the perimeter fence, sending me flat on my stomach under the cover of a gorse bush. I watched him as he stopped some way from the fence and ducked down behind the bank of an old rabbit warren, long abandoned since the building of the airfield. Thank goodness I had come out tonight without Bess. Ponsonby's furtive scurrying would have been irresistible to her strong instinct for pursuit; she would have been on him in a flash and given us both away. Because that is exactly what Ponsonby looked like: prey. Crouched low, his head turning this way and that, he dropped to his belly and lay still before squirming forward, pausing for a second, almost as if to sniff the air.

Mr. Ponsonby, retired solicitor from London, was not quite as bland as he first had seemed. His arrival in Little Buffenden at the end of last year as the land had been leveled for the airfield was not a coincidence. His secretive and clandestine behavior was itself a giveaway. His reluctance to join in the simple village pastimes in our community was for a good reason. This was no bird-watcher! I could have hugged Mrs. Glossop a hundred times for her suspicious mind. How many nights had I walked past this man in the lane as he had crouched in hiding? I looked up again to find that my quarry had disappeared. If I was to find out what he was up to, I must not fall behind.

I went forward, keeping close to the ground, pausing every so often behind a clump of stiff uncropped pasture grass to lift my head. I saw his lean shanks only once before he disappeared completely. I wriggled up to where his rump had disappeared behind a clump of gorse and found myself at the entrance of a badgers' sett underneath the spread of a mature beech tree.

The sett was concealed under the lee of the bank and, though wide, was low in height. I craned my neck over the top of its grass-covered parapet: there was no sign of Ponsonby. Could he have possibly gone into the sett? European badgers are large creatures with robust bodies; short, powerful claws; and strong jaws; and although reserved in nature, would be formidable if you stuck your nose through their front door. Grandad had told me that badger baiting, although illegal, is still considered great sport in the out-of-the-way parts of Wales and Ireland. If Ponsonby had had the gall to cram himself into a badgers' lair, he must know that it had been deserted.

I raised my head again and looked toward the fence. I couldn't see Ponsonby at all, and this made me nervous. The last thing in the world I wanted was to turn around and find him standing behind me.

There was a spinney of birch trees on my left. Perhaps he was in there? If he was, he was most certainly watching me. Sweat broke out on my upper lip and my scalp prickled with fear. The thought of being watched by this man made my mouth as dry as cotton. Pull yourself together, I instructed. It was too late to worry about being caught by a man who had apparently vanished into thin air. I took a long breath to steady my nerves, switched on my torch, and shone it into the opening of the sett. It was quite empty.

I took off my helmet and inched forward on my stomach until my head and shoulders were inside its opening. A few more inches farther in and I noticed that the tunnel widened—considerably; its sides appeared to be squared off with small sharp chops in the clay and sand walls. There was an unnatural look to the squared-off walls. No animal could possibly have excavated these runs. Tunnels created and used by badgers would be more rounded, brushed smooth by the countless passings of hairy bodies. This passageway looked man-made, or at least enlarged by man. And if it was, then Ponsonby could easily have crawled through it just minutes before my arrival. I turned my torch upward; I could see the roots of the beech tree arching overhead, providing a strong support for the roof. This was an entrance into the airfield, created from an old badgers' lair and made useful.

I desperately wanted to follow Ponsonby, but not into this airless passage. A trickle of sweat ran down the side of my cheek and my hand trembled, causing the frail beam of light to dance along the tunnel as it stretched away into darkness. Was it my imagination, or did a cool shower of sand from the roof sprinkle down on the crown of my head? I had only my shoulders in the entrance, but before I could stop myself, I was inching backward until I was lying outside in the blessed cool night air, sweat dripping and chest heaving as if I had run for miles.

We often wonder if there is a limit to what we expect of ourselves when it comes to physical discomfort. I had just met mine. Nothing at all would ever make me venture into that network of dark tunnels. If Ponsonby had gone into the sett, even now he might be worming his way back down the main tunnel toward me! I must retreat as far away as I could so that I could watch to see if he reemerged.

Doing my best to be calm, I crawled and slithered on my belly into the shelter of the spinney and lay there, watching the entrance to the sett. I waited as the moon went behind a bank of cloud and emerged again. And just as it was about to repeat the whole business a second time, my tired eyes picked up on an outline above the entrance to the sett: the head and shoulders of a man as he emerged from the darkness of the bank below and got slowly to his feet. It was a fleeting moment, and then the shape sank below the brow of the bank and disappeared.

Ponsonby *had* gone into the tunnel! I waited a good few minutes until I judged he had retraced his steps into the wood and then crawled toward the sett. Ignoring its entrance, I went over the top of the bank above it and forward toward the American airfield.

Six yards, ten, I have no idea how many feet I crawled. I made my painful way on bruised knees until I came up close on the wire fence stretching away to my left and my right. I rolled over onto my side and looked around me, and as the moon swung out from behind a bank of cloud I saw the back entrance of the badgers' den: a dark shadow half-concealed by a thick gorse bush, and as I had hoped, it was on the other side of the fence. My hands shook with the excitement of my discovery: Ponsonby had used the abandoned sett to gain entrance to the airfield! He had widened it knowing that the roots of the tree would provide an overhead fortification that would prevent the tunnel from caving in.

I pressed my face against the wire of the fence. Smooth concrete runways shone pale in the moonlight, and squatting on their surface were the hulking silhouettes of American bombers. They were large machines, about the size of our RAF Lancasters. I smiled as I remembered facts and figures about the great British Lanc that I had had to listen to as Sid and I had walked our patrols together. What did the Americans call their bombers? Fortresses—we had seen them fly over the village most nights, escorted by the smaller, swifter Mustang fighter planes: the type that Griff flew. On the ground the bombers looked massive, so heavy it was impossible to imagine them airborne. I pressed my cheek up against the wire of the fence. There appeared to be even larger planes farther back on the field, but however hard I squinted and pressed my face against the fence, two gorse bushes obstructed my line of sight. Frustrated, I turned and made my way back to the wood. I knew that if I wanted to find out what Ponsonby was up to at the airfield, then I had to follow in his footsteps and brave the black stuffiness of the tunnel to reconnoiter on the other side of the fence, as he had done. But a more exciting thought brought me to a standstill as I retraced my steps through the wood: if a human body could crawl down the badgers' tunnel, then what was Ponsonby's secretive business at the American airfield? The first word that came into my head was: "spy." But, more important, if the tunnel was a viable thoroughfare, then anyone could come or go from the American base without being seen, whether there was a curfew and a heavily patrolled perimeter or not.

I couldn't decide which was the greater discovery: that Ponsonby made a habit of trespassing in the American airfield, or that anyone from the base, or the village, could come and go undetected.

TWELVE

I ALMOST MISSED SID'S COMPANY AS I SET OFF ON MY PATROL
the following night with Bess. At least if he had been with me I
wouldn't have been drawn into a conversation with Fenella Bradley. Both the Bradley sisters were on home leave from their arduous
life in London, and whereas they might condescend to talk to me,
they would never have deigned to pass the time of day with the local schoolteacher's son beyond a polite hullo.

" 'Lo, Poppy!" Betty hailed me as we met up on the village
green. Betty is the more agreeable of the two Bradley girls: she's not
quite as full of herself as Fenella. But, honestly, a little bit of Bradley
goes a long way.

"What are you up to, Pops?" Fenella chimed in as she gazed
thoughtfully at my helmet. "Patrol? I mean, is it really necessary?"
She shook her head and giggled. "I simply can't imagine an air raid
in Little Buffers, can you, Bets?" Betty shook her head.

So, we were safe, then—no air raids likely to happen in dear
old Buffers! I smiled and nodded my hullos and said absolutely
nothing.

"Do you have time to join us for a drink before your patrol?" Betty asked. "We are meeting a couple of American chaps at the Rose. Why don't you come along for a quickie with us—they are such fun!"

"She actually has an American boyfriend, don't you, Pops?" Fenella as usual was immaculately turned out—her shining black hair was arranged around her shoulders in soft waves, her perfectly plucked eyebrows arched as she looked me over. "Half the village are dating Americans, apparently—hasn't been so much going on in our dear little village for centuries."

I couldn't believe that she could refer to girls dating Americans without mentioning the horrifying incidents that had every one of us on edge. There is something remarkably cold about Fenella. I wondered if she had been staying up at Bradley Hall when Doreen and Ivy had been murdered. And since I found my dislike of her almost overwhelming, I wondered if she might possibly have a motive for murdering the prettier members of our village community.

"How's life in London?" I said the first thing that came into my head, and it was stupid of me to ask, because of course now I would have to put up with all sorts of bragging about nightclubs and ripping-good times at the Admiralty with senior officers. Talk to Fenella for two minutes and you would think this war had been arranged exclusively for her social life.

I was right. After a rundown of her busy and exciting nightlife, she ended with, "For heaven's sake, Poppy, you simply can't stay here buried in this little backwater for the duration. There must be *something* we can find for you to do in London—the Admiralty is desperate for help." Her cool blue gaze rested briefly again on my helmet as she tried to think of what that something could possibly be.

By the time she had finished making me feel thoroughly inadequate, my duties as ARP warden particularly futile, and yes, let's admit it, utterly green-eyed about her fabulously exciting London life, we had reached the pub. I was glad to see that neither of the two Americans the Bradleys were meeting was Griff, but rather Captain Maxwell and the tall, Nordic-looking Captain Peterson with the colossal shoulders and white-gold hair of a Viking, both of whom I had met at the Reaches dinner party and who had come to our last Sunday lunch.

It was gratifying to be greeted with such enthusiasm; it certainly gave Fenella something to think about.

"Miss Redfern—Poppy!" Captain Peterson cried as he got to his feet to tower over everyone standing at the bar. "Great to see you again—we were just saying what a delicious lunch we had at your place. Now, what'll you ladies have?"

"Unfortunately, Poppy can't stay," Fenella put in hurriedly. "She's on *duty*!"

Peterson had engulfed my hand in his and was still holding it. "Perhaps when you are off duty some night, you would join us for what you Britishers call a 'pint'?"

I said how lovely that would be, and then, wishing them all a pleasant evening, I left. More than anything I wanted to mull over my conversation with Griff earlier today when I had rashly filled him in about my adventure in Bart's Field when I had tailed Mr. Ponsonby.

"You followed Ponsonby?" He hadn't looked too pleased. "What made you do that?"

"He had no idea I was following him—I stayed well back."

"But he could be the Buffenden Strangler"— his name for our murderer.

"I am quite sure he isn't! But he *was* behaving suspiciously. Don't you want to know where he went?" I have to say I was surprised at his rather cross response. After all, this was real news and I wanted a good reaction, not this cautionary elder-brother stuff.

"Where?" He folded his arms and frowned.

"He went *under* the perimeter fence of the airfield."

Now I had his attention—though most fighter pilots like to think they have ice in their veins and are capable of a perfect poker face, Griff's head whipped round in a most gratifying manner. "*Under* the fence?"

I gave him a detailed rundown of the exciting events of last night in Bart's Field.

"A badgers' den?" he said as I ground breathlessly to a halt. "Are you sure? That would be a tight fit . . . for a man." He looked skeptical, almost disappointed.

"Do you have badgers in America?"

"We do. They're mean little things." I felt a moment of childish victory: here, for the first time, was something we English had, albeit a badger, that was bigger than its American version.

I drew myself up and looked him squarely in the face. "Our badgers are far from little—in fact, they are large. Most of them weigh in at fifty pounds, the males even more." I stretched my arms wide. "And their dens are extensive. But what is far more interesting is that this sett looked as if the underground passageways had been widened—widened by a human with a spade, not an animal with claws." I felt sure that this would get the response I was looking for, but Griff was being careful now: his face was quite expressionless. The sort of concentrated blankness when someone is determined not to reveal that they are thinking hard. "Ponsonby definitely went into the sett, because I saw him come out," I added, so he would understand the single-minded intention of my quarry.

He collected himself and smiled his undeniably charming smile. "Poppy." He put both hands on my shoulders and looked into my eyes. "A man has strangled two girls in Little Buffenden. Neither you, nor I, are quite convinced that it was Perrone, and yet you followed this Ponsonby into a wood, on your own, at night. Don't you see how crazy that was?"

I stepped back so his hands fell away.

"So, are you going to do something about him, or not?"

"You said he was a bird-watcher, right?"

"So, why would he crawl down a man-altered badger tunnel into your airfield, d'you think? Don't you see that *if* he can get in and out, *anyone* else can too? I think *that's* significant." I was not only irritated by his dismissive attitude; I was confused by his feigned disinterest.

"Yes, it was a great find, it really was."

How bloody patronizing could he be? I did my best not to get too hot under the collar. He took my silence as acquiescence.

"I want you to promise me you won't follow this man again." His face was so set, so closed up, that I had difficulty believing that this was my friend Griff O'Neal, the man who had positively egged me on to start my own clandestine murder inquiry.

He turned away to search for a stick for Bess, leaving me feeling as if my find was a threat to my personal safety and nothing more.

"Oh, for heaven's sake!" I erupted with my hands on my hips.

"Don't tell me that a man who has probably spent weeks scrambling in and out of your airfield might be the Little Buffenden Strangler, because that doesn't make sense at all."

"It most certainly does! Could you please find it in yourself to just stay away from this man—for me?"

"Bloody hell!" I said, because I was furious. "There has to be more to this than your stay-away-from-him-for-me answer. There must be a reason. Could *you* find it in *yourself* to tell me why?"

But he was having none of it. He smiled at me and shook his head—his hands in his pockets, his face regretful. And I ungraciously stumped off with a miserable Bess trailing at my heels.

"I don't know why I bother with this stupid investigation," I said to Bess as we clattered over the bridge. "I think I'll just stick to writing."

I GAVE GRIFF a wide berth; or rather, he gave me one. They were running missions day and night now as we stepped up our air raids on Germany. I heard their planes take off some afternoons as I hid out in the orchard and wrote about Ilona. It only took me three chapters to restore my sense of equilibrium and stop huffing over Griff's unreasonable and stodgy reaction to my triumphant find. When I had written away all my annoyance, I was ready to continue with my investigation. I needed fodder for my plot and I needed to find out more about my next suspect, Percy Frazer, and his dubious history. I went in search of Mrs. Glossop. If anyone knew about Percy, it would be our garrulous postmistress.

Once again, I was met with reluctance—this time from our village scandalmonger, of all people. She wasn't just reluctant either.

"No, we don't talk about Percy Frazer, Miss Redfern, because by and large he did his time, and his is a sad story. The past is the past; best leave it at that." Mrs. Glossop is the last one to let a subject drop. So, I waited her out.

"Well, I suppose there's no harm done in telling you that Percy was only a little lad—about eight years old he must have been—when he found his dad, as dead as a doornail, in the woodshed." I remained silent, and true to form, she redoubled her efforts.

"Ned Frazer was a drinker and a mean one. One Friday night, when he had been paid by whoever was stupid enough to give him work, he drank it all away at the Rose and Crown. Nothing unusual in that, and neither was there anything unusual in him going home to take his miserable temper out on his wife. Many's the time Mary Frazer wouldn't come into the village because Ned had given her a black eye. But that particular Friday evening, after he had come back from the pub, he must have decided to clean his shotgun, because he shot hisself—right through the head—and it were poor little Percy who found him."

I sort of knew all this about Percy's dad. There were two schools of thought in the village: either he had committed suicide in a fit of drunken despair, or he had accidentally shot himself cleaning his shotgun. Mrs. Glossop, I remembered, favored the second group: her view of most men was that they were a feckless and rather careless bunch who would dwindle away and die without the strength of a strong and practical woman in their lives.

I kept my face impassive and she fixed me with her uncompromising stare and continued with her story. "Mary Frazer had always been a bit of a strange one herself. Perhaps a life of poverty married to a brute of a man who one day ups and leaves you destitute can unhinge you. Anyway, she took to wandering, and when Percy found her, would refuse to come home. She was often found miles from where they lived, wandering haphazardly around the countryside, talking to herself, with no idea of who she was or where she was. Sometimes she would disappear for days. In the end, the Wilkes family looked out for Percy, who was slow for his age—he never did learn to read or write. A timid, undersize boy he was, poor mite. When his mum died of the pneumonia, Percy was about seventeen. The Wilkeses took him in and he lived permanently in that little one-room cottage next to their cow barn and helped them around the farm."

She paused to serve Mrs. Angus, who had come into the shop for twenty Senior Service cigarettes for her husband. "Poor Percy," Mrs. Angus pitched in. "I think he's as touched in the head as his mum was."

"Percy most certainly isn't touched!" When Mrs. Glossop sticks up for someone, you had better think twice about taking an opposing view. "I'll have you know there is nothing wrong with Percy. He was and still is a shy man, never has two words to say to anyone. And yes, he might be a little bit slow, but he is a decent, hardworking individual." Having settled Mrs. Angus's incorrect thinking, Mrs. Glossop turned back to me. "But the thing about Percy was he was never interested in girls of his age—or any age, come to that. At least we thought that was the case."

"Yes, we did, and how wrong we were." An undefeated Mrs. Angus leaned an angular hip up against the counter and folded her arms over her flat chest. "One night, old Mrs. Herrick who used to run the haberdasher's remembered she had forgotten to bring in her washing. Out she goes, and there's Percy standing under the window of her youngest daughter Gail's bedroom. She said he was just standing there watching Gail brush her hair in front of her mirror."

Mrs. Glossop wasn't going to have anyone telling her story.

"Gail was in her *nightdress*—and hadn't the decency to pull her curtains closed. Mrs. Herrick bustled Percy away and then went up and gave Gail a good box round the ears for making such a spectacle of herself. Herrick gave Percy what for, I can tell you."

Mrs. Angus snorted with derision. "That's not the way I heard it. Gail was still *fully* clothed. All she was doing was brushing her hair: lovely hair it was, thick, glossy, and such a beautiful golden yellow. I think it reminded Percy of his mother—she had a beautiful head of hair before all that trouble over Ned shooting hisself. And it didn't end there, this gazing up at women's bedroom windows. One night, Gladys Pritchard was pulling her bedroom curtains closed and saw Percy peering up at her from behind the laurel hedge that separates their house from the rectory. She was in her nightie: tiny, little flimsy thing, she said it was. Bert and her had just got married, and what a magnificent bustline Gladys had then. Though Bert in his day was a handsome man too."

"What with one thing and another," Mrs. Glossop interrupted unnecessary descriptions of the Pritchards in their heyday, "the police were called in and Percy was sent down for six months, first offense as a Peeping Tom. And if Percy was a bit odd before he went to jail in Wickham, he was a good deal odder when he came out." She shut her mouth tightly and didn't say another word, but the glare she directed at Mrs. Angus carried far more meaning than any good-bye.

"Good Lord above, would you look at the time." Mrs. Angus put the cigarettes in her shopping basket. "I have to pick up some more yarn. Me and Gracie are knitting socks for soldiers."

Mrs. Glossop picked up a duster and flapped it up and down the counter until she was quite sure that Mrs. Angus was on her way. "The rest of Percy's story is not common knowledge, by the way—so don't *you* go repeating it. About seven years ago, young Doreen came home one summer afternoon and told her mum that Percy had been hiding behind a hedge while she, Audrey Wilkes, and Ivy Wantage had been swimming in the river. The details were not ones I could bring myself to repeat." She tucked her chin down into her neck as she glanced at me to see if I understood. Obviously, she didn't think I had. "If I had a daughter who went swimming in just her knickers and brassiere, the little hussy, I would be the last one to point fingers at a man for taking notice and behaving indecently. Good box around the ears is what I would give a daughter of mine, I can tell you.

"Mrs. Newcombe called in Constable Jones, and he talked to Doreen and Ivy. Doreen said that Percy was hiding in the bushes watching them, and Ivy, after a lot of hemming and hawing, agreed. Then Jones went over to the Wilkeses' to talk to Audrey." She paused and nodded as if this next bit of information would be significant. And it was. "Audrey said that she had not seen Percy behind any hedge along the river and neither had Doreen nor Ivy told her that they had seen him. She said she was wading in the river with her skirt tucked up into her underwear and that she had a much better view of the river's edge than the other two girls. She was very clear about it."

"So, Ivy was just corroborating Doreen's story?"

She shrugged. "Who knows what was going on—girls in their

teens are untrustworthy to say the least. Jones went to talk to Percy—luckily, he was helping Mr. Wilkes with the evening milking. Mr. Wilkes heard everything Jones asked Percy, and when Percy had stopped crying he said that he had never been near the river—for months. Wilkes wasn't going to have Percy bullied by a policeman. He called Audrey into the cowshed, and she confirmed again that she hadn't seen Percy by the river—and that she thought Doreen had just been making up a story!" Mrs. Glossop walked to the door of the shop and shook her duster outside before folding it up and putting it away in a drawer.

"I suspect, since you asked me about Percy, that there is talk going around that he might have murdered Doreen and Ivy. Am I right?"

I put on my innocent face and she nodded. "Yes, I thought so. Just remember that there is *always* talk in a village; most of it's idle speculation that over the years has become what *some* people take for truth. Percy is a natural scapegoat. But"—her fierce little eyes bored into mine—"he is one of life's unfortunate casualties too, and the last thing he would ever do is harm anyone, let alone strangle them. He just doesn't have it in him. Just you remember that, when you go poking about asking questions."

I PONDERED THE Percy story as I walked over to the vicarage to discuss Little Buffenden's first air-raid drill with Mr. Fothergill. Part of me wished I hadn't heard the full story of what amounted to Percy's victimization by two adolescent girls. But it did give him a motive for revenge. More than anything it was not Doreen's, but Ivy's behavior that puzzled me.

"Do you think it is at all likely that Percy Frazer might have, you know, murdered Doreen and Ivy, as revenge for that business by the river?" I asked the reverend when we were finished with ARP business. What I like most about our vicar is that you can just come right out and say a thing; you don't have to beat about the bush.

"Interesting you should say that; Inspector Hargreaves was asking the same question. And he hasn't arrested Percy, so I am assuming that his inquiry turned up an answer that made sense to him."

"I expect Percy was the first person everyone in the village suspected."

"Oh, I don't doubt it at all." He slapped his pockets and looked around for his tobacco pouch and found it. "Every village has a Percy." He began to fill his pipe. "Or at least in the days before the last war they did. Poverty, drink, physical abuse—it's a vicious circle and it doesn't make for very sound mental health." He sighed as he drew on his pipe. "Ignorance and lack of education round out the tragedy of families like the Frazers. And as you know, memories are long in small communities, and gossip makes life difficult for the likes of those who don't quite fit in." He waved his pipe toward the sherry decanter. "There are some glasses somewhere. Ah yes, there they are." He poured us two generous glasses. I'll say this for our Rev—his sherry is exceptional.

Lifting his sherry in salute, he continued. "It was Davey Wilkes and I who persuaded Constable Jones to drop the business of Percy spying on Doreen and her friends by the river that summer. What was it, about five years ago? Percy was probably just walking along the towpath and Doreen saw him: girls can be a bit fanciful in their teens, some of them. But there again we mustn't disbelieve them just because they are going through a silly phase." He sipped his sherry for a moment. "I was called in simply because I am the vicar, and Jones felt uncomfortable talking to both the girls alone. We thought very hard about Doreen's account of what happened. I know you didn't run around with girls of your own age in the village, because you were away at school. But"—he paused and fiddled about with his pipe—"Doreen was rather a spoiled and vengeful little girl, if she was thwarted. I suspect she was pretty cruel to a boy like Percy, and the others in her group followed along. When we talked to Ivy, her account was a little different. It was Audrey being so sure that Percy had been nowhere near that part of the river that convinced Jones not to take it further. So, Jones let Percy off with a warning. And after that Mr. and Mrs. Wilkes made sure he didn't wander about at night, kept him busy on their farm. Good people, the Wilkeses. Yes, Poppy, I understand your concern, but for once Mrs. Glossop is right: Percy doesn't have it in him to be violent. Poor chap saw enough of that when he was a child. And if you would like another glass of sherry, I'll tell you something else that exonerates Percy Frazer."

THIRTEEN

ONCE I GET SOMETHING IN MY HEAD, IT IS HARD FOR ME TO let it go, and I was still annoyed with Griff and his offhand response to my information about Ponsonby. As I walked down the lane that night, I slowed down at the stile into Bart's Field, and there to my pleased surprise I saw a familiar figure walking rapidly toward the wood. It was Ponsonby! I called Bess to me and made a leash of my belt. "No barking, Bess," I whispered into her alert ear. "We must be *very* quiet." And we set off through the long, dry grass at the edge of the field and followed our bird-watcher into the wood. Bess is not used to being restrained—I put her on a leash only when she is being particularly unruly—so she walked obediently at my heel, looking up at me every so often as if asking what she had done wrong. I reached down and stroked her head to reassure her that all was well and then concentrated my full attention forward.

Mr. Ponsonby strode ahead, a dark shadow in the dappled cold gray light of the moon. He took the same route as before, and I made sure that I stayed well back. When he broke the cover of the wood, I paused to see which way he went before walking forward.

And to my delight he made for the badgers' sett. Bess caught my excitement and began to forge ahead, straining against the short length of my belt. I reined her in as we came out of the wood and into the open and then dropped down next to her to crawl through the meadow grass. She was panting so loudly in my ear I couldn't hear a thing. "Shush," I whispered, and she covered my face in lavish kisses.

We crawled up the slope, settled ourselves behind a nice thick gorse bush, and waited. Against the pale light of a star-filled sky, Mr. Ponsonby's shadow made its way toward the entrance of the sett and was lost in the darkness of the beech tree. I pulled Bess down close beside me and snuggled her under my arm. Always responsive to being close to me, instead of cuddling up she started to squirm and wriggle. "Bess, stay," I muttered, trying to pull her back to me, but she resisted with all her might. I could feel her little stump of a tail wagging frantically. Worried that she would start to bark, I hauled her back toward me as a strong hand clamped down on the small of my back, pinning me flat in the grass.

I heaved upward, my heart racing, as an even stronger hand cupped my mouth. Why wasn't Bess barking? I started to panic that she had been hurt by my attacker. A heavy body rolled half on top of me, crushing the breath out of me. Ponsonby! He must have circled around out of the shadow of the beech tree. What a fool I had been. Why on earth hadn't I listened to Griff? I struggled with all my might, but I was helplessly pinned.

"Will you lie still, for God's sake?" a familiar voice grunted in my ear.

It was Griff. I went limp and he rolled off me. "What the hell are you doing here?" he whispered in my ear and released his hand from my mouth.

I turned my head to his. "I might ask the same thing of you," I hissed. Bess had wriggled herself between us and had settled in to enjoy this new game.

"Be quiet." Griff lifted a pair of field glasses to his eyes.

"Ponsonby's in the badgers' sett."

"Yeah, I know, but not for long." He lifted his head above a tussock of grass and so did I. Against the sky on the other side of the wire fence I thought I saw the long shadow of our nocturnal birdwatcher. And then another and another. I strained my eyes, wishing for more moonlight so I could see him. Surely that was him standing upright on what must be the edge of the runway?

A large shadow broke into separate shadows and moved forward. There was a reception committee waiting for Ponsonby. I held my breath and waited, staring into the dark.

I was dazzled by the glare of headlights from a jeep parked on the runway.

Griff put his hand on my shoulder. "Now, for once in your life, listen to me, please. Stay right here. When we have gone, then you can leave."

"Please don't tell me that you are arresting Ponsonby for trespassing." I didn't spare the sarcasm.

"Yes, that's about it." And he got up and walked toward the entrance to the sett.

As he left I raised my head and shoulders above our hiding place. The slender figure of Ponsonby—he had not brought his campstool—was standing upright with his hands raised above his head. A group of three helmeted men—US Military Police—were gathered around him, their dogs crouched on the ground. Bess growled deep in her throat as she watched.

Griff emerged on the other side of the fence as the moon came out from behind the cloud. He strolled over to the group of men and appeared to have a few things to say to Ponsonby. He had joined them by using *my* badgers' tunnel! One of the MPs was handcuffing Ponsonby's hands behind his back. Another was searching through the bag he always wore over his shoulder.

"Bess!" I said, pulling her intent little body close. "They're arresting Ponsonby—he has to be a spy!"

Another jeep raced across the runway and pulled up: Ponsonby was stowed away in the back with a police escort, and Griff got into the other one. They dimmed their headlights and I heard them drive away into the night.

As I got to my feet, I realized that I was trembling from head to foot with the excitement of it all. But it was nothing to the jubilation I felt as Bess and I tramped back to the lane—through the wood and to the stile, where I sat for a moment or two to collect myself. If Fenella Bradley could have witnessed that scene, it would have been a coup to end all coups. "So much for boring Little Buffers," I said aloud and heard Ilona's answering silvery peel of laughter in my head. *I wouldn't mind being rolled around in a flowery moonlit meadow by Lieutenant O'Neal, darling. Not one little bit!*

MRS. PRITCHARD SET down a frothing pint of bitter in front of Captain Bill Peterson and a glass of sherry for me. And then she set up three more pints on the oak bar top.

Griff lifted his pint to me in silent salute and took a long swallow.

"Best beer in the world," Hank Dexter said as he lowered his tankard and smacked his lips. "And I love it that you serve it in . . . what's this called again?" He waved his tankard.

"A pewter tankard, ducky, that's the right way to serve a pint." Mrs. Pritchard clearly enjoyed the company of handsome young Americans in her pub. She winked and laughed her loud, happy, publican's laugh, her cheeks as rosy as the sweater she was wearing.

Bill Peterson drained the rest of his pint in two swallows and wiped his mouth with the back of his immense hand. "That's it for me," he said as he set his empty tankard down on the bar. "I have a date in Wickham with a stunning young woman who I must not keep waiting." He spun some coins down on the counter. "That's for the first round. Poppy, are you on patrol this evening?"

"No, it's my night off. I get two a week now we have recruited another ARP warden."

"Recruited another ARP warden?" Griff put his beer down on the counter. "That sounds very official."

"It isn't really. Mr. Fothergill enlisted Sid's help so I can have a day off occasionally."

"Sid Ritchie," Griff explained to Hank Dexter as Peterson left the pub, "is an interesting sort of guy—a real English eccentric. He's the one who wouldn't come over to join us for a pint." And he explained about Sid's passion for the Royal Air Force and his devotion to Biggles. I had to admit when you hear Sid described by someone who has never spent a minute in his company, he sounded even more idiotic than he was in real life. "Bananas" was the term Griff used.

"And now I am taking Miss Redfern to a movie, and we must leave now, or we'll miss . . . what are we seeing again?"

"*Mrs. Miniver*—with Greer Garson."

"And who else?" It was a leading question and I laughed.

"Walter Pidgeon."

"See, Dexter, the Brits call their leading men after birds—the entire country is obsessed with birds." He was so delighted with his joke that I didn't like to tell him that Walter Pidgeon was a Canadian actor.

"ARE YOU GOING to let me in on what was going on at the airfield?" I asked as we drove down dark lanes at white-knuckle speed, hopefully toward Wickham.

"No need to clutch at the door handle. There is nothing to fear. If I can fly a plane at night, I can certainly get us to town without landing us in the ditch." All pilots, Griff had explained many times, have something the rest of us mere mortals don't have: natural night vision.

"But if you can see in the dark, why did you have your night-vision binoculars up by the badgers' sett?" I teased, because I was just as pleased as he was that we had returned to our easygoing ways with each other. He laughed, and I immediately pursued my quest for information. "Don't try and avoid my question. What was going on at the airfield?"

"Ah yes, you want to know about your local bird-watcher. But I'm going to have to disappoint you there, Poppy. I'm not being stuffy; it's classified information. Unfair, I know, because we would never have caught him so quickly without you . . ."

You might not have caught him at all, was what I wanted to say, but I bit down on the hot words: I didn't want to fall out with him again. Instead I said, "It can't be classified if everyone in the village knows Ponsonby was arrested. We're not that gullible. This business about him having to return to London because his mother is sick is a laughable cover story. Why don't you just say you arrested him for spying?"

He slowed at the crossroads before turning right toward Wickham, and on we sped. "When you say 'everyone in the village,' you really mean Mrs. Glossop, don't you?" He slowed to negotiate a cyclist wobbling along the narrow lane in the dark.

"She just puts two and two together—"

"And makes five. And I am sure you told her about your involvement."

I hadn't, of course, and the fact that he thought I had was irritating. "You should know better than that. All I want to know is whether he was a German spy, or worse, an English traitor. You don't have to tell me exactly what information he was after at the airfield."

"Thank you."

"Will he be shot for espionage?" I asked, hoping to surprise him into giving me a straight answer.

He laughed and shook his head. "You're so quick, Poppy, so darn quick. Now, let's talk about our suspects—who in this village could possibly be the Buffenden Strangler, I wonder? You haven't been distracted from our mission by ole Ponsonby, I hope. Are you going to update me about the village flasher? I think my money's on Percy."

I laughed at his flippant reference to our murderer, even though it was said with a completely straight face. "Has it occurred to you that since your base has been proved to have a violable security system that any man who wanted to could leave, after curfew or even if you were all confined to base? I mean, the badgers' sett has really been an unpatrolled gateway between your world and the village, hasn't it? We really, at this point, should be looking at every man on the base as suspects for the murders of Doreen and Ivy."

He said nothing about Ponsonby at all, which I found supremely annoying and rather arrogant.

"How is our inquiry going in the village? Any developments there at all?" He took his attention off the road for a moment to turn his head to me. "Percy Frazer, for instance?" And because I am the cooperative type, unlike Griff O'Neal, I filled him in on my now non-suspect: Percy.

"However much he appears to be a perfect suspect for this sort of murder, Percy is simply not the type: both the vicar and Mrs. Glossop have assured me that he is too timid to do something as aggressive as killing two girls. He is a sad man, and we shouldn't make fun."

"I am not making fun. You just think that because I am an American and we tend to be more lighthearted than you Anglo-Saxons. What you call our flippant attitude is how we cover awkward situations, whereas the English just clam up and look grim. So, even though Doreen made up a story about Percy hiding behind a bush and watching them while they were swimming—and her friend Ivy corroborated it—that wouldn't be a good enough motive for their murder? You see, although I am just an American, I would have thought that strangulation was the least they deserved for making up such a poisonous story and pinning it on a vulnerable male like Percy Frazer."

I sighed, because of course his theory made complete sense. And considering Percy's sad history, Doreen's false accusation was a particularly vicious one. But even if Percy had had a sort of breakdown and had sought revenge after all these years, it still wouldn't wash.

"Not in this case," I said. "You see, after all that business years ago when Doreen made up her story about Percy, Mrs. Wilkes had him come and live with them at the farmhouse, so they could keep an eye on him."

"With a thirteen-year-old daughter in the house—they must need their heads examined."

I could understand his reaction. Surely no one in their right mind would have a man who had been convicted as a Peeping Tom sleep in the same house as their teenage daughter.

"The Wilkeses have been looking out for Percy since he was a boy. They obviously know and trust him, and they did everything they could to stop him from being sent to prison because they understood his little peculiarities."

A whoop of laughter from the driver's seat. "Little peculiarities! That's rich—you English are really eccentric, aren't you?"

"If you call looking after the defenseless and the weak eccentric, then, yes, I suppose some of us deserve to be called that. Do you want to know why Percy is no longer a suspect, or not?"

"I do," he begged. "I really, really do!"

"Good. You see, Percy had the perfect alibi for when Doreen was killed, the vicar told me. He had injured his foot the night before Doreen was murdered—cut it on the blade of a plow. It sliced right through his boot, and he had to have stitches in his foot. Reverend Fothergill was clear on that point because Dr. Oliver did the stitching. Percy was still unable to walk without a pair of crutches when Ivy was killed. It was the first thing Dr. Oliver told Constable Jones and Inspector Hargreaves when the girls were murdered."

I heard him sigh as he changed gears to negotiate a corner. "Damn. I had my heart set on Percy."

"You wouldn't say that if you met him."

"Okay. So, who's next on your list?"

I tried to match his lighthearted mood: "Every single man on your base."

And we were still arguing about village versus air-base motives as he parked the car at the back of the Gaumont cinema and we joined the long queue to see Greer Garson and Walter Pidgeon in a romance set on the home front.

FOURTEEN

T HE ENDING OF *MRS. MINIVER* WAS SO TERRIBLY UNEXPECTED
and so devastating that I had difficulty not breaking down as
we shuffled out of the cinema, surrounded by a crowd of tear-
streaked faces, and walked to the car.

Griff reached out a hand and took mine. "You expected the pilot
to be killed, didn't you? I know I did."

I didn't want to say anything about pilots being killed; it was all
too tactlessly close to home.

"I was so shocked when *she* was killed . . . She was so . . . so in
love . . ." I stumbled along in the dark trying to see through welling
eyes. Griff put me into the car and by the time he got in beside me,
tears were streaming silently down my face. "But I didn't want him
to die either—it's all so terrible. I really *hate* this war."

He put his arm around me and drew me to him. Well, at least he
drew me as close as he could, because the hand brake got in the way
and jabbed me viciously in the ribs, and I pulled back slightly. He
must have taken my not leaning in any further as reluctance to be

held too close, because he released me and sat back in his seat, and sadly the moment was gone.

"Good fighter pilots don't die, Poppy."

"They don't?" I asked, knowing this wasn't true. RAF pilots were killed all the time, in frightening numbers. Everyone knew it, and however dashing the Americans are, they are certainly not invincible.

"Nope, the good ones live forever," he said and started the engine.

We drove home in silence, a complete departure from our usual teasing banter. He stopped the car outside the lodge, got out, and came around to open my door.

"Thank you for a wonderful evening," he said in such a gentle voice that I almost started crying again. It was a beautiful night, and I'll say this for the blackout: I have never seen the night sky so thick with stars so bright that a moon would have paled into insignificance. I hoped he would put his arms around me again, but he didn't.

He cleared his throat. "We are going to be a bit busy for a few days." He always called missions "being a bit busy." "When I get back I'll come and find you on patrol," he said, and then he laughed. "If you promise me that Sid won't be escorting you."

"I promise. Thank you for taking me to the pictures, Griff. I can't imagine that you could have enjoyed the film as much as I did."

"I thought it was a clever movie in its own way—the best bit of propaganda I've seen in a long time."

"Propaganda? I thought it was a film about the heroism of the English on the home front—and it was wonderfully romantic."

"Exactly," he said with finality. "That's good propaganda for you. There's no need to bash everyone over the head about how evil

Hitler's Germany is. Just show a decent, law-abiding English family struggling to adapt to the horrors of war and selflessly doing their bit, and you have the making of a perfect propaganda movie. That part when Mrs. Miniver tries to help that wounded German paratrooper and he repays her by demonstrating just what unpleasant bullies those brainwashed by Nazism really are. That was well done. I am sure *Mrs. Miniver* convinced lots of Americans that we had done the right thing by joining the war."

And in that moment, I saw how clever the plot of the film had been. There had been no frantic flag waving, no grand speeches, just, as Griff had said, a decent family doing their best for their country in a time of war. I watched him jump back into his car and shoot off down the village High Street and realized that there was a good deal more going on under the surface of Griff's often playful exterior than I had at first imagined.

FOR THE NEXT three days I gave my novel everything I had. Egged on by the soft drawl of Ilona's patrician voice in my head, my plot left matters of murder to concentrate entirely on affairs of the heart. I wrote furiously, pausing every so often to weep into Griff's handkerchief, with Bess looking anxious or bored by turns as she devotedly washed my hands and polished off my unfinished lunches.

Three nights later, before I left to go out on patrol, I read through the pages I had written. I had to admit my story was moving forward. The romance part was, I prayed, not slushy or sickeningly sentimental, but, hopefully, deeply and tragically sad.

I don't want to spoil anything in case it's published, but the gist of this part of the book is that the love of Ilona's life, her editor, Tom

Hartley, announces that he has joined the Royal Navy. It's the least he can do, he says, after the catastrophe of Dunkirk. Ilona is devastated but does a tremendous job of covering up à la *Mrs. Miniver*. She doesn't even break down on their final evening together: they go to a nightclub, drink champagne, and dance every dance—and of course Tom is a superb dancer and Ilona looks ravishing in an ivory silk dress that I borrowed from a Ginger Rogers film. In the small hours Tom Hartley walks Ilona back to her flat, and as they stand by the river to watch the sunrise, she says good-bye to him, careful to preserve an affectionate but self-contained shop front.

He kisses her: a kiss so tender and lingering, so full of love and desire, it leaves her breathless and in no doubt that if he doesn't come back to her she will simply die. They walk on together to the front door of her flat. They kiss one last time and then he walks away. At the end of the street he stops, turns, and gives her a farewell salute—he is standing in a patch of early morning sunlight, which she takes as an auspicious omen. She lifts a hand to wave, and now that he can't see her, she allows herself to cry.

After I had blown my nose, bathed my eyes with cold water, and washed all the dog lick off my hands, Bess and I set off on patrol. The evenings were beginning to draw in, and there was that distinct chill in the air that tells you that autumn is not far off.

We walked fast in the cold evening and stopped only once to remind Mrs. Angus—who was becoming more forgetful by the week—that her parlor blackout wasn't completely covering the window. "An air-raid drill will do this lot nothing but good," I confided in Bess as we came up toward the Wilkes farm.

I slowed down, hoping to catch a glimpse of Audrey taking a solitary walk along the lane. But there was no sign of her and I decided to drop in and simply say hullo. If I had made a promise to myself that I would no longer pretend I was too busy to spend time with the most overlooked young woman in our village, then I needed to keep it.

Mrs. Wilkes opened the door and I was surprised to see that Audrey was not sitting at her kitchen table studying her movie magazines.

"Do you have time for a cuppa? Must be chilly out tonight." Mrs. Wilkes was already setting down blue-and-white cups and saucers: three of them, I noticed. And sure enough, the door into the kitchen opened and there was Audrey—a wholly different woman from the one I knew. Instead of being confined in a long tight plait down her back, Audrey's loosened hair framed her large pale face in soft, thick, shiny bay brown waves. It was a magnificent sight: thick and lustrous, the sort of hair a film star would have envied. She was wearing a jade green floral blouse cut quite low to reveal a deep cleavage and satiny smooth ivory skin. Around her shoulders was a dark green cardigan. She wasn't wearing much makeup, but the little she had on emphasized the blue lights in her dark gray eyes and gave her cheeks an almost silky glow. But wonder of wonders, instead of her old corduroy dungarees she was wearing a skirt and—my eyes nearly popped out of my head—high heels!

She looked what Granny would describe as Junoesque: an Edwardian term reserved for big and beautiful women. I nearly said, Audrey, you look absolutely smashing! But an admonitory frown made me pick up my cup of tea and blow lightly across its surface. Audrey, I remembered just in time, didn't go in for flowery compliments.

"Tea's on the table, dear," said Mrs. Wilkes, as if Audrey always swanned into the kitchen looking sensational and not scuffing along in broken-down slippers with slumped shoulders in a shapeless old cardigan that had belonged to her dad.

She joined us at the scrubbed pine table, and Mrs. Wilkes poured. I knew how much Audrey loved films, so I told her all about *Mrs. Miniver*. She listened politely and then she yawned, and I had to laugh. "Not your cup of tea, then, Richard Ney? After all, he is a British actor."

"No, he's not; he's American." She smiled because she was the expert. "But he does a pretty decent accent. I like the American stars more than ours—they have more oomph." She sipped her tea and said no more, and when we had finished I thanked them and got up to go. As I walked to the door, Audrey joined me and said she would walk me down the drive.

As we strolled along in the cool of the evening, she said, in the most offhand way, as if she were discussing the price of livestock in Wickham market, "I don't miss either of them, you know. Doreen and Ivy. It's funny, but it's as if they never lived here, that I never saw them every day when I was a kid. They've simply gone—just like that."

I let her remark lie there uncommented on and waited.

"The only thing that I found hard to forgive Doreen for was that she led Brian Chambers on. She wasn't happy until he had proposed. You know something, Poppy? She was that spoiled and in need of attention that she had to have a proposal from the one hero in our village. I hated the idea that Brian would come home, marry her, and find out how third-rate she was. She wasn't fit to wipe the dust off his boots."

This was pretty condemning stuff from Audrey, considering what had happened to Doreen.

"Brian was wonderful," she said softly. "Far too good for the likes of Doreen, but he's gone now, so he'll never have to find out how rotten she was."

If I had been Constable Jones, I would have taken her in for questioning right then and there. But I wasn't Jones, and anyway, if she had strangled Doreen, what reason could Audrey have had for bumping off Ivy? And then it came to me. I didn't need Ilona to prompt my thinking: Audrey had murdered Doreen, and then Ivy had found out and Audrey had had to kill her too. Ivy's death was a cover-up, as Griff would have called it.

I was so preoccupied with these thoughts that it took me a moment to realize that Audrey was waiting for me to say good night and go. There was nothing particularly subtle about her demonstrated need to be alone. She sighed, shifted her feet, and then said, "Nippy for the time of year, isn't it? How much more of your patrol do you have to do?"

"I am halfway through."

"Right then, you'd better be getting on, then, hadn't you? Looks like rain's coming in." I took the hint and, calling Bess, set off toward the village.

As I paced along lanes and across bridges, I wondered why Audrey had taken the time to walk me down the drive—dressed to the nines—to tell me quite baldly that she didn't miss either Ivy or Doreen and that she had found Doreen particularly unpleasant. And when she had got that off her chest she had then pretty much told me I could go. What a confusing woman she is, I said to myself as we walked up Water Lane. *She most certainly is. And why is scruffy old Audrey so groomed and dressed in her best?* Ilona's voice chimed in, because things like appearance matter a lot to her. *Did you notice that she was wearing stockings?*

I stopped so abruptly and stood for so long that Bess came running back to me. "Stockings!" I said aloud to my little dog. "Audrey was wearing stockings!" She wagged her tailless rump and danced around me.

There is not one woman in Little Buffenden whose legs are sheathed in sheer nylon. Either we wear ankle socks (it had become fashionable in the last two years), or, if they are going dancing, some girls shave their legs and then ask a girlfriend to draw a dark line with an eyebrow pencil from the back of the ankle on up past the knee to give the effect of seamed stockings. Granny would never tolerate me drawing lines on my legs; she is very clear on what Redfern women do and don't do.

The only girls in our village who had worn stockings recently were Doreen and Ivy. Was my new friend Audrey, who wouldn't be caught dead running around with a Yank, dating an American? Is this why she was all dressed up and had wanted me to leave—so she could meet him privately? I spun on my heel and started to walk back to the Wilkes farm.

Hold on a moment. Ilona's voice stopped me from being rash. *Darling, you are dating an American too, aren't you? Oh, come on, don't deny it. The only difference between you, Doreen, Ivy, and Audrey is that your chap hasn't given you nylon stockings. He is far too much of a gentleman,* she said, as if I needed these things explained for me.

As usual, Ilona had come to the point with deadly accuracy: the most incriminating evidence about both murders was that Doreen had been strangled with nylon stockings and Ivy with an American Air Force tie. If Audrey was secretly dating an American, she would have had access to both.

FIFTEEN

M Y GRANDPARENTS WERE WAITING UP FOR ME WHEN I GOT
home. Granny was busily dropping stitches in her knitting.
Grandad's eyes were glued to a newspaper advertisement for baby
food. They both threw their props to one side as I came in through
the door.

"How was your evening, dear?" Granny patted the space between them on the sofa.

"Cold night. I was just thinking of having a whiskey and soda."
Grandad rarely drank this late at night. They were nervous. Something was up. Granny would not look me directly in the eye, and I
prayed we weren't in for another discussion on ARP patrol being
too dangerous for nice young girls of my age. I dutifully sat down,
and Granny put her hand over mine.

"Hank Dexter . . . popped over this evening . . ." She stopped and
made a silent appeal to her husband.

"Ahem, yes . . . always best to come straight to the point." Grandad groped for my free hand and held it in a bone-crushing grip
that brought tears to my eyes and a strange tingling sensation in my

fingertips. "Now, there is no need for alarm, but Griff didn't make it home this evening with the rest of his squadron."

No need for alarm? There was a ringing sound in my ears. Random images flashed through my mind: Griff peeling potatoes; throwing sticks for Bess; tinkering with the engine of his beloved Alvis.

But he had told me that good fighter pilots live forever.

I stared at Grandad and he plunged into more explanation. "He was shot down over the Channel. Managed to bail out before . . . before his plane crashed into the drink." He cleared his throat. "His dinghy inflated when he was in the water, so they know where to look for him. Dexter says they will find him soon."

But those yellow dinghies—the Americans called them life rafts—were notoriously unreliable. Packed flat for month after month, and now year after year, if they were inflated too quickly they exploded. Not to mention how leaky most of them were. And without a life raft, how could they spot one tiny human head in those miles of choppy gray water? Were they searching with aircraft or boats? How long had they been looking—hours? All day? But I couldn't get out the words to my questions. My mouth was as dry as sand.

"We are having a particularly warm end to summer," Granny pointed out. Rain that had threatened all day had finally arrived and was lashing down. People died of hypothermia in the stretch of freezing water that separated England from France. No one swam off the south coast, even on the hottest day in August, unless they were a health nut.

I couldn't bear the expression of kind concern in Grandad's eyes; neither could I begin to believe that Griff O'Neal wouldn't make it back. Bess jumped up on my lap, breaking Granny's rule about dogs on furniture. I held her to me and for a moment was comforted by her warm doggy body.

My mouth was so dry my tongue felt too big in it. "Did he come down closer to our side or the French coast—do they know?"

Grandad couldn't take it anymore; he got up and poured two whiskies. I heard the familiar hiss and gurgle of the soda siphon before he put a glass into my hand. "Sip this—slowly—it will do you good." I nodded and held the drink untasted in my hand.

I repeated my question. "Which side?"

"Hank Dexter said they had just flown over the French coast when they came across a squadron of Messerschmitts. They came up from the west with the sun behind them."

Then he could just as easily be picked up by Germans as by our navy search team. Griff was probably a prisoner of war right now, his injuries tended to by a German nurse in a prison hospital. That is, if he had survived the drop. I put my untasted whiskey down on the low table in front of me.

"Then we must hope for the best," I said, no doubt echoing what my mother had said when my father went missing in action almost twenty-four years ago. And I settled in to what so many women did these days: the uneasy business of trying not to unravel as we waited.

WITH NO NEWS of Griff by the end of the next day, I was grateful for the distraction of our air-raid drill. The rain that had been falling on and off since last night had finally let up, and as Bess and I left the lodge, a mist was settling heavy and thick in the meadows

down by the river, and the pungent, sharp smell of rotting vege-
tation scented the damp air. It was a little after midnight as Bess
and I stationed ourselves at the bottom of Smithy Lane and waited
in the shadows for the air-raid siren on the base to sound its
warning.

There is something about the damp cold of our island that seeps
deep into your bones. I shivered and pulled the collar of my old
tweed hacking jacket up around my ears. How long had Griff had
to wait, burdened by his heavy boots, flight suit, and leather jacket,
in the chilly waters of the English Channel? Trembling with cold
and anticipation, I switched on my torch and looked at my watch
for the hundredth time. Three minutes to go to half past twelve.
The village was darkly silent around us. I looked up at the sky; the
cloud cover obscured all light from moon and stars.

The seconds ticked slowly by, and then the silence of the night
was shattered by the loud mechanical wail of the air-raid siren. In
that split second, I was back in the East End of London. I looked up
at the sky and expected to see searchlights, but the sky remained an
implacable black. An air-raid-warning siren has to be one of the
most awful sounds in the world. There is a dire note of melancholy
portent in its warbling wail, almost as if it is signaling doom. It was
a sound I had never wanted to hear in our peaceful village.

Bess, sitting quietly at my feet, leapt up, barking frantically, and
then answered the siren with a howl of her own. There was no time
to calm her as I started up the slope of Smithy Lane to the village.

The siren was still going when we arrived on the edge of the village green to find everyone out in the High Street, standing in
groups and staring up at the sky. What on earth did they expect to

see? I fumed. If German fighter planes were to arrive, it would take them seconds to strafe the entire street. I blew my whistle, but of course no one could hear it over the wail of the siren.

"Fast as you can," I shouted to Mr. and Mrs. Angus, who were standing side by side gawking at the empty sky. "Go to your assigned shelter at the Rose and Crown or the crypt." I went on to the next group.

There was something both demented and comic about the surging group of villagers, as if they were taking part in a scene with the Keystone Cops. They were all heavily laden with an odd assortment of belongings grabbed at random as they left their houses. Mrs. Angus, her hair in curlers, was carrying a carriage clock and a canary in a cage and shouting instructions to her heavily laden children. Her butcher husband, in pink-and-white-striped pajamas, was clutching his fly-fishing rods and a bag of golf clubs. It was clear what was important in Mr. Angus's life.

Mrs. Glossop, holding the hands of two sobbing children, was yelling at Mr. Newcombe, who, still in his apron, his hands covered in flour, was standing in the doorway to his bakery in a pool of bright light. "Close that door, you fool!" I heard her shriek as I pushed past her.

I felt like an overactive border collie as I divided the crowd into two lots. One group started up the High Street to the church crypt, as Bess and I chivied the rest of them across the green toward the pub.

The siren finally stopped. "Eight minutes!" I shouted. "You have to move more quickly! But don't run!" A little girl went sprawling on her stomach, sobbing and clutching her teddy. Her pregnant mother was carrying her two-year-old brother. "Come on, you must get to the church as quickly as possible. Don't stop!" I said to her as I picked up the little girl and walked ahead of her mother up the street to the church. Normally it takes five minutes to get from one end of the High Street to the other. Tonight, it seemed to take hours. People were toiling up the middle of the street with suitcases, bundles of bedding, prams laden with children, and household treasures. Little Buffenden was so heavily burdened with their property it was amazing they could move at all.

I shooed the last of my neighbors through the church door to find the marvelously efficient Mrs. Martin counting heads and ticking off names on her list. The vicar was helping mothers with their children, which meant he could not go down the street to assist our elderly villagers, which is what we had planned. "Where is Audrey?" I asked Mrs. Martin.

"Twenty-two, twenty-three—yes, Mrs. Pearson, your daughter and her three are already here, not to worry. Miss Wilkes did not turn up, Poppy."

Why had I depended on the community's most antisocial member to help if there was an air raid? "Perhaps she went over to the Rose." Mrs. Martin ticked off the last of her names. "That's the lot—all accounted for."

"I am going over to the Wilkeses now. Will you tell the vicar I've borrowed his bike?" And with Bess running at my side, I sped back down the High Street and bumped across the green's uneven grassy surface to see how many people had made it to the pub's cellar. I thought at one moment I saw Audrey shouldering her way through a group of giggling and shrieking Girl Guides, but it wasn't her. She was probably with her family in their farm's Anderson shelter, which is where those who could not get into the village were to go if there was an air raid. The noise in the pub was overwhelming: everyone was gathered in a tight knot around the bar.

"Don't stop in 'ere—you need to get down them stairs to the cellar." Bert Pritchard was brandishing a shotgun. I prayed it wasn't loaded.

I directed Mrs. Angus with her birdcage to go down the stairs into the cellar, followed by a stream of flustered and unkempt villagers. "The animals went in two by two," Mr. Angus said in his wheezy, asthmatic voice.

"Watch who you go calling animals." Mrs. Pritchard shrieked with laughter. She was wearing a cherry-colored dressing gown over something lacey and pink. Mr. Pritchard followed her and closed the door to his cellar behind him.

For the first time in fifteen minutes all was gloriously quiet.

I went outside and stood alone on the green and looked at my watch, and even though I knew it was just a drill, I scanned the sky for the first planes. According to our schedule, the Luftwaffe would have dropped their first bombs three minutes ago, eliminating half the village as they ran up and down the High Street. And if they had been in the mood for a bit of strafing, their Messerschmitts would have finished off any stragglers on the green with the greatest of ease.

"Poppy." I turned to find Sid standing next to me, Sten gun in his hands.

"Sid, why aren't you with your mum in your Anderson shelter?" I was staggered to see him standing there, scanning the night sky.

"Mum's all right. She was in that shelter with Dr. and Mrs. Oliver before you could say Jack Robinson. Seen anything yet?"

"No . . . nothing."

As always, Sid was fully armed with the facts. "It takes fourteen minutes for the Luftwaffe to fly from the south coast to London. Give them another four at the most to get to Wickham. We should have heard them by now." He turned to me with none of his usual diffidence. "What are you doing out here, Poppy? You should be down there"—he jerked his head toward the Rose and Crown—"keeping order."

"What about you?"

"I am waiting for Jerry—I'm going to shoot him out of the sky."

The all clear sounded and Sid turned a face toward me that was so shocked I almost laughed.

"What happened? Why the all clear? Where are the Germans?"

"It was a drill," I said and watched his face fall. "An important one, because if it had been a real raid, half the village would be dead and the rest badly injured." It started to rain, a thin, cold drizzle. I turned to go back into the pub.

"You mean everyone had to get out of their beds in the middle of a night in the rain for a drill?" He sounded incredulous.

"Yes, Sid, because the next time the air-raid warning goes, it will be the real thing and everyone must know exactly what to do. This drill was a fiasco."

But he wasn't listening; he was running ahead of me toward the pub porch to get out of the rain. His heroic gesture on the green minutes ago as he readied himself to wipe the German air force from the heavens had gone completely. After all, God knows what would happen to his delicate system if he caught cold.

———

I WAS GREETED by a hubbub of outrage as I walked into the village hall at ten o'clock the next morning. Cedric Fothergill was standing on the dais, his right hand lifted in an ecclesiastical plea for silence. Mrs. Glossop was standing in the middle of her group of Women's Institute friends holding forth, with condemning accuracy, on everything that they had done wrong during our air-raid drill. Every one of her sentences started with "What were you thinking?" or ended with "What's wrong with you?"

The talk and exclamations finally died down, and the vicar could make himself heard.

"Now, settle down, please, settle down. There now, that's better." He looked at my grandfather, who was standing with his hands behind his back frowning at everyone. "Anything you would like to say about last night, Major Redfern?"

Grandad cleared his throat. "Like all of you, I believed it was the real thing. My wife and I went immediately to our Anderson shelter. And I wish I could say the same for all of you. If that had been a real air raid last night . . ." He glared around the room and waved his swagger stick at us. "The whole bally lot of you would have been wiped out." I could see why Grandad was so popular with his Home Guard, who were all in uniform and standing to attention down one side of the hall, their faces stern with judgment. He emanated authority and his timing was perfect.

"How many of you thought to put on your gas masks?" he barked. A few tentative hands were raised in the air, their owners looking smug. "Keep your gas masks handy at all times."

His frown deepened. "I don't know what use fishing rods, caged birds, and perambulators full of family photographs would be to anyone during or after an air raid." He stared at Mr. Angus, and the butcher's face deepened in hue.

"The reason you leave your house for the safety of a shelter is that it wouldn't take much to flatten this village in an undefended attack. So, don't waste your time loading yourself down with useless possessions. When you hear the air-raid siren, pick up your gas mask, get your children out of bed and wrap them in something warm, and make your way to the shelter designated to you in an *orderly* fashion. And absolutely *no* running; you will have time to reach safety if you leave your house the minute the siren sounds."

He stared at us for a moment as if we were particularly slow. "Now, if you live next door to a woman with small children, be neighborly. Help her carry them. I do hope that I am being clear. That's all I have to say, Reverend, thank you."

The vicar nodded and glanced at a piece of paper handed to him by his housekeeper. "Mrs. Martin said that once you were all in the crypt, everything was all very orderly. But we need more blankets as we go into colder weather. If any of you can donate a blanket or two for the duration, please let Mrs. Martin know." He looked around the room and nodded at Bert Pritchard. "Anything you have to add, Mr. Pritchard?"

"Apart from the fact that it was bloo— excuse my French, pandemonium? The most important thing is to help each other get to safety. I didn't see much of that last night. Women and children first, in an orderly fashion!" He glanced at his wife and she gave him an approving smile.

The vicar cleared his throat. "That was our one and only drill. So, remember: the next time you hear the air-raid siren, don't stop to ask if it is the real thing—pick up your gas mask and get yourself and your neighbor to safety. Thanks to all of you for coming!"

"But we're not all here for your debrief." Mrs. Glossop's voice was critical. As the leader of the Women's Institute, she often goes head-to-head with our vicar on points of accuracy. "Where's Audrey Wilkes? Isn't she in charge of the kiddies that go to the church? Where was she last night? That's what I want to know."

"All the farms and outliers have Anderson shelters," Mrs. Pritchard corrected her. "They don't need to come into the village."

"Of course the Wilkeses are not here; they aren't village!" called out Mr. Angus in his wheezy voice. "It's only village that use the crypt or the Rose as an air-raid shelter." He was right, of course. If there was an air raid, Audrey would go with her parents and Percy to their Anderson shelter. Her helping Mrs. Martin had only been for the drill.

Perhaps Audrey had forgotten that it was a drill. I walked over to Mrs. Martin. "Audrey didn't turn up at the vicarage after the drill, did she?"

"I didn't see her all evening. I thought she might have gone to the Rose and Crown."

"I didn't see her there. Not even after the all clear."

As I pushed my way through the crowd to the door, I wondered how Mrs. Glossop knew about my enlisting Audrey's help at the church crypt for the air-raid drill.

"OF COURSE, WE had no idea it was just a drill. Audrey told us she was on her way to the vicarage to help Mrs. Martin organize for the jumble sale. Then when the siren went, I thought at least she's safe down in that crypt. It was raining heavily when the all clear went, and we assumed she was spending the night at the vicarage—she does that sometimes if she's been helping Mrs. Martin." Mrs. Wilkes was chopping carrots and cabbage at the kitchen table.

"But Audrey didn't turn up at the crypt for the drill, Mrs. Wilkes. When did *you* last see her?"

"She had her tea as usual, and just as it was getting dark she said she was off to help Mrs. Martin with the . . ." I watched the color drain from her face as she realized what she had just said. She slumped down into a chair, her face as white as chalk. "Oh dear God," was all she said.

I quickly poured her a glass of water from the pump in the kitchen sink. "Where is Mr. Wilkes?"

"Him and Percy are mending the fence up at the north end of the cow pasture." The expression on her face was so distressing I couldn't think of a thing to say, other than I needed to use her phone. I left her sitting there alone at her kitchen table, with her heart full of dread, and went into the stuffy narrow corridor and telephoned Constable Jones. It took me seconds to get through to him and seconds more to let him know that Audrey Wilkes had been missing since seven o'clock yesterday evening. Then I went back into the kitchen and sat down at the kitchen table next to her mother.

SIXTEEN

WAITED IN THE KITCHEN WITH MRS. WILKES AS MORNING turned into afternoon. For such a laborious and slow-moving individual, our local police constable had been quick to summon the people he needed to turn out on a cold, wet autumn day to search woods, fields, farms, and their outbuildings for Audrey.

I had wanted to join the search party too, but I knew I couldn't leave Mrs. Wilkes alone in her kitchen. As the afternoon hours crept by, she did not move from her chair by the kitchen table. It was as if she had been frozen into immobility and would remain rooted there until she heard news of her daughter.

At about four o'clock, as I made yet another pot of tea, she looked up at me. "Thank you, dear. It is very kind of you to stay with me," she said. "Audrey always liked you." She smiled. It was a poor specimen to be sure, but my heart lifted to see it. Mrs. Wilkes is one of those cheerful, busy women, as farmers' wives so often must be. It was awful to see her silently waiting to be told that her daughter would not walk through her kitchen door again.

"They'll find her soon, Mrs. Wilkes. It will be all right." I tried to block the image that had insidiously crept into my head, of Audrey lying dead in a ditch, ever since Mrs. Martin had said she had not turned up at the crypt even after the drill.

I had callously made Audrey my prime suspect based on some careless assumptions. Now I knew that far from being Doreen's and Ivy's murderer, she had possibly joined them as the killer's next victim.

I murmured the usual things we say to comfort and encourage as I poured more tea. But Mrs. Wilkes wasn't listening. She was looking at the kitchen door, and Bess, who had waited patiently under the table for fallen scraps, was up and standing to attention, her head cocked on one side. I got to my feet as the three of us listened to the heavy steps of what sounded like a small army of people tramping up the crazy paving path to the Wilkeses' kitchen door.

"OH GOD, OH dear God." Her tightly held self-control had vanished; Mrs. Wilkes wept in the arms of her husband as, gray with fatigue, he patted her gently on the back.

"She'll pull through, Doris," he reassured his wife. "She'll be all right—she's a healthy, strong girl."

"Did she say anything?" Mrs. Wilkes lifted her tearstained face.

"No, love, she was unconscious. Now, put on your coat and I'll drive us over to Wickham General."

"Where was she?"

"The old lambing hut on the edge of Bart's Field."

"How long had she been there?" Her daughter was not dead, but she was badly hurt—on her way to hospital, perhaps already there. Mrs. Wilkes was desperate for details.

"Dr. Oliver thinks she was there all night. She must have crawled into the hut and then blacked out. They'll take care of her at Wickham General, you'll see. She'll be as right as rain in no time." But Mr. Wilkes didn't look too convinced. After all, he'd been one of the first on the scene when Jones had found his daughter.

As I listened with half an ear to Mrs. Wilkes's frantic questions, my mind went to the old lambing hut on the edge of Bart's Field—not far, I remembered now, from the badgers' sett. I stored this nugget away for later consideration. The Wilkeses, struggling to understand how and why their daughter could have been so brutally attacked when the Little Buffenden Strangler was locked up on the American base, were still standing side by side, their hands clutched together, as the search party gathered in their kitchen doorway, desperate to reassure them that their daughter was in good hands and that she would pull through.

Mrs. Glossop's pale face, screwed up with determination to bring comfort, peered into the kitchen. She saw me and nodded as if she was confirming something to herself. It was Constable Jones, hero of Little Buffenden's most triumphant hour, who ushered the well-wishers down the drive in a steady downpour and the failing light of day.

I knew I was intruding on the constable's inquiry—ordinarily he would have asked me to leave too—but I had waited the long hours with Audrey's mum, so in a way I was almost family. Percy Frazer came in through the kitchen door, hat in hand, and crept into a corner of the kitchen next to the Aga, where he meekly held out his hands to warm them and then took a seat out of the way. I caught his eye and felt even more guilty for considering him as a possible suspect when he gave me a shy, tentative smile before concentrating his surprised gaze on the large puddle of rainwater growing at his feet.

"Now then." Jones stood before us, a comforting and solid presence with water still dripping off his nose. "Detective Hargreaves will have some questions for you, and he should be here momentarily."

Mrs. Wilkes started to protest. "Tonight? But why can't he wait until tomorrow? We have to go to Wickham." Of course she didn't want to talk to a policeman; she wanted to be at her daughter's bedside in Wickham's general hospital.

"Audrey's in good hands, Mrs. Wilkes, and they wurn't let you see hurr till tomorrow marnin' anyways." His soft West Country burr had a reassuring effect. Mrs. Wilkes sat down at her kitchen table again and drank a glass of what her husband called "something a bit stronger." It was parsnip wine, the old country standby— every farmer's wife in England knows how to make the stuff: strong and thick, with a treacly consistency. I accepted a glass but couldn't bring myself to take even a polite sip.

"What had he done to her?" Mrs. Wilkes, fortified by alcohol, was almost belligerent. "What had the beast done to her?"

"Best as I could judge . . ." Jones was cautious, and his accent thickened. "He had tried to . . . probably tried to . . . urr. Well . . . our best guess is that Audrey 'ud managed to fight him off. And . . . so, more than likely . . ." His eyes wandered over to Mr. Wilkes as if asking for help in explaining the next part, and then, pulling himself together, he finished in a rush. "Her attacker had hit hurr over the head with a brick, or probably summat like it."

Mrs. Wilkes groaned and, clenching her hands into fists, lifted them to her forehead. Mr. Wilkes was at her side, his arm around her shoulders. "She'll be all right, love, just you wait and see." He turned an anguished face to Jones and shook his head. But Jones had steeled himself to finish. "It looks like she 'ud crawled into the old lambing hut, which wurr a good thing, because otherwise she woulda died from the exposurr. Dr. Olivurr says they'll exur-ray her at the hospital." Mrs. Wilkes began to sob, and we were saved from any more of Jones's floundering explanations by the arrival of Detective Hargreaves.

I WAS SPARED the inspector's interview. As he came into the kitchen, he didn't look in the least bit surprised to see me. All he said was, "It's getting dark out, Miss Redfern. Constable Jones will see you home."

"Please don't worry about me—I'll be fine," I said, getting to my feet, anxious to be on my way.

"No, Miss Redfern, you can't go home alone. There's a very dangerous person at large. Constable Jones will see you home."

It had stopped raining, and I picked up Bess and stowed her in the bike's grocery basket strapped to the handlebars. It made the going slower, but I found the silhouette of her round head and upright ears in front of me soothing.

Jones was silent as we biked up Water Lane, past the now empty building where our German spy Mr. Ponsonby had once lived, and then Dr. and Mrs. Oliver's house. We were both out of breath as the gradient steepened past the Ritchies' house. Their kitchen window was open, the blackout tightly closed behind it, and we could hear England's favorite radio program, *It's That Man Again*, or *ITMA* as it was affectionately referred to. I heard a burst of laughter from Sid, and his mother called out something to him and he laughed again and imitated the program's popular catchphrase: "After you, Claude—no, after you, Cecil." Hearing him from outside, I could have sworn it was the radio and not Sid.

Constable Jones laughed. "He's got them down to a T. You know, he told me that's what RAF pilots say to one another now, before they go in for an attack! Bet they don't do it half so well as our Sid, though—that boy's got real talent. You should hear him take off Tommy Handley—really good, he is."

I realized, with a mixture of exasperation and affection, that I would be patrolling with Sid again, now that, in the parlance of Hargreaves, there was a "dangerous person at large." How will our village receive that news? I wondered. Will they feel guilty that they had lumped all our allies in together as a "bad lot"? I was too tired to be bothered thinking about what the outcome of the day's events would be. I got off the bike and lifted Bess down. "Thank you, Constable Jones, for finishing my patrol," was all I could manage.

"Don't mention it, Miss Redfern. Your grandfathurr would have something to say if I didn't—and it shouldn't take me that long—everyone is worn out what with the drill and then the search for young Audrey. And don't you fret yourself about hurr neithurr—she'll be as right as ninepence in a couple of days—you'll see."

I watched Jones's solid shape cycle off into the night as I wheeled my bike up the front path. What on earth had Audrey been doing up at Bart's Field? My tired mind couldn't help but run through the few men in the village who might be strong enough to tackle Audrey: Mr. Angus and Bert Pritchard both had arms like tree trunks and could overpower any woman, even Audrey. I was so exhausted and disturbed by the attack, I even considered Cedric Fothergill, who though slender was undoubtedly fit, as he is captain of our cricket team and is an athletic batsman. It was laughable to imagine our vicar hiding in bushes and then jumping out and strangling young women. And even though he was getting on in years, hadn't Dr. Oliver wrestled for Oxford in his distant youth? And what about Sid—while I was at it, why not consider Sid, who wouldn't be caught dead in Bart's Field or anywhere he might fall into a ditch full of stinging nettles or catch a terrible cold.

The gossip mill would be hard at work tomorrow morning. I could almost hear Sid quoting Mrs. Glossop's latest opinion that the village would never be safe with the American Air Force base as its neighbor. And perhaps she was right. If Griff could crawl through the badgers' tunnels, then anyone under six foot two could have done the same. I counted back. Had it been seven or eight days since Ponsonby's arrest? Surely the badgers' sett had been filled in by now and the perimeter secured.

I remembered Bud Sandusky, who had dated Doreen. Could he have pretended his food poisoning and left the airfield using the badgers' sett? It was such a harebrained idea that I almost laughed, and so did Ilona: *Give it up, darling. You are simply not thinking straight. Go inside and have a stiff shandy or whatever it is you drink,* she ordered.

I opened the scullery door and a grateful Bess skittered over to her food bowl to polish off the scraps from supper, leaving me to blunder into the comforting light of the drawing room. Now that the search for Audrey was over and she was safe in hospital, my other worry emerged. It had been nearly three days since Griff had been reported missing, and so far we had heard nothing. As I opened the drawing room door I decided that if there was no news from the base tomorrow, I would ask Grandad to go up to Reaches and talk to Colonel Duchovny.

The first fire of the season, blazing on the hearth, lit up the two joyous faces of my grandparents in a golden rosy glow. Grandad got to his feet—he was smiling. "Nasty night out, come and warm yourself—it was good of you to wait with Mrs. Wilkes. Thank God young Audrey is safely tucked up in hospital."

Granny tossed her knitting to one side and said, as if she could hardly contain herself, "Griff is back, darling, just a few small injuries!" And I put my head on Granny's shoulder and wept. Sometimes life is just too overwhelming for words.

SEVENTEEN

B ESS HEARD HIM FIRST. WHEN I LOOKED UP, HE WAS STANDING in the entrance to the orchard trying to fend off her joyous welcome. How I envied her doggy honesty. I would have loved to run across the orchard into his arms, but my restrained upbringing together with our island reserve kept me planted, straight-backed, in my old wicker lawn chair.

"Go easy with me, girl," Griff said. As wan and battered as he was, he was still the most vital being I had seen for days. But even though his cap was perched back on his head at a jaunty angle, I noticed that he was listing to the right as he tried to fend off Bess's high-spirited greeting. "And what have you both been up to while I was away?"

"Quite a bit, actually. When did you get back?" I flinched at my polite maiden-aunt tone.

"On the evening of your air-raid drill. I was in the infirmary—recuperating." He straightened up from Bess as if it hurt and leaned up against the gatepost. "Impossible with that air-raid siren howling away half the night."

I had been sitting in the orchard all morning, too tired to write, as I waited for him, and now here he was and all I could come up with was the attack on the night of the drill.

"Did you hear about Audrey?" I asked.

He nodded. "Yes, I did. Is she conscious yet?"

"She wasn't last night, but apparently she is doing better this morning. She was found in that old stone hut—the one in Bart's Field." He looked puzzled. "The top of the wood cuts through Bart's Field, the lambing hut is on its west side, and our badgers' sett is on the east side." He ignored the reference to our badgers' sett.

"How did she get there? Did someone take her to the hut?"

It had not occurred to me that someone might have the gall to try to take Audrey anywhere, but something else did, and it was that Audrey's brush with the Little Buffenden Strangler could wait. Here was Griff O'Neal propped up against my gatepost and looking all in. Feeling less tongue-tied, I got to my feet. "I am so very glad you're back, Griff. How long was it before they got to you?"

"I think I was in the water for about six hours before they fished me out. Told you the good ones are hard to kill," he said, and winced as he pushed himself upright from the gatepost. "Three broken ribs," he explained, "so please don't rush over here and hug me."

"You have a pretty spectacular black eye too." I stayed where I was, and to my disappointment, he looked relieved.

"Never jumped for real before: no one told me how much a parachute bounces around if there's a strong wind." Bending so I couldn't see his face and careful to guard his left side, he fondled Bess's ears and talked loving nonsense to her. "I'm grounded for the rest of the week. So I thought I might come with you on patrol this evening. I could ride shotgun," he said as he straightened up again.

Nothing could have pleased me more—so why on earth didn't I show it? "Thank you, that would be nice, but only if you're up for it. It's getting chilly out here. Let's go into the kitchen. I'll make you a nice cup of ersatz coffee, and as a special treat we'll open a tin of Carnation."

"Gee, thanks—nothing better than a splash of the old evaporated."

I made Camp coffee, and to his credit, he didn't wince or shudder as he took a tentative sip. "See what you mean about Carnation being a treat," he said. "How did your air-raid drill go? And I want to hear all about Audrey."

I told him about our flop of a drill. About Mr. Angus in his pink-striped pajamas, and the rest of them struggling up the High Street with their cuckoo clocks, fishing rods, and birds in cages. About Mrs. Glossop's voice being the only one to be heard above the air-raid siren. "That Mrs. Glossop." He was holding his side and trying not to laugh. "I can just see her shrieking at the Girl Guides to stop messing about—I love the way you tell it."

Encouraged, I told him about Sid standing at the ready to shoot Jerry out of the sky, and then we stopped laughing, and I settled down to fill him in about Audrey.

"I think she was meeting someone on the night of the drill," he said when I had finished. "I just remembered you telling me that she was all dressed up when you last saw her. I mean, *really* dressed up—right?"

The same thought had occurred to me—that Audrey had a secret admirer. "Yes, but just because a woman gets dressed up, does it have to be because she is meeting a man?"

He looked puzzled for a moment. "I don't know. I'm just going by what you told me about her. If she usually scruffs about in old clothes and her dad's sweater, and then suddenly she is dressed up to the nines and wears lipstick, what does that mean? What would make you put on lipstick and curl your hair?"

I wasn't going to answer that dangerous question. "I can't imagine that she was meeting anyone from the base. Audrey told me she would never date an American."

"She might *say* that—she might *pretend* she's not interested, but I bet you anything you like she was meeting a Yank. You British girls are so reticent—you never like to let on if you are smitten." I glanced up to see if he was joking, but his face was quite serious, and I blushed. Flushed cheeks on a brunette are enchanting; on a redhead they are a disaster. "Unless of course she has developed a crush on Sid Ritchie." He seemed to find this thought inordinately amusing because he laughed in a most uncharitable way.

"I suppose she could have been meeting someone from the base. She *was* found up there by Bart's Field."

"Curfew is at midnight."

"And the badgers' sett was filled in when?"

"That's classified information." He must have seen the incredulous look on my face because he added, "It was filled in after Ponsonby." He put down his coffee cup and got to his feet. "C'mon, let's go talk to Audrey. We can drive over to the hospital right now."

It must be their diet, all that beef, eggs, and milk. Americans have this boundless energy. Even after being ditched in the icy waters of the Channel for hours, Griff was ready for action. I almost hated to quell his enthusiasm.

"Her parents went over to the hospital this morning and she was still very woozy—no visitors except family, even tomorrow."

"Okay then, we'll go over tomorrow: visit Audrey and then have dinner. What do you say?"

I tried not to say, "Yes that would be very nice," too eagerly.

I HAD TIME to finish a chapter before Griff and I set off to visit Audrey at Wickham General Hospital. The love of Ilona's life was missing in action. It wasn't difficult to write about how devastated she was—the words simply poured like water from a faucet. Anxious and heartbroken, Ilona threw herself into her work, filling her hours and days with the lives and adventures of others. She could hardly eat; she barely slept. I paused. Griff had been missing for only three days and I had enjoyed a heap of toast and jam for breakfast after the air-raid drill and slept for hours that night. Perhaps I wasn't in love with Griff after all. Perhaps I was merely infatuated. I was so absorbed in trying to sort out the difference between infatuation and love that I didn't hear him arrive until he called out, "Aren't you ready yet? We have to leave in five minutes; otherwise we'll miss visiting hour."

THERE IS NOTHING quite as delightful as a drive in the country on an early autumn afternoon. The Women's Voluntary Service girls had brought in the harvest weeks ago, and the rich, nutty smell of cut wheat fields scented the golden air as we bowled along the narrow, hedge-lined lane to town. Griff had put the top of the Alvis down, so any conversation below a shout was impossible. But I was merely content to enjoy the glories of the world as it flashed past me.

"Do we go right here?" All signposts were removed two years ago to confuse any stray German paratroopers, should they ever invade.

"Yes, three miles to Wickham. At the bottom of the hill take the left fork. Thank you for doing this, by the way."

"Doing what? You mean taking you to Wickham hospital? I promise you my motives are entirely selfish."

WHATEVER GRIFF'S MOTIVES were, the moment we were ushered down the long ward to Audrey's bed at its end, he appeared to lose all interest in whatever she had to tell us. He stood at the foot of her bed with his hands in his pockets. He had taken off his cap at least and smiled politely as he mentally absented himself from Women's Ward 2B and let us get on with our girls' visit.

"Hullo, Audrey." After being driven along country lanes with the sun on my face, I found myself almost monosyllabic. A complete disadvantage if you want information from a naturally taciturn woman who had been unconscious for twenty-four hours and was now lying between sheets of pristine white with a face to match.

Her voice was low and hoarse. " 'Lo," was all I got.

"No grapes, I'm afraid," I said, referring to the curse of food rationing.

"Don't like 'em." She was at her most reticent.

An awkward silence, and I bit my lip. Should I just wade in? I glanced at Griff, and he gave me a brief nod of encouragement.

"So, Audrey, what on earth happened?" I stupidly adopted the sort of Bradley heartiness, the vigorous exhuberance they commonly used at church fetes.

She sighed as if I was being particularly thick. "Someone bashed me."

"Any idea who?"

"Let me think." She made me wait. "Dark . . . wake up . . . half . . . village asking . . . same stupid question."

"I'm sorry, Audrey. I was just wondering what happened."

"Splitting head. Come to . . . point."

"Where were you when . . ."

"You know where."

"*Before* you were hit on the head." Silence as Audrey closed her eyes as if begging for divine intervention. "Audrey, please."

"Last . . . remember . . . saying good night."

"You met someone up at Bart's Field?"

Annoyance made her eloquent. "Blow me down, you haven't worked that one out yet? Yes! I was going to meet someone." I was pleased to notice that her voice was less feeble and her tone louder.

I glanced at Griff out of the corner of my eye. He was humming softly as he jangled small change around in his pocket. Audrey frowned at him and he apologized.

"Griff, there's a canteen somewhere if you want a cup of coffee," I said.

"I'm fine, thanks. Audrey, may I tell your . . . friend that you're doing just great?" He perched on the side of her bed, ready now to participate.

"No sitting on beds!" The directive came like the lash of a whip, and for a man with broken ribs, Griff was up off Audrey's bed like a rocketing pheasant in October. An angular, grim-faced woman with iron gray curls glued to a high forehead and eyes like black ice sprang up out of nowhere. She was dressed in the uniform of a QAIMNS ward sister: the elite military nursing corps founded by Queen Alexandra. A quick glance at the fob watch pinned to an apron crackling with starch, and she launched into the attack. "Are you family?"

"Brother and sister," said Griff. "I was given two days' leave to come and see our younger sister, Audrey. Ain't that right, sis?" I was grateful that he wasn't doing his beloved cockney accent.

Audrey smiled. But the ward sister didn't even look at him as she smoothed and tucked in the turned-down bedsheet tightly across Audrey's chest, for added protection against her fake brother. "Young man, it doesn't matter to me if you broke out of a German POW camp to come here today. Five minutes and then you must leave. This patient needs her rest. Am I clear?"

Griff said she was as clear as crystal and gave her one of his special smiles. There was a minimal thaw as Sister turned and marched on to the next bed.

"No need to be scared, Lieutenant. Underneath that starch and corsetry beats a heart of gold." Audrey was smiling now. Is there anyone in the world who can resist Griff? "Looks like *you've* seen some action." She was flirting with him; it was quite wonderful to see. Audrey was not only playful; she was fully aware she was flirting and reveled in it.

As Griff regaled her with a lively account of his bailing out over the English Channel, I sidled over to the bedside table to admire a dozen red roses with long straight stems and no thorns (they must have cost a fortune) in a glass vase. Surely only an American could afford these, I thought, as I squinted my eyes to read the card: "Hope you're recovered enough to go dancing on Friday! All my love, Bill."

All my love. The American Air Force had been here just over six weeks and Audrey had managed to secure all of Bill's love?

As Griff and Audrey bantered back and forth—he volubly, she sparingly—I realized that Audrey was one of those women who preferred the company of men. We girls were apparently an irritant, an unfortunate necessity of life. Audrey was happy to flirt with Griff, but I had to beg for her attention. "Audrey, please, we have less than four minutes . . ."

She switched her gaze from Griff to me and frowned. "Told the police. Now you?"

"Come on, Audrey. Tell Poppy. Tell her everything you can remember. Why? Because she cares more about you than some overworked cop from Wickham does. She spent the morning, afternoon, and evening with your mom as they waited for news of you. Least you could do, don'tcha think?"

Audrey considered him for a moment and then turned her head on her pillow to me. "I met my friend at the lambing hut. He left, and I was going to go up to the village to help Mrs. Martin."

"What time do you think that was?"

"I had to leave at a quarter to twelve."

"Do you know who attacked you?"

Her look was derisive.

"What do you think happened to you, Audrey, up at Bart's Field?"

She closed her eyes for a moment, and Griff and I looked at each other. "Go on"—he made a circular motion with his hand. "Audrey, what happened to you?"

She pulled aside the collar of her nightdress to reveal a thick bandage; her face was the color of whey, and I realized what an effort this conversation was for her. Her hand lifted to indicate her thickly bandaged head.

"Was it a man?"

"Dunno." She pointed a tired finger at me. "Don't stir . . . it up . . . don't want another Yank in . . . lockup." Her voice faded, and she closed her eyes.

I put a reassuring hand over hers, and she slid it out from underneath mine. "Don't . . . get sloppy," she warned me.

"I'm glad you're pulling through, Audrey," was all I dared say.

"I'm not stupid Doreen, or daft Ivy." Her voice was barely a whisper.

Sister's voice warned us we had seconds left.

"Smell," Audrey said. Her eyelids flickered and then closed. "Attacker . . . strong smell. Camphor smell."

I froze—camphor? The only person I knew who smelled like that was Mrs. Glossop. Doreen used to call her "Old Mothballs."

"Camphor? Are you sure?"

"Yes . . . course I am."

EIGHTEEN

G RIFF AND I WERE SHOWN TO A TABLE IN A LITTLE CORNER of the dining room at the Red Lion Hotel—Wickham's only posh restaurant. A candle was lit in the center of a cloth-covered table adorned by a single red carnation in a stem vase. The lights were low and, for some reason, a dusky pink, so everyone looked as if they were suffering from pernicious anemia.

As soon as he had seated me, the maître d' flourished two menus in front of us and left us to it. A band was squeaking out a barely recognizable Gershwin tune, and a very young woman with a paper gardenia in her hair was doing her best to sound like Billie Holliday, which is difficult to do if you come from Surrey.

Ordinarily, I would have been swamped with shyness at having a candlelit dinner with a man I found irresistible. But from the moment Audrey had said "camphor," my mind had immediately gone to Mrs. Glossop.

"I know it sounds ridiculous, but Mrs. Glossop has a distinctive reek of camphor about her. Do you think that tiny woman could tackle two healthy young girls like Doreen and Ivy—let alone someone of Audrey's intimidating height?"

I was feeling particularly heady for two reasons: one, Audrey had survived her attack and had information to share, and two, here I was alone with Griff, and however bad it was, there was a band, and that meant dancing.

"Mrs. Glossop." Griff considered. "How tall is she? Five feet at a pinch. I suppose she might take a woman of Audrey's height and build by surprise. But isn't camphor used for other things? I think we put it in liniment, but that's for horses." He leaned back in his chair and smiled across the table at me. "What will you have to drink? I seem to remember you like martinis. Do they know how to make them here?"

"Probably not. This isn't London." I remembered that the sherry in the Red Lion was that sweet stuff they call cream sherry. I suddenly felt sophisticated and rather daring. "I'll have a gin and tonic, please."

Before the war, the Red Lion was a pleasant place to have lunch or dinner after a day of shopping in Wickham. But in the last three years it had become *the* place to go if you were a serviceman looking to, in Griff's parlance, "live it up," because it is the only restaurant in town that has a dance floor.

One of the things snobby girls' boarding schools specialize in is equipping their pupils for the ballroom, and I love to dance. I wanted to be taken onto the dance floor by a man who knew how to dance, the sort of thing you see Fred Astaire doing with Ginger Rogers: the Hollywood version of what we call the foxtrot.

"Do the English use liniment?" Griff asked.

"I *think* we use liniment on horses, and embrocation on humans. But I expect they amount to the same thing. What's in liniment?"

"Menthol usually, and wintergreen—which is what might have made Audrey think of camphor. I would say that the smell of either or both is what she's remembering." He turned to the waiter and ordered two gin and tonics—with ice.

"It doesn't sound very much like the sort of thing one of your fellow pilots would use if he was courting."

"Pilots?" He frowned.

"I think I'm safe in saying that no one in Little Buffenden, or anywhere else around here, could, or would, send a dozen red roses to Audrey. So, they were probably from an American. An American with the first name of Bill. I read it on the card to Audrey, the one from whoever sent those roses."

He whistled, and his eyes narrowed. "Bill? There's only one Bill up at the base. Bill Peterson."

I remembered an evening at the Rose and Crown. Bill Peterson, massively tall, Nordicly blond and nice-looking, in a sort of Labrador retriever kind of way, had said that he was dating a wonderful woman who could not be kept waiting. "Bill Peterson is courting Audrey!" Bill Peterson was an exceptionally good-natured man: well mannered and kindly. I was so pleased for Audrey, I sounded quite triumphant.

His answer horrified me. "Who said Bill was *courting*?" He laughed, the sort of laugh that men make when they are with their male friends. "Sounds like he was looking to have a good time to me—in Bart's Field in the old lambing hut."

His answer was so offhand, and at the same time so revealing, that I was not only shocked; I was angry. "A good time—with a girl who happens to be one of the most vulnerable people I know?" I snapped.

I have no idea why I was so angry with Griff; after all, he knew Bill better than I did, and if Bill Peterson was a carefree womanizer, it didn't reflect on Audrey, only on him. But I felt in the way he said those words that he was being dismissive—dismissive of a girl who had gone out of her way to be attractive, a girl who had been laughed at, ridiculed in our village as Big Audrey. And who was now dating an American officer who had referred to her as "wonderful." I also hated to hear that offhand and rather crude phrase on the lips of a man I was hopelessly in love, or maybe now just infatuated, with.

He reached a placatory hand across the table to take mine. But I wasn't having it. I put both my hands in my lap. Childish, I know, but I was genuinely shocked. A gin and tonic was put in front of me, without ice, and I took a tentative sip. It was awful. The tonic made it taste terribly sweet in a bitter sort of way, and the smell of warm gin was nauseating. I put it down and stared down at the cloth.

"You've got the wrong end of the stick, Poppy. Of course he was out to have a good time. I don't think we mean it quite the way the English do, by the way. I wasn't being disrespectful; really, I wasn't. It's just that Bill has always had lots of girls hanging on his arm. He's one of nature's flirts."

For some reason this made me even more angry. "And he couldn't *possibly* be *in love* with someone like Audrey."

"Of course he *could*." He didn't sound too convinced.

Our waiter brought sardines on toast as an hors d'oeuvre, but I was so angry I could barely bring myself to eat them. Were we English girls just something to pass the time with to these worldly men who spoke our language but always seemed to mean something else? And if we were not prepared to "give them a good time," was one of them capable of whacking us over the head or strangling us with their gift of stockings?

And what was worse, had I mistaken Griff's attentiveness to our investigation as interest in me when he was only trying to find out whether the Little Buffenden Strangler was an American, or which one of us was interested in spying on his precious bloody airfield?

They say that lack of self-confidence can make for suspicion and doubt. I picked up my knife and fork and stared down at my greasy sardines, too miserable to eat. It was as if the members of the band understood my misery, because they launched into "Let's Call the Whole Thing Off."

"Will you put your knife and fork down and dance with me— please, Poppy?" I looked up and saw his face across the table: his hazel eyes glowing, his smile persuasive. "C'mon. Let's shelve this mystery for a while and do what everyone else does these days. Let's dance and pretend we haven't a care in the world. After all, you say to-mah-toes and I say to-may-ters, so this tune is meant for us."

And for every other American serviceman looking to have a good time with some little girl from an English village, I couldn't help thinking, as he got up and came around to the back of my chair and helped me to my feet. As we joined other couples on the dance floor, I made a supreme effort to push away my doubts and relax. It was so easy to follow him, because Griff O'Neal is a natural dancer.

IT WAS THE smell of camphor that woke me up the next morning, long before dawn. Not the actual smell but the realization that it was not only Mrs. Glossop who fills her chest of drawers with mothballs; there are other dedicated camphor and embrocation users in our village too.

Our vicar liberally slathers on lashings of the stuff for his cricket knee when the weather is damp and chilly. Mr. Angus, our butcher, uses something similar throughout the winter months for a stiff shoulder. Even Len Smith, who found Doreen under his church-yard hedge, uses wintergreen on his back after a long day in the garden. Lumbago, old cricket injuries, tennis elbow, a wrenched shoulder from hacking up raw meat: embrocation users in the British Isles at this time of year must be endless in their numbers.

Our villagers had probably dug out their favorite nostrums from their medicine chests as soon as the weather had changed. I counted back to the three rainy nights that had heralded the onset of autumn before our air-raid drill and Audrey's attack. By now I was thoroughly awake and giving up on sleep. I moved a heavy Bess off my feet and put on my dressing gown. I needed tea.

Downstairs, as I waited for the kettle to boil, I thumbed through the pages of my exercise book to my first list of able-bodied men in our village, the one I had written the day after Doreen's death.

Not bothering with my grandfather, who uses some infinitely foul ointment for a stiff neck the moment the thermometer sinks below thirty-five degrees, I worked my way methodically through my list.

Cedric Fothergill. How disrespectful, I thought. He is our vicar, for heaven's sake, and one of the most decent men I know. And he is far too self-contained to strangle women in the dead of night—or at any other time.

Mr. Angus. Unfortunately, I had no difficulty in seeing those red, powerful hands tightening on smooth white skin, and embrocation was one of our butcher's standbys no matter the season.

Len Smith. How ludicrous of me to have written his name. Gentle Len? He had been sick with distress when he had found Doreen under the hedge. But he was a great fan of a very strong camphor-scented embrocation that he used unsparingly in the autumn and winter months.

Mr. Newcombe. I just crossed his name through.

Bert Pritchard. Now, Bert did have a bit of a wandering eye—or so I had been told. In his youth he had been considered Little Buttenden's Lothario, disappointing all the available village maidens when he had married the outgoing Gladys Wilcox, a city girl from Wickham. Who had told me all about the Pritchards in their courting days? Mrs. Glossop, of course.

I wrote her name down. I mustn't be put off by the fact that Mrs. G. is too tiny to effectively tackle Doreen, Ivy, or Audrey. Our postmistress is particularly judgmental, and sometimes the spry are stronger than we imagine. And she always has been extravagant with the mothballs.

I stared down at my list as I sipped strong tea. There was a pattering of feet and I was joined by Bess. She sprang up into my lap: the tiled floor was ice-cold and there was a penetrating draft coming from the scullery door. I hugged her to me to keep warm.

"I have widened my list of possible suspects, Bessie. All based on smell—something I know you will appreciate." She wagged her rump and stared at the hardtack we refer to as a ginger biscuit. I handed it over.

"I should ask myself what possible motive any of them could have for killing or wanting to kill three girls." I looked at the first name on my list. "Could our vicar be a religious fanatic, obsessed with original sin? Perhaps he believed that Doreen, Ivy, and Audrey were wantonly infatuated with Americans?" It was an amusing thought, and that's all it was. But I did not cross through his name; I put a question mark to indicate that I must follow up.

"Has butchering all that raw meat sent Mr. Angus round the bend? I could see him hacking through joints of meat, seething with rage that no one finds him attractive anymore, as he lusts after young girls—who laugh at him. History has had its fair share of murderous butchers; look at that man who made his victims into pies." I put an asterisk next to Mr. Angus because he was the most likely of all my suspects, and I must find out where he had been on the three nights in question. It should be easy—especially for the night of the air raid.

"What about poor old Len Smith? Dedicated to the hallowed sanctuary of the church and churchyard. Perhaps he had come across Doreen and her boyfriend behaving outrageously on a grave-stone, and before he could stop himself, he killed her. Perhaps Ivy saw something or suspected something, and he had to kill her too." Clearly the man or woman who had set out to kill three girls was mentally unstable, but Len was as sane as they come. I put a question mark next to his name.

And while I was on the subject of mild-mannered men, I had to include Sid Ritchie on my list. Every winter he slathered on cam-phorated oil as a preventative against bronchitis. But I hadn't no-ticed that he had been reeking of it when he had joined me on the green on the night of the air-raid drill, which would have been after Audrey had been attacked. I jotted his name down. Then I remembered that Sid had been thirty miles away in Wickham doing his Home Guard small-arms training when Doreen had been killed.

I tapped pencil on paper as I considered Sid Ritchie. His dislike of the American Air Force was tedious, but it was also rather obsessive. Did he have what it took to kill the girls he had grown up with? I was tempted to both cross him off and put a question mark by his name. My conversations with him on our patrols convinced me that he was a bit on the neurotic side, but he was too docile in temperament to kill, and completely lacking in imagination to prevaricate so consistently. I put a question mark next to his name.

A sleeping Bess started to slide off my lap, and I hitched her back into place. "You know something, Bess? I think my favorite suspect is Bert Pritchard. He always has had a rather lecherous look about him—perhaps underneath all that professional cheerfulness beats the heart of a predator." I remembered the night of the air-raid drill. Bert had been very prominent: shepherding people down into his cellar and then standing everyone a drink when the all clear went. Would he have had the time to run up to Bart's Field and try to strangle Audrey before the drill? It was well-known that Mrs. Pritchard was the workhorse of the Rose and Crown. Bert played darts or disappeared down into his precious cellar to take an inventory and to test his vintage brandy. It was only during the rush at opening time that he would be at the bar playing host. I should check Bert Pritchard's movements between a quarter to twelve and when the air-raid drill had started at half past. And I should make sure that I checked with Audrey that she was sure of her times, too.

A thought struck me. How had Audrey's attacker known that she would be up at the lambing hut? She was so cagey I couldn't imagine that she had mentioned her date with Bill Peterson to anyone. Not even to her mother.

I jotted down my estimated time for Audrey's movements that night. At seven o'clock she had left the farm to walk up to Bart's Field. Her attacker, having decided that she would be his next victim, must have been watching the farm and followed her. Just as I had followed Ponsonby. He or she had hidden while Audrey had spent time with Bill Peterson, and at a quarter to midnight, when Bill had left and Audrey was setting off for the vicarage, her attacker had made a move. Would Bert have the time to lurk in waiting from seven o'clock until nearly midnight? I put a question mark next to his name.

Which brought me to the Americans. Of the two men known by Doreen and Ivy, Bud Sandusky and Joe Perrone, Sandusky had been too ill from food poisoning to leave the base on the night Doreen had been killed, and Joe Perrone still wasn't completely in the clear. He could have left the base via the badgers' sett and killed both Doreen and Ivy. But he could not have attacked Audrey, because he was locked up in prison. That left every man on the base who had not been flying a mission on the nights of Doreen's and Ivy's murders and Audrey's attack as possible suspects. We had been told before they arrived that the American Air Force population for our new airfield was well over a hundred and thirty men, maybe even more. I had no idea how many of that number had been killed or wounded in action since their arrival, and still less about replacements. And it didn't matter if the gates to the base were closed every night at midnight, or if their perimeter fence was a mile high; anyone from the base could have used the badgers' sett to come and go at will, until Ponsonby's arrest.

My heart rate picked up considerably at my next thought: perhaps Audrey's attacker was not the same person who had killed Doreen and Ivy. I felt my tired head spin.

Concentrate on one thing at a time, Ilona instructed. *Take a nice deep breath and just focus on what you know about Audrey's attacker. Your problem is you're a wee bit prejudiced, darling, and it's clouding your thinking. You are aware, aren't you, that everyone in the village calls you the Yank-lover?*

NINETEEN

I HEARD THAT YOU WENT TO WICKHAM TO SEE AUDREY."

"Mm . . ." I was so lost in my thoughts that I had been nodding along to a string of Sid's complaints without listening.

"Nice of that American to give you a lift in his car." His voice was a bit too admonishing for my taste, so I ignored him. Would this rift between our village and the base never resolve itself?

"And why do you invite all of them to lunch every Sunday?"

I sighed, loudly, as a warning that I was fed up with all this anti-Yank business.

"No, really, Poppy, I don't understand why they are so favored."

"We don't invite *all* of them. We invite *some* of them and *some* of the people in our village! And you were asked to come last Sunday, when we invited your mum, so why did you pretend you had another engagement?" He stopped and shot me a look in the moonlight that was so shocked at my curt tone that I reined it in. "Honestly, Sid, you might at least give them a try. Once you get to know them, they are not that much different from us."

"Yes, they are! They have more money and they never stop

splashing it about. And they're . . . they're . . ." He racked his brain. "They're cocky know-it-alls. Mum came back after lunch with them and said they all couldn't stop bragging about their baseball games and their hot dogs, whatever they are—sounds disgusting to me."

It was all so ludicrous I knew I shouldn't take him so seriously. "They weren't bragging; they were trying to explain why they were called hot dogs."

But Sid hadn't finished airing his frustration. "And"—he was scowling at me—"you didn't tell me you were going around with a Yank. I thought we were friends; I thought we could tell each other everything!"

I can't remember when I told Sid anything personal. Our conversations were one-sided: he did the talking and I thought of something else. I must have looked annoyed because he was instantly contrite. "Their coming here has ruined our village— nothing's the same." His lower lip jutted in protest, and he turned away from me. "We don't need *them* to win this war."

Of course, he was jealous. Unable to join up to fight for his country, he had felt out of place and inadequate. Then Grandad had rescued him by recruiting him into the Home Guard: finally, he could be a soldier and forget the shame of not doing his bit for the war effort. And then the Americans flew in to their new airfield to rescue us from a German invasion, and Sid's village had been invaded by what he saw as cocky Yanks, splashing their money about and charming all the women. He felt threatened and he believed that the Americans were responsible for the deaths of his childhood friends.

I put out a hand, took his upper arm, and gently turned him to me. "I know what you mean, Sid. It does seem as if terrible things have happened since the Americans arrived. Please try to see that underneath their cultural differences they are just like us. Just get to know them a bit, and you'll see how much we have in common with them."

He shrugged off my hand and adjusted his Sten gun. "We'd better get going." His voice was grumpy. "I'm usually on my way up Streams Lane by now when I'm doing ARP patrol."

If he was determined to be touchy, then the best thing to do was change the subject. "Audrey sent you her love." She hadn't, of course—I only said it to appease—but I was astonished by his reaction.

His head whipped round, and his scowl deepened. "There's another one," he said. "Everyone in the village is saying she was seeing a Yank too. I can't believe it—she was never interested in them, not even when they first came." Except for Hollywood movie stars and Bill Peterson, I thought.

His voice broke. "But I thought better of you, Poppy, really I did. I thought you cared more for this country and this village. One of those fun-loving Yanks up there"—he nodded his sorrowful head in the wrong direction—"is a mass murderer, and you say there is no difference between us all."

I felt nothing but exasperation, when all Sid was doing was telling me how he felt. I summoned patience. "But Joe Perrone was put in jail after the slimmest of inquiries, and now it's quite possible that he is innocent. The only other American who knew Ivy and Doreen was Bud Sandusky, and he had a very strong alibi for his girlfriend's murder: food poisoning. And are you quite sure that

Audrey is dating an American?" I knew she was, but how had the village found out?

"I don't know." He looked worried. "But that's what everyone's saying, except you." He paused as he heard himself. "You don't believe it was one of us, do you?" His face was so incredulous, so shocked at my possible wrong thinking, that if he hadn't been so devastated about what he believed was happening to us, it would have been farcical. "You don't really believe that *one of us* killed Doreen and Ivy and put Audrey in hospital?"

I had never seen him this distressed before. And I realized that he was probably just echoing the sort of rubbish he had heard in the village—from Mrs. Glossop. "Does everyone think this way?" I asked him. "Does everyone think that it was an American?"

"Yes, they do," he said. "Crikey, Poppy, wake up!"

"No, I mean *everyone*, not just Mrs. Glossop and your mum."

This gave him pause. "The Pritchards do; so do the Newcombes and the Wantages."

"I know Mr. Fothergill doesn't, and neither do my grandparents, and I never heard the Wilkeses laying blame on the Americans after Audrey was attacked."

He was shaking his head again. "They may not say it, but they think it. Everyone deep down thinks the murderer is an American. No one can remember a time when there was murder done in our village—until *they* came. It's all *their* fault." His voice was muffled with emotion. "I can't understand you, Poppy. I really can't. How could you think it was one of us? How could you believe that someone we know would want to kill those girls? I wish the airfield had never been built, I really do."

He was so distressed that I put out my hand to him and he took it. "It's all right," he said. "I mean, I'm all right. Really, I am." He dashed away tears with his free hand. "I just feel so helpless. And I don't want you to be . . . you know, hurt in any way."

"Why do you think I would be harmed?"

"Because you are seeing an American."

"Not in that way; not in the way Doreen and Ivy were seeing Americans. Lieutenant O'Neal just helps me with the Sunday lunch."

He sighed—a deep, gusty sigh of misery.

"I see every single girl in this village behaving like fools because some American takes her out dancing and to the flicks, and then just when everyone is friends and saying how nice the Americans are, just like that"—he waved his hand in the air—"terrible things start to happen. But I never expected *you* to act that way. I thought you were different—more sensible." He turned away, his face stricken.

"I am not behaving foolishly. Neither am I dating an American."

"Oh, really. Why do you keep saying that when you see him all the time? And if you knew what I knew about him, you'd ditch him pretty quickly."

I was so shocked by this that I switched on my torch and shone it on his face.

"Who?" I demanded so hotly that he looked almost scared. "Just *who* are you talking about?"

"Your American."

"And what is his name, since you know so much about him? Go on, tell me."

He cocked his head on one side and looked at me as if I were a simpleton. "I can't remember what his name is. But he drives that red car about—so you know who I mean because he took you to Wickham in it. Even during their midnight curfew I saw him driving that sports car in the direction of Lower Netherton. Now do you see?" He looked miserable. "I wasn't going to tell you, because I know you like him. I didn't want to hurt you . . . but I don't want you to be the next victim." He looked away. "Now I've said it, and I'm sorry, but it is for your own good, Poppy. I couldn't stand it if you were . . ." He couldn't finish he was so choked up.

"This is bloody ridiculous," I shouted, sounding just like Grandad in one of his thunderous moods. "I don't want to hear another word about Americans, Sid. I think you've lost all sense of proportion about them. It's the shock of what's happening in the village." He turned away from me in a huff. "And I don't want your company if you're going to sulk. So please pull yourself together." And of course, it worked. Sid, if anything, was the obedient type—after all, his mum is the village schoolteacher and used to keeping order in crowded classrooms.

On we tramped in silence. Sid kept his shoulder turned away from me like a sullen schoolgirl. The heat in my cheeks cooled and the anger left me, but I kept hearing Sid's voice: "He drives that red car about . . . Even during their midnight curfew I saw him driving that sports car in the direction of Lower Netherton."

We turned into Streams Lane, with Bess yards ahead because she hates arguments and raised voices. As we came up to the bridge, I offered up a flag of truce. "You're twenty-one next week, aren't you, Sid? I would like to buy you a drink at the 'Sheaf to celebrate."

"No, thank you, Poppy. I'd rather not. I don't hold with smoking and drinking, but thanks all the same."

Despite his refusal to celebrate his birthday, at least he was less sulky. When we got to the narrow bridge, he made a great effort. "After you, Claude." His imitation of Jack Train on *ITMA* was flawless, even down to the intonation.

I was only too happy to respond: "No, after you, Cecil," and I heard him giggle. *Phew,* said Ilona as I walked over the bridge that we had found Ivy Wantage lying under in what seemed like another lifetime. *I'm glad all that's sorted out and you can be friends again.*

I LAY AWAKE staring at the ceiling all night with a sleeping dog on my stomach and a head full of ridiculous fantasies. I couldn't get what Sid had said out of my mind. Why was Griff allowed to leave the base when everyone was restricted from leaving? There was no doubt that he had left with permission, because he was in his car, which meant he had had to go through a well-guarded gate. Had he been off base on the nights that three girls from our village had been attacked?

I had almost confided in Grandad—or at least I had asked him for information, which is the same thing, because he always knows when I'm rattled.

"Do you think they do some sort of intelligence work up at the base? You know the sort of clandestine stuff our Navy Intelligence gets up to—like spying?" In my mind I saw a red sports car driving down Smithy Lane to Lower Netherton.

"I shouldn't think so, but they probably have a counterintelligence officer or two up there. Most military installations do; they must protect themselves from espionage, you see. But I can't imagine that they actively gather intelligence—their job is to attack the enemy and defend us by counterattack. Are you thinking about Ponsonby and all the gossip circulating about him? You shouldn't bother yourself; you know what the village is like. He probably does have a sick mother." I hadn't told my grandparents that I had seen Ponsonby's arrest, or my involvement in discovering how he could get onto the airfield, because Griff had asked me to keep it to myself, and if they thought I was putting myself in the slightest danger, my ARP patrol would be a thing of the past. "I like Griff. He is a very decent, straightforward sort. If he is in counter-intelligence, it shouldn't be something you should worry about."

He was right; there was nothing dishonorable in protecting your country's military secrets. But still I couldn't sleep. I tossed around, disturbing Bess, who groaned theatrically and jumped off the bed to sleep in her basket. *I thought Sid was color-blind. How could he be so sure it was a red car?* Ilona put in as I thumped pillows and searched for a cool spot to lay my head. I smiled in the dark: all the American Air Force vehicles were a sort of muddy green, easily confused with red in the dark. But at night when you are overtired and agitated, the slightest thing becomes important and takes on all sorts of dire portents, so it was at least an hour later before I dropped off into a deep and exhausted sleep.

TWENTY

I AWOKE HEAVY-EYED AND LOW IN SPIRITS: THE SORT OF FEELING
I used to get when my trunk was packed and it was time to go
back to school. I brushed my hair and put it up in a victory roll the
way Fenella Bradley wears hers, and then shook it down and left it
the way I always wear it, which is in no particular style at all. I decided that I wasn't going to examine what Sid had said about Griff
until I had had a chance to talk to him.

I have a lot to do today, I told myself as I made my bed. There
were several chapters to write, and Audrey had given us a very useful clue that I would start to work through. I got out my list of villagers plagued with rheumatism, stiff joints, and bad backs and read
it through.

Cedric Fothergill was at the top of my list, and whether I liked
the idea of him being our strangler or not, he was known to be lavish with Foster's Embrocation, which made the church vestry reek
of wintergreen.

Bess and I arrived at the vicarage just in time for a prelunch
glass of our vicar's excellent Amontillado sherry. I pray his cellar is

never depleted before the end of the war, because a good glass of sherry has a very civilizing effect during difficult times.

"Sid seems to be shaping up as our assistant ARP warden—you have done a good job of training him. Do you think his nerve would hold up in an air raid?"

"He seemed pretty calm on the night of our drill." I was fed up with Sid and his ridiculous fancies.

"Bert Pritchard told me that Sid was pretty hard on him showing light on his patrol last week. Threatened to close the pub down." Mr. Fothergill smiled into his generous glass of sherry.

I could see Sid's earnest face as he shouted through the door of the pub at Mr. Pritchard and giggled. "He doesn't hold with the demon drink," I said in Sid's Biggles voice as I sipped my sherry. Its nutty warmth trickled down my throat. "Actually, he doesn't hold with much at all—except perhaps the Royal Air Force and Biggles."

I hadn't noticed a particularly strong smell of wintergreen hanging about the vicarage hall when I was blown through the front door by a particularly rough autumn wind. And even though I had accidentally dropped my keys on the floor as Mr. Fothergill took my coat, there was not the slightest whiff of Foster's hanging around his knees.

It is always pleasant passing the time of day with our vicar. He is one of the most relaxed clergymen I have ever met and enjoys a good gossip just like any other country bachelor. He once told me that vicarhood in a comfortable rectory with a few pleasant neighbors is a perfect way to live a country life. I honestly don't think he lets ecclesiastical stuff bother him much. He is the sort of vicar who appreciates the architectural glories of the church rather than worrying about his congregation's relationship with their maker.

"Bitterly cold out," I said, and he obediently poured me another glass of sherry.

How on earth do you ask your vicar how his knee is doing? I wondered as I brought the conversation around to the change in the weather.

"And wet—hope it's not going to be a hard winter," he dutifully replied, because according to Griff, we English know a thing or two about a proper conversational exchange on the elements.

"I hope it isn't as wet as it was last year," I observed. "ARP patrol won't be much fun if it is." And thanks to the miraculous way a glass of sherry loosens inhibitions: "This damp weather hasn't given you any trouble, then, with your knee?"

He looked rather surprised at my inquiry after his physical person but answered quite readily. "Dr. Oliver diagnosed arthritis."

"All that cricket up at Cambridge, I expect."

"Cricket?" He laughed. "Oh no, I wasn't really good enough for the university team. I enjoy playing, but I was hardly a Cricket Blue. My passion was the theater in those far-off days. Did I tell you that I was the star in *HMS Pinafore* for May Bumps?" I shook my head. The only thing I knew about what Cambridge called its week of rowing races was its wild parties in celebration. "Ah yes, I was quite good at comic opera." He took a breath, and to my surprise, he warbled in a rather faulty baritone:

When I was a lad I served a term
As office boy to an Attorney's firm.

I cleaned the windows and I swept the floor,
And I polished up the handle of the big front door.
I polished up that handle so carefullee
That now I am the Ruler of the Queen's Navee!

I was grateful he treated me to only one verse. "Somewhere . . ." He looked around and picked up an old well-worn photo album that was lying on a low table. "Where is it, now? Ah yes, here we are. *That* was me in *HMS Pinafore*. Brought the house down with that one." And there he was, looking like a younger, brighter, and more chipper version of himself, wearing a theatrical navy uniform. "And here is another of me, when we did *The Mikado*. Just for a lark, I played one of the Three Little Maids. That was awfully good fun." I nodded, my face stretched in an approving smile that was beginning to ache with the effort of trying not to laugh at a photograph of our vicar dressed in kimono and a full black wig smiling coyly over his fan. "It wasn't all Shakespeare at Cambridge in those days!" He smiled at his joke. "Anyway, the doc has had me off embrocations for a couple of years now, says they are a waste of time. Just two aspirin in the morning and two again at night. It's astonishing what a difference it makes. Whatever you do, Poppy, don't get old." I finished my sherry and he got up from his chair to walk me to the front door.

"Oh dear," he said as he threw it open—it was hammering down outside. He handed me an umbrella. "I think Mrs. Ritchie left this one in the church hall when she came to help Mrs. Martin get ready for the jumble sale. That woman has a passion for jumble sales, doesn't she, Viv?" he asked as Mrs. Martin came through the baize door from a kitchen that smelled of warm apples and cinnamon.

"She's a jackdaw; she buys all sorts of useless things," his housekeeper said. "In the end I gave her her own key to the village hall storage, so she could come and go whenever she wants to, so she can earmark all her coveted treasures. Tell your granny that I'll have a couple of jars of crabapple jelly for her when it sets."

They stood together in the hall. "No need to return it, the umbrella, I mean. I notice that they have a way of circulating among the village at this time of year," Mrs. Martin said as they ushered me out into a day probably reminiscent of the one when Noah decided it was time to start building his ark.

WHENEVER I GO into Mr. Angus's shop I try not to look at his hands—especially if he is holding a meat cleaver. I have always been a bit squeamish about raw meat, and Fred Angus's hands look like two immense mutton chops. Not that we see many of those these days.

"Mrs. Redfern has already picked up your meat ration, Poppy." The butcher was stuffing ground pork and bread crumbs into sausage casings, a repulsive sight, so I looked away to say good afternoon to Mrs. Angus.

"I was wondering if you could spare some marrowbones—I am making stock for Sunday's lunch." She was sitting at her little desk in a corner by the door that leads into their house with her coupon ledger open in front of her.

Mrs. Angus is narrow where her husband is wide, pale and fair in contrast to his ruddy complexion and black hair. It's rumored that she was a nut cutlet girl before she met Mr. Angus and he converted her to meat.

"I am so sorry, dear, but we can't let you have anything without your ration book, and strictly speaking, marrowbones count as meat. But we really are looking forward to joining you and your grandparents for lunch." Even though the Anguses eat better than most of us do, roast beef is a rare treat even for them.

A thwack as Mr. Angus lifted his cleaver and cut through a pork shoulder lying on his chopping block—to my delight he winced.

"Looks like you have a sore shoulder, Mr. Angus. The vicar swears by aspirin to ease arthritis."

"Not me." A short, wheezy laugh. "I have my Elliman's Embrocation."

A loyal user! Did he have an alibi for the nights of the three murders? I reminded myself to tread carefully. Rather than go back to the night of Doreen's death, I decided it would be simpler if I dealt with the night of Audrey's attack and went on from there. Where had Mr. Angus been at eleven forty-five, when Bill Peterson left Audrey in Bart's Field? I had seen him in the High Street at the time of our air raid drill in his natty pajamas, which meant he had either been in bed or was about to go to bed. He could have easily followed Audrey up to Bart's Field and hidden there until Bill Peterson left and then returned home to change.

Remembering that he was a stalwart member of Little Buffenden Cribbage Club, which got together at either the Wheatsheaf or the Rose and Crown, I posed an idea I had had about inviting the Americans to become more involved in our village. "Good idea," he said with panting brevity as he took another whack at the mound of bone and gristle in front of him. "Except that we have two full teams already." He reached for a towel and dried his hands. I could see bits of raw pork still stuck to his meaty knuckles and looked away.

"And o' course they probably don't play cribbage over there in America. They play . . ." He thought for a moment. "They probably play poker." A short, breathless laugh. I remembered that Mr. Angus was not overfond of Americans.

"*Anyone* can play cribbage," piped up Mrs. Angus from her corner. It was well-known that Mrs. Angus and Mrs. Pritchard both thought the Americans were charming boys. "Anyway, it's not really about the game, is it? It's about making those boys feel welcome. No harm in asking them, is there?" She raised her thinly plucked eyebrows.

I beamed across at her. "What a good idea! How often do you play, Mr. Angus?"

He shrugged his shoulders. "Now and again."

"Every night, except Sundays, Mondays, and Thursdays, from six o'clock in the evening until half past whatever time they stop playing." Mrs. Angus pursed her lips and sharpened her pencil.

I couldn't imagine any of the poker players up at the base being the least interested in cribbage. "Who *is* in your club?" I asked.

"Len Smith, Tom Wantage, and Davey Wilkes and me, and some of yer grandad's Home Guard chaps, Mr. Edwards and Mr. Wilson. They *never* miss a night," said Mrs. Angus with some resignation. It was also known in the village that Mrs. Angus liked to keep her husband on a short leash. Was it because he had a wandering eye? "They normally play at the village hall, but on Fridays they play at the Rose, so Bert Pritchard can join them."

"That's right—every Friday," said Mr. Angus virtuously.

Friday night. It was the night of the air-raid drill and Audrey's attack.

"Wait a moment, Fred, you said as Bert Pritchard couldn't play with you last Friday."

"No more he couldn't. Too busy clearing out his cellar, and Mrs. Pritchard was run off her feet, so we had to cut the evening short. I was home in time to listen to *It's That Man Again* on the radio, with *you*, wasn't I, dear?" His watery eyes fastened themselves on her face, as if he was making a point.

"For once," she replied, and I realized that I was witnessing an argument between the butcher and his wife about how much time he spent with her as opposed to his cribbage mates.

If they had listened to *ITMA* together, he wouldn't have had time to run up to Bart's Field and back before the air-raid drill.

Mrs. Angus returned to her figures and I couldn't help but put Mr. Angus on the spot. "You might like to ask your club if they would be willing to invite some of our Americans."

Mr. Angus started to shake his head, his eyes on his wife as she added a long column of numbers. "Like I said, we already have two..." Mrs. Angus wrote down her total and looked up—straight at her husband. "Course I will, Miss Redfern, be glad to ask," he added.

I LEFT THE butcher's shop and walked across the green to the Rose and Crown. I was Bert's first lunchtime customer. And as he put up my half a shandy on the polished oak of his bar, I opened our conversation with thanks for his help during our drill.

"Glad to be of use, Miss Redfern. But it looks like it would have been a fiasco if it had been a real one." He wiped down the countertop.

"Yes, but you were well prepared, and that matters more than anything," I flattered as I took a sip of shandy and put it down carefully on the cardboard beer mat on his gleaming countertop.

He laughed. "Just between us, the vicar tipped me the wink. The wife took care of the customers while I was down in the cellar. There was a lot of stuff that had to be shifted to make room for them all. Len Smith and a couple of the cribbage lads gave me a hand."

"Is Len supposed to be lifting things with his bad back?"

"He just helped me with the light stuff." He winked at me. "Dr. Oliver has got him on some sort of medicine—little white pills— that stops his back from flaring up too badly. So, I went along to the doc about my lumbago, and he told me that all those embrocations are rubbish. Put me on those little white pills and you wouldn't believe the difference. Mrs. P. has never liked the smell of Foster's."

No embrocation for you or Len Smith, then, I thought, which put him in the clear, thanks to our doctor's passion for aspirin.

Bert set about polishing glasses. "I think we should do another drill; they should practice until they get it right."

"If we do too many drills, they won't react quickly enough when a real raid happens. They need to know that the next time the siren sounds, it will be the real thing."

"So, you think there'll be a real air raid, then?" He looked disbelieving. "I thought the Germans only bombed industrial cities, like Coventry, or London and the south coast."

"I hope you are right, Mr. Pritchard, but you never know. We have an airfield, so that increases the chances."

"More's the pity. Course, it would be different if we had our fly-boys up at that airfield and not a bunch of Americans." He caught himself and looked embarrassed. "Begging your pardon, Miss Redfern. I didn't mean to cause offense." He bent down to stack glasses under the bar, and I realized that here was another one who thought I was "seeing a Yank."

I took my shandy over to a table by the window and watched the leaves on the oak tree that spread its boughs over the pub roof fall in rain-drenched twos and threes to join a thick russet carpet on the grass, as I finished my drink.

TO MY SURPRISE, Mrs. Wantage was in the kitchen, mashing potatoes for lunch. She looked up as I came in through the door. "Lunch will be ready in a jiffy; I was about to lay the table," she said. "Wasn't sure if you would be back in time."

"How are you doing, Mrs. Wantage?" She had lost weight and her skin looked dull and papery.

Her eyes welled. "Some days are better than others, but it's best to keep busy. This terrible business with Audrey has brought it all back. Poor girl, thank the Lord she wasn't too badly . . ." She finished mashing and bent down to open the oven door. Before the war, Mrs. Wantage had her pick of great houses to work at, but she prefers to help us out. She and Granny are good friends in the way of women who have nothing in common whatsoever, but respect and like each other, and I knew Granny had been over to Mrs. Wantage's cottage several times since Ivy's death.

"It's good to see you here again, Mrs. Wantage," I said rather awkwardly. "I am so sorry about Ivy."

"Thank you, my dear." Her smile was shaky, and she turned

away. The subject was closed, and I wandered into the dining room and set the table to give her time to collect herself. She came in to fill the water glasses, her face determinedly cheerful.

"That American chap popped in here earlier on, wanted to know if you would like to go to the pictures with him in Wickham. Said it was the one with that cowboy in it. Can't remember the name. He left a note for you." She handed over a folded slip of paper.

"Looks like I'm going to miss Sunday lunch this weekend. Want to catch a Bogart movie tonight? Pick you up at six? G."

I decided to say no when he turned up. I would tell him what Ilona always says when she refuses an invitation: *How kind of you, darling. But not tonight; I have to darn my socks.*

I went into the drawing room and pulled out my list of embrocation users. Every single one of them was in the clear, except for Mrs. Glossop and Sid Ritchie. I wrote another name down on it. Supposing Bill had said good night to Audrey, left her, and then doubled back and surprised her as she was leaving the lambing hut? He is a large man; he could easily overpower Audrey. But if Bill Peterson was our murderer, he would have had no difficulty at all in strangling her, so surely there would have been no need to hit her over the head with a brick? Almost as soon as I had written his name, I crossed it through.

Was I being a bit too gullible about the Americans?

TWENTY-ONE

H ULLO THERE, POPPY!" IT WAS FENELLA BRADLEY—AGAIN—
hailing me from the other side of Streams Lane where it forks
left to go up to the Bradleys' Victorian redbrick country house. For
a girl who had a fascinating life in London, Fenella was spending a
lot of time in our dull little backwater these days. She was driving
her father's Daimler and looking ravishing in a deep red suit the
color of garnets. After the bruising I had received at her hands the last
time we met, I approached with caution.

"Just popped down to see the Aged Ps." Fenella loves to churn
out bits of Dickens; it's what sets her apart from other girls who
are merely gorgeous. "Everyone's talking about your Sunday
lunches—I would love to come. Can you squeeze me in?"

And of course, I fell for it, completely forgetting that it doesn't
do to be too complacent about Bradley attendance at village func-
tions because they always manage to let you down if a more entic-
ing invitation crops up. "Of course, we would be delighted for you
and your sister to join us," I said.

"Do you really do all the cooking? How clever you are, Pops." When Fenella isn't being patronizing, she is quite charming.

"Actually, Lieutenant O'Neal is the cook. We invite three men from the base and one or two couples from the village. It is part of our—"

"Oh, please count me in!" she said carelessly as she turned large blue eyes on me with that imploring look she does so well, especially when she is quite sure her wishes will be granted. "I would love to come, really I would. I can peel potatoes, you know." Then she remembered a little too late: "Who is on your guest list from the village this coming Sunday?"

"Sid Ritchie," I said and watched her eyes wander away to the road ahead. "And Bert and Mrs. Pritchard. And since we are one short from the American side, I can fit you in quite easily." She managed not to flinch at the thought of sitting down with the Pritchards and Sid Ritchie. But she looked almost afraid when she asked, "Short of who on the American side?"

"Lieutenant O'Neal. Duty calls, apparently."

"Oh, but he's the cook—you can't do without him, surely?"

I watched her bright smile fade at the thought of lunch without Griff O'Neal after she had begged for an invitation. "Delighted you can come, Fenella. Arrive early if you can, and I'll show you how to make a wine reduction!" I smiled my most winning smile.

"I'd love to, Poppy." She returned my smile with one equally winning. "I'll confirm as soon as I check with the Ageds about their plans." She pulled a wry face at the domineering old couple who ran her life, released the hand brake, revved the engine, and then shot off down the lane in what I would have called reckless driving in anyone but a Bradley.

It was of course inevitable that Fenella could not after all join us for lunch. "Wish I could join you on Sunday, but my parents have included me in their plans. Please invite me again—some other time," she had written on a little card that plopped through the letter box onto the coir mat promptly on Saturday morning. Mrs. Wantage brought it to me and was quick to fill me in on the rest of the scenario.

"The Bradleys are entertaining on Sunday." She smiled with the suspicion of a wink. "I'm making one of my mutton curries for them. They are having lunch for Colonel and Mrs. Smithers, Lord and Lady Kingsbridge, and Fenella has asked that nice Lieutenant O'Neal to make up the numbers. I'm glad she thought to tell you she couldn't make it, because I didn't know whether I should inform you of their plans or not. Especially since they invited your nice American chap." Mrs. Wantage looked at me out of the corner of her eye to see if I was upset that Griff would not be slogging away in my kitchen but sitting down to luncheon in the Bradleys' baronial dining hall. "Not that it will be a patch on roast beef and your lovely Yorkshire," she said as a consolation, and flicked her duster at the Bradleys and their snooty friends.

I didn't know whether to laugh or grit my teeth that Griff was lunching at the Bradleys with Fenella. Why on earth hadn't he said so in his note to me? It is all too ridiculous, I decided, as I went upstairs to change for patrol. Why on earth shouldn't he have lunch with the Bradleys? I kicked my shoes off across the room. When this wretched war was over, he would go back to America anyway.

SUNDAY LUNCH WAS a tedious affair, especially as Sid was at his most self-conscious. The Pritchards did their best to divert some of his more searching questions of our American guests about their Mustang fighter planes.

"If one of your Mustangs was in a dogfight with a Spit, I think the Spitfire would win because of its superior attributes, like speed, climb, and maneuverability," he said in his Biggles voice. The only reason it didn't come off as downright patronizing is that he is so genuinely proud of his beloved Spitfire.

"Probably," Lieutenant Hawkins, who piloted a Mustang, agreed. "But they were built for different purposes. Your Spitfire is an interceptor, while the P-51 is a long-range escort fighter."

There was a pause as Sid decided whether or not he was being put in his place.

"So, you see," Lieutenant Hawkins added in a neutral voice, as he glanced at his navigator, who was busily cutting up meat, "you can't really compare them, can you? Although I would give anything to fly a Spitfire."

Sid stared at him for a moment and then shrugged his shoulders. "It was just a hypothetical question," he said.

Without Mrs. Pritchard and her happy laugh, and Bert, with his determined mine-host jocularity, it would have been a disaster. Granny looked tired and Grandad tried to jolly Sid along, but he was at his most obdurate. As I watched him I thought how much fun he was when he was imitating his favorite comic characters from *It's That Man Again,* instead of being stuffy about aircraft. Poor Sid. At least he was trying to get along with our Americans.

As soon as coffee had been served and all our visitors had made a beeline for the front door, Sid followed me into the kitchen and insisted on helping me with the washing up. He was particularly bad at it, and it was depressing watching him make a sudsy mess when it was usually Griff and I who did the washing up together.

"I've been thinking about what you said the other night. And I'm sorry that I got so angry about what's been going on in the village. You are right about the Americans; they are here to help us. And if one of them is a murderer, it doesn't mean they are all bad." He glanced at me to see how I was taking his about-face.

"Good, I'm glad you feel that way."

He swirled soapy water with his dish mop, and I could tell there was more to come.

"What is it, Sid?"

"I just feel I should . . ." He stared down at a dish covered in suds. "What I mean is . . . I think . . ."

"Sometimes it's easier to just say a thing."

He cleared his throat. "Right then . . . I want to warn you about your friend Griff O'Neal." My heart sank. "I sort of lost my nerve the other night when I told you about seeing him in his car after curfew. But since you are not involved with him or anything . . ." I nodded and tried to breathe. "You should know that on that night, when I saw him in his car, it was pulled over to the side of the road and a young woman in a yellow dress got into the passenger seat." I dried knives and forks very carefully, so I wouldn't have to catch his eye.

"Why are you telling me this, Sid?"

"I don't know. I just thought it was something you should know."

"Even though I have told you that there is nothing between Griff and me, other than my grandparents' Sunday lunches?" He slopped water down the front of his shirt.

"What about all those walks with the dog, trips into Wickham to the flicks, and to visit Audrey? And all those patrols he did with you when he was off flying? Everyone in the village thinks he's sweet on you." A nauseating expression, which made me harrumph and fold my arms.

"Everyone? You mean Mrs. Glossop and her pals? Well, they are utterly wrong, aren't they?" I said. But I could feel a lump building in my throat and I felt humiliated and silly standing in my kitchen being informed by Sid Ritchie that Griff was not the man I thought he was.

"She had dark hair," said Sid. "Tallish. Slender."

I acknowledged each detail with a nod. "When was this?" I heard myself say with a calm I was far from feeling.

He handed me a plate to dry. "I can't remember exactly. After Doreen, though . . . and before . . ." He heard himself and turned to look at me, his face horrified. "Oh no, it couldn't be. Poppy, it couldn't be."

"Couldn't be what?" I asked.

"Because it was the night before we found Ivy, that's why. Cripes, Poppy! Dark hair, tallish, slender, that's . . . that's Ivy." His face was pale, and his large brown eyes were wide with the horror of what he had said.

"I hope you told Inspector Hargreaves about all this, Sid."

"Why . . . ? No . . . I haven't. Of course I haven't. It only just came to me."

Did I believe him? I thought over what he had told me, and a cool voice in my head told me that I should pay very close attention. "Sid, I don't want to be an alarmist, but this sounds very serious." I made my voice as flat and dispassionate as I could. "If you really think you saw Lieutenant O'Neal giving Ivy a lift the night before she was murdered, you must go to the police. You certainly don't want to be withholding information from them, do you?" I watched his face flush.

"But supposing it wasn't the night before Ivy was killed? Supposing it was several nights before? You know how bad I am about things like that."

"Are you saying you are not sure?"

"Yes, I think I am. What shall I do?"

"Sid, it's up to you. If it was the night before Ivy died, then you must speak out. If you are not sure, then . . . you're not sure."

I honestly don't know how I got him out of the kitchen and on his way home with a little packet of cold roast beef for sandwiches, but I managed it without losing my temper, or being unkind, which was the main thing.

"I can't be *sure*," he kept wailing as I escorted him to the front door. "I mean, it could just as easily have been after we found Ivy. It's so long ago now. And it might not even have been her."

"So, if it wasn't Ivy, who else could it have been—what did she look like?"

"I only saw her from behind. She was wearing a yellow dress and high heels. So, she might have been shorter than I thought. It was so long ago."

So long ago? It was three weeks since we had found Ivy. I fumed as I thanked him for half doing the washing up.

"Poppy, I'm so sorry about the washing up."

"Sid, please don't worry. I'll finish it."

I returned to the kitchen and started the laborious business of rinsing all the soapy dishes left in the sink. Granny came in and picked up a tea towel. "Weren't you a little bit sharp with poor Sidney?" Evidently, she had heard only the tone of our conversation and not its content. Otherwise she would have agreed that he was being particularly half-baked.

"No, not really," I said, wishing I could be alone for just five minutes. "He does talk such rot sometimes."

"Yes, I know, dear. I'm sure he can be very trying. But the poor boy means well, and he doesn't have much confidence."

I wanted to scream: I don't have much confidence either, and apparently the man I am "sweet" on is not only secretive, but also might be a liar or even a murderer. And then, very unfairly, I wondered how I would know anything at all about this confusing world when I have been overprotected all my blasted life. But I bit my lip and finished rinsing the dishes.

"Are you upset because Fenella Bradley invited Griff over for lunch?"

"No, not really."

"I am afraid that Fenella is not a very straightforward girl." I put down the dish mop and drained the sink. There are many character traits that Granny rates highly in young women, but being straightforward is at the top of her list. If Fenella was not straightforward, that meant she, in Granny's parlance, was cunning, sly, and not truthful.

I took off my pinny and hung it on a peg by the door. "I think she's rather keen on Griff," I said in a whisper, because it hurt like anything to say the words, even if it was to this kindly, sympathetic soul. Granny has always listened and given me practical advice on all my woes, until I turned fifteen and realized that there were things I could no longer ask her about.

She came over to me, lifted my chin, and stroked my hair back out of my eyes. "Yes, dear, I'm sure she is. If only because she knows he likes to spend time with you. But you don't seem to have much faith in yourself, do you, darling? Don't underestimate yourself, Poppy. You are a lovely and intelligent young woman, and, most important of all, you are compassionate and kind." She put her arms around me. "And what about Griff? Surely he has something to say about all this. I'm sure there is some rational explanation why he had lunch at Bradley Hall and didn't tell you."

His lunching at Bradley Hall was the least of my concerns, because if Griff O'Neal had stopped to give Ivy a lift in his car the night before we found her under Streams Lane bridge, it didn't really matter where he had breakfast, lunch, tea, or dinner, did it?

I MADE MY escape into the orchard with Bess. I wouldn't walk up the lane with her toward the airfield, in case I ran into Griff. And I didn't want to walk through the village because now everyone believed that he was two-timing me with Fenella. I wanted to pack a bag, catch a train up to London, and volunteer to be a real ARP warden and not one who walked around a village every night checking that everyone had the blackout curtain tightly drawn as I worried where the next dead body would turn up.

I do wish you wouldn't be so fatalistic, chimed in Ilona, which reminded me that I hadn't written a thing about her for days. *Why don't you ask him outright?*

Honestly, for such a smart woman, Ilona can be an awful nitwit sometimes. I remembered how deftly Griff had avoided all information about Ponsonby. He never answered disconcerting questions, I realized, as I threw windfall apples for Bess. He skated lightly through life, relying on his ability to make things smooth and pleasant for everyone. I scowled and kicked a few dandelion clocks with my toe, sending showers of seed heads into the air. Bess ran after them, snapping and sneezing, and her clowning made me laugh.

" 'Ello, 'ello. Fought I would bump into you two if I walked good and fast." It was Griff, striding through the orchard gate toward us, brandishing a stick for Bess and talking in his terrible cockney accent.

"Hullo." I stopped and stood there, completely uncertain of how to behave or what to say.

"How was Sunday lunch without me? Did you overcook the beef—and the beans? I know how much you English love to boil your greens to death." He turned and threw the stick for Bess. "You look like you've heard some bad news." How right he was. "Everything okay?" His face was concerned. Not pretend concern, but what I prayed from the depth of my desperate heart to be simple, honest concern.

I shook my head and laughed. "Everything's fine," I said.

"Aha, so you did overcook the beef. You have that look on your face." He was laughing. "C'mon, you can tell me."

"No, I didn't—it was delicious."

"Lucky you—I had to have lunch up at Bradley Hall. Me and Colonel Duchovny. Boy, was it heavy going. Never had lunch with such a stuffy bunch." He winced as he threw his next stick, and half lifted his hand to his ribs. "They all looked as if something smelled bad. Not enough gin in the world to loosen those people up. So, how were the Pritchards? Why am I asking? I bet it was a breeze."

"The Pritchards, three *lewtenants*, and Sid," I reminded him.

"Ah yes, Mr. Ritchie—well I guess life isn't all fun and games."

The last thing in the world I was going to do was ask him for any details of his blasted lunch or refer to Fenella.

"Come on." He took my arm. "Let's stroll down to the pub and have a nice pint—shandy for you and bitter for me—and chew over this liniment business, and then we can go into Wickham and see a movie."

"I can't," I said and pulled my arm away. "I promised Granny I would help her with the mending. I can't put her off anymore, 'specially since most of it's mine."

"Well, okay. I could come and keep you company and enjoy a glass of Jasper's scotch."

"Not tonight, Griff." I whistled for Bess, and to my utter relief, she appeared almost immediately.

TWENTY-TWO

HAD TWO EMBROCATION SUSPECTS LEFT TO CHECK ON—MRS. Glossop and Sid Ritchie—and I felt downright silly about pursuing both. One was an interfering old lady with too much time on her hands, who was about half Audrey's size. And the other: even at his most irritating, Sid was loyal, had a strong sense of right and wrong, and was far too squeamish to commit murder, not to mention he had a solid alibi for Doreen's murder.

My mood was gloomy as I walked up the village High Street toward the post office. As soon as I had tackled Mrs. G., I would drop in on Audrey, now that she was out of hospital, and see if there was anything else that had come back to her from the night of her attack.

Questioning Mrs. Glossop would be easy. All I had to do was bring up the subject of coughs, colds, and sore backs and she would be ready with a string of instructions and long lists of home remedies and the sufferers they had cured. Then I could steer the conversation around to the night of our air-raid drill.

"What's the matter with you? Are you coming down with something?" Mrs. Glossop's eyes searched my face. It was a relief to see a concerned expression rather than a critical one. "You've got rings under your eyes." Her voice was chiding but not unkindly, as if my dark circles were a cause she was prepared to fight for.

"Just a bit of a scratchy throat," I said as hoarsely as I could manage.

"Elliman's Embrocation, that's what you need. Don't use Foster's, it's rubbish. I've heard it causes breathing problems if you use too much of it. Destroys the lung tissue."

"I can't stand the smell of either of them," I told her. "And anyway, it's for sore backs and stiff joints, isn't it?"

"What rubbish. Elliman's has simple clean ingredients: wintergreen and other natural things. Mr. Glossop used to swear by it when his throat got ticklish. Rub some of that on your chest and you will be as right as rain. And wrap up when you go out at night. That uniform of yours wouldn't keep a cat warm. Do you have a nice Chilprufe vest or a Liberty bodice?"

I refused to be drawn into a chat about my underwear, and instead asked her a bold question of my own. "Do you use Elliman's?" I asked.

"I don't use anything. I never get colds and bad chests. I don't have time to get sick. There's this post office to run for one thing—and the mail has to get through: all those letters going to our boys overseas." She pursed her lips and, turning, looked along the rows of jars that lined the back of her shop. "What about a throat lozenge? Fisherman's Friend is good for sore throats, and they don't count as sweets in your ration book, which is a very good thing. I sometimes suck on one if I have a yen for sugar. Take a bag of Friends with you."

She opened a glass jar and smiled at my enthusiastic grin as a strong camphor-like aroma filled the shop. "Never had a Fisherman's Friend before? You don't know what you're missing."

My eyes were watering as she put the open jar down on the countertop. "Good heavens, what on earth's in them?"

She cocked her head on one side and read from the label on the jar. "Licorice extract, menthol, ewcally-iptus oil, and pepper tincture. Good combination for a sore throat. Made for fishermen in the North Sea. Go on, take a couple. See if you don't come back for more. The vicar loves them." She twisted two white pastilles up in a bit of paper and slapped them into my hand.

I thanked her and was immediately instructed to put a Friend in my mouth.

"There." She laughed at my horrified expression. My mouth felt as if someone had lit a fire in it. I was about to spit it out when she said, "Keep it in, keep it in. You'll get used to the heat. And anyway, heat's good for a sore throat. You should wear a woolly scarf at night."

"I'm on my way to see Audrey," I said in a voice that sounded as if I had been adrift on the seven seas all winter on a life raft. "She's out of hospital but has to stay inside convalescing for a few days." I gasped in a cooling draft of air.

"Then wish her a speedy recovery from me and tell her I'll pop by tomorrow afternoon when I'm done here." I almost expected her to come up with some instructions as to the quickest course Audrey should take for her recovery, but she didn't.

"When did you know she was missing—was it before or after the air-raid drill?" I asked her and caught a sharp look.

"Back on that old bandwagon again, are you?" Her eyes were

shrewd. "Well, someone needs to be asking questions; the police don't seem to have the time or the inclination. They say crime's shot up in the last two years, what with the blackout and so few policemen. For your information, I got a message from Mrs. Martin just after eleven thirty, when Audrey didn't show up at the vicarage. And I know you are not going to like this, but she told me about the air-raid drill—no, don't look like that! She had to have *some* reliable help, poor woman—and I know how to keep my mouth shut." I could have laughed out loud at this Glossop pearl of inaccuracy. "Anyway, over I went to the vicarage. Mrs. Martin was that worried about it being too cold in the crypt for the kiddies." She paused only to glare at me. "Why you had to plan that drill for after midnight I can't imagine. They do have air raids in the daytime, you know." She paused for another scowl at my awkward planning. "We scrounged up blankets and shawls from the stuff put by for the jumble sale and carried them down into the crypt. Of course, if there was a real air raid—which there will never be—then we would all have to put up with a bit of cold, wouldn't we?"

And there it was. Mrs. Martin had told Mrs. Glossop about the drill. Had Mrs. Glossop popped a Fisherman's Friend in her mouth to stave off a craving for sugar and then stopped at Bart's Field to whack Audrey on the head before she arrived at the vicarage? But I knew that Mrs. Glossop was clearly not my suspect. She was an interfering old bat, but she was not the Little Buffenden Strangler.

"So, now you know where I was and at what time." Her eyes were shining with pleasure as she informed me she knew what I was up to. "And before you go thinking the worst, the last person in the world I would harm is our Audrey—so don't you jump to any conclusions, Miss Redfern. Doreen, now"—her mouth came down at the corners—"she was another matter entirely. Oh, go on with you." Her eyes were two dark crescents of laughter. "You are taking your inquiry far too seriously, my dear. I've known all three of those girls since they were babies."

"Thank you, Mrs. Glossop," I said and made for the door. My mouth was on fire from the Fisherman's Friend. I spat it out in the gutter and walked up the High Street in the direction of Streams Lane for a nice cuppa tea with Audrey.

"STREWTH!" AUDREY BACKED away as I walked into the kitchen. She groped for the back of a chair and, holding on to it with one hand, raised the other to her throat. I was used to Audrey's implacable silence, but this reaction seemed rather an overly dramatic swing in the other direction.

"Audrey, what on earth is the matter? Come on, sit down." Alarmed, I pulled out a chair with a high back and arms and helped her into it. She had been fine when she opened the door to me, almost cheery. And here she was backing away from me as if I were the devil.

I filled a glass of water from the kitchen pump. "Sip slowly." She did, but I noticed that there were beads of sweat on her upper lip and that her hand was shaking as she took the glass from me. I cupped my hand around hers to steady the glass in it. Then I took a seat next to her and waited.

"Fine now. Not your fault, but you gave me such a fright." Her voice was low—almost a whisper. I had come to welcome her back from hospital and had caused this?

"Oh, Audrey, I'm so terribly sorry."

"What on earth have you been eating?"

Now I understood. "A Fisherman's Friend, but that was when I left the village. It was so strong I couldn't finish it."

"Do you have any more?" I pulled out the little twist of paper, opened it up, and held out a lozenge. Audrey cautiously sniffed. "Oh God, that's it. That's what I could smell when I was attacked."

"A Fisherman's Friend? Audrey, really?"

She nodded, waving her hand in front of her face. I put the lozenge back into the paper, twisted it closed, and stowed it in the pocket of my cardigan.

"Your attacker had one of these in his mouth?" An awful understanding was taking shape, as I remembered who Mrs. Glossop had said enjoyed these peppery lozenges.

"I'm sorry, Poppy, but I have to get some air." Her face was the color of parchment.

Standing in the scullery porch with her, and gulping down lungsful of the damp afternoon air, I realized that all my checking on embrocation hadn't been an exercise in futility. It had led me here; the murderer wasn't a liniment or embrocation user at all. It was someone who, just like Mrs. Glossop, enjoyed a lozenge to soothe a craving for sweets. The list of possible sufferers might be as long as the number of residents in our village, but Mrs. Glossop would know exactly whom she had sold Fisherman's Friends to.

"Are you up to doing a test for me, Audrey?"

She turned her head and smiled. "Don't tell me you want me to sniff a mothball and then that nasty little lozenge," she said. "No need, Poppy. When you walked through that door with that smell on your breath, it was as if I was back in Bart's Field." Her eyes were dark, her lips still pale. "What do they say about smell? That it fixes in your memory more strongly than sight or sound?" I shrugged my shoulders. I had no idea. But then I hadn't been the victim of a vicious attack on my life in the dark of night with only foxes and owls to call on for help.

Audrey took a grateful gulp of the mild afternoon air. "That smell brought that awful night back, as if he was with us right now. I felt the most terrible pressure on my neck as my head was wrenched backward. His mouth was level with my ear. And that dreadful reek filled the air. It wasn't a woman, Poppy; it was a man. He was tall, or at least as tall as me, and strong."

"Come inside, Audrey, and I'll make you something hot to drink. Or would you like a glass of parsnip wine?"

She sat down at the table, and her eyes were so fearful that all I could think of was that if it was me in her place, I could only hope to be as brave and as courageous as she had been when she was set upon in the dark.

I squeezed her hand with the full force of the approval and affection I felt for her, and she winced. "Go easy," she said under her breath. "That's only my bloomin' hand, and I'll need it tomorrow morning for milking. And tea will be fine, thank you."

The kettle rumbled to a boil on the hob and I got up to make us tea.

"Be as angry with me as you like, Audrey, but I want to rule out Bill Peterson right off the bat. I can't bear to think that another American will be unjustly accused."

She snorted. "Of course it wasn't Bill, stupid. He may be an American, but he is a decent, kind man. Not a mean bone in his body."

I nodded in vigorous agreement. "But you had spent the evening with Bill . . . up at the lambing hut . . . and then you said good-bye.

And the next thing you knew . . ." I tried to find the right words and failed.

She burst out with protestations that Bill would rather die than hurt her. "It was never Bill. I am quite sure of that. And there are just two things that bear out that he was not my attacker. The smell of that disgusting cough lozenge has made me remember that the man who tried to kill me was wearing a coat or jacket of some rough sort of wool material—like tweed. The Americans' uniforms are made of smooth fabric: worsted or serge. And Bill is large: he has broad shoulders; strong, thick arms, and a chest like a barrel. The man who attacked me was whippy, and his strength was . . . how can I describe it? It was wiry. I was attacked by a lean, wiry man. I would stake my life on it."

She nearly had, I thought, as I mentally filed away her description.

"How tall?"

"Not as tall as Bill, but taller than me. Probably about six foot."

So, I was looking for a tallish man in a tweed-type jacket who was strong enough to take her by surprise but not completely overpower her and who enjoyed Fisherman's Friends.

I saw the most civilized man I knew in our village, sitting back in his leather armchair with a glass of fine Amontillado in his hand, enjoying the company of good friends. "It can't be!" I cried out, conscious as I did so that I would make a terrible poker player.

"For God's sake, what now? You really are on edge today."

"I have to go!" I said, getting to my feet and making for the door.

"You could at least tell me what's going on!" Audrey called after me as I walked down the path to join Bess at the gate.

"I will, Audrey, really, I will. I just have to think things through for a bit first." I tried to cover the elation I felt. Griff O'Neal certainly wasn't my suspect! He might be unreliable and not particularly straightforward, but he was not a murderer!

My elation didn't last long, though. The thought of our vicar strangling young women was so disturbing that I was almost up to the stile that led into Bart's Field before I stopped to order my thoughts.

I must not reach for the easiest conclusion based on new information, I told myself. Audrey had mentioned that her attacker was wearing a harshly woven type of fabric. Tweed is the first woolen material that springs to mind if you are English and live in the country. *Oh, come on, sweetie,* Ilona chimed in, *your little village is swarming with chaps who wear those dreadful uniforms. What do you call them, the Home Guard?*

TWENTY-THREE

I TRIED TO MEASURE SID'S HEIGHT AS WE WALKED DOWN Streams Lane. I estimated he was about six feet: easily tall enough to be Audrey's attacker. Had Home Guard training turned round-shouldered, cave-chested Sid into a young man with what Audrey described as sinewy strength and a "whippy" build? It was hard to tell; I was so used to thinking of him as a sickly weakling.

Sid was carefully dressed for the chill of an autumn evening. Underneath the coarse wool of his battle dress he was wearing a sweater in a dark cable knit made by his mum; I could see the wool cuffs sticking out of his jacket just above his bony wrists. Around his neck he was wearing a thick wool scarf, the ends of which were tucked into the front of his jacket. The coils of the scarf came up to his ears. Balanced on the top of his meticulously combed and Brylcreemed hair was a field cap, and on his hands were dark gray knitted gloves. He was so thoroughly bundled up it was hard to tell what sort of physique he had. His eyes slued over to me and I looked away, embarrassed to be caught out. He smiled: Sid was still in an apologetic mood.

"Did you talk to Hargreaves?" I asked.

"No, but I did talk to Constable Jones."

"And what did he say?"

"Poppy, I can't tell you. It's police business now."

I was so annoyed I wanted to biff him one. "Police business? But I was the one who told you to go to them."

"Yes, I know. Please don't be like that. I hate it when you get annoyed with me. It's just that I gave my word to Constable Jones." It was the boys-only thing all over again. You take the time to counsel some silly twit who hasn't a clue what to do. He follows your advice, and then lo and behold you are immediately barred from any more information—simply because it's boys only. If the Luftwaffe had flown over at this point and dropped a bomb on Sid Ritchie, I would have cheered.

"Hi, there—I was hoping I'd bump into you . . . two!" I breathed a sigh of gratitude for the interruption, until I realized that the friendly voice in the dark was that of Griff O'Neal, the other man in my life who led a blessed and exclusive male existence where women were only welcomed to enjoy moments with them in the kitchen or hop in and out of their sports cars.

"Hullo," I said, careful to keep my voice neutral in case I sparked off some sort of rivalry between a defensive Englishman and an oblivious American. "Sid, have you met Griff O'Neal? Griff, this is Sid Ritchie."

Griff lifted his right hand in that lazy and informal gesture that Americans call a salute, and Sid snapped one back in return, his back parade-ground straight. "No, we haven't been introduced, but I am familiar with the lieutenant *and* his red sports car," he said, with what I supposed he imagined was subtlety, and then in a miffy sort of way, over my head, to Griff: "My job is to escort Miss Redfern, but now that *you're* here . . . I'll be getting off home." And having handed me over to the enemy, Sid stalked into the night, leaving us both standing outside the Wheatsheaf.

"Funny sort of guy, isn't he? We've seen him when we go to the pub, but he never responds when we call out to him to join us for a pint. Must be one of the Little Buffers who disapprove of Uncle Sam."

Oh, you don't know the half of it, I thought.

"Haven't been into the Wheatsheaf before. Shall we have a drink?"

I walked with him up the path feeling self-conscious and, for some reason, annoyed, not just with him, and with Sid for stranding me, but with myself too. An awkward situation had become even more so because for some reason I couldn't get over the fact that Griff had evidently been seeing something of Fenella Bradley. He had even used her favorite term for the village: Little Buffers. And why not? I thought as I ungraciously said I would have a glass of sherry. It was hardly as if there was an understanding between us, and his behavior toward me was almost brotherly. We were evidently, in his mind, simply friends.

Just keep things light, I told myself. Light, as if I couldn't care less.

He brought over our drinks and set them down on the table. "You know, back home, when we go out to a bar for a drink and we sit down at a table, they come over to you, take your order, and bring you your drinks. When we first went into the Rose we all sat down and waited and waited." He laughed. "And then Mrs. Pritchard called out, 'There's only two of us serving, so come on up to the bar and tell me what you want,' and she laughed that big, loud laugh of hers. And we realized that it was our mistake and we weren't being ostracized."

"Yes, well, England is very different from America." I didn't mean it to come out in quite such a prissy way: it was the strain of trying to make small talk, when I wanted to take Ilona's suggestion and just ask him outright about Fenella. But I knew I would never be able to say with light unconcern: So how was lunch at the Bradleys? It would come out like a nosy question from a disapproving maiden aunt.

"Any developments?" He raised his glass and took a sip.

"None at all."

"Oh, I see." He cleared his throat. "So, that was Sid Ritchie. You know, I think he rather likes you."

"No, he doesn't," I snapped, abandoning my decision to keep things light and breezy. "I have known Sid all my life. He is just a boy from the village."

"Takes himself pretty seriously."

"No, he doesn't. He's a very sweet boy—he's just not as casual as you are."

The landlady called closing time and I leapt to my feet. Being polite in a pub with half the farmers' wives and their Land Girl friends in the area enjoying a night out and covertly gossiping about us was a strain, and I felt tired and dispirited.

"Something's up," said Griff as we got outside, and he stopped to put on his cap. "Come on, out with it." I was already marching up the lane, as far away from the farmers' wives coming out of the pub as I could get.

"Hold up a minute, Poppy." He caught up with me. "Something's wrong. Won't you tell me what it is?"

"Nothing's wrong."

"Well, yes, there is something. You're all stiff and starchy, which is far worse than just being mad. C'mon, let's get it out in the open.

Are you about to announce your engagement to Sid Ritchie?" He laughed uproariously at the idea. And I bit my lip. "That wasn't okay," he said. "I'm sorry, really I am. What have I done to offend you? I know it's something."

Ilona wouldn't have had any trouble speaking out—she would have done so days ago—but I don't have her wonderful confidence. "You were seen on what was possibly the night of Ivy's murder. In your car, on the road to Lower Netherton, stopping to give someone who looked like her a lift."

"I didn't give Ivy a lift anywhere." Was it my imagination or did his answer come too quickly, too defensively?

"A dark-haired girl was seen getting into your car. Not many *young* women with dark hair in our village, and, come to think of it, not many red sports cars around here either."

"You've been listening to village gossip about me?"

"It was you who encouraged me to listen to it—so that we could identify the Little Buffenden Strangler. 'We are in a perfect position to investigate,' remember? 'You know everyone in the village and I know everyone on the base.'"

"Seems to me you just added two and two and made five. Are you seriously accusing me of being Ivy's killer?"

"Why don't you just tell me who you stopped to give a lift to? Oh, by the way, you were all confined to the base when you were seen. That's sort of interesting, don't you think?" I had tried to keep my voice neutral, as if I was merely following up on a new clue, but I am a redhead after all, and the last bit came out more harshly than I had intended. I might have crossed Griff off my list of suspects, but I was quite sure that he was seeing Fenella Bradley and now he was lying about it.

He went very quiet. I couldn't see his face, but I could feel how angry he was. After a long pause he said, "Well, in that case, you're running a bit of a risk, aren't you?" His voice was ice.

We were standing glaring at each other in the dark, and Bess, who had been loitering in ditches, came racing up to see what the holdup was.

"I just want to know who you gave a lift to," I said. "If it was Ivy, then . . ."

"Then what?"

"Then I'll have to take it further."

"Take it further to who? God, you English!" He was furious now. "You are so darned self-righteous, aren't you? Well, lemme tell you something: it's none of your darn business who I gave a lift to. Okay?"

"I'm so glad we cleared *that* up," I said. "It's none of my damned business what Ponsonby was doing in your stupid airfield either, is it? Not that you would have known about it if I hadn't told you. And now it's none of my business who you gave a lift to on the night Ivy was strangled with an American officer's tie. How arrogant can you be? You're right—it is none of my business—so I'll say good night. I'm tired and I want to go home. Come on, Bess." I pushed him to one side and whistled to Bess, who simply gazed at me as if I was a complete idiot.

Not waiting for her, I marched off, seething with rage.

"Hey! Wait up!" Griff called after me. "C'mon, don't be mad!"

"Come, Bessie, come on, girl." And to my utter relief she peeled away from Griff and ran up the lane toward me. "What a good girl, Bessie," I said, relieved that I didn't have to go back for her. "Let's go home and have a nice ginger biscuit."

TWENTY-FOUR

A LARGE BUNCH OF ROSES WAS WAITING FOR ME IN THE kitchen when I came down to breakfast. An almost overwhelming mass of them, filling the whole ground floor with their fragrance, which mingled, quite unpleasantly, with the smell of Camp coffee. Granny was arranging them in several vases.

"What a sweet young man your lieutenant is." She smiled gaily at me. "He must have been up with the lark to pick these; look, they are still dewy. The last of the roses before the frosts come. Don't they smell exquisite?"

I filled the kettle at the kitchen sink and put it on the hob. "Lovely," I said and reached into the pantry for the oatmeal. It would be a complete waste of time to tell her that Griff was not my young man.

"And he left a note for you." Granny, at her most winsome, put down an envelope next to the cups and saucers on the kitchen table. "Your grandfather has asked him over this evening. Did you know that Griff plays bridge? We were talking about getting up a four."

"I can't play bridge this evening, but I bet the vicar would love to make up a four."

"Of course you can, Poppy; it's Tuesday and one of your nights off."

"No, Granny, I swapped with Sid. I am on patrol tonight. I have the night off tomorrow."

She put the last rose into the vase. "When Jasper invited him for bridge it was quite touching how pleased he was. I'm sure it wasn't simply because he wanted to play cards with *us*. He wants to see you, dear." I said nothing, which is dangerous because Granny always interprets my silences with unerring accuracy. "Apart from this business with Fenella trying to insinuate herself, has he offended you in some way, or has there been a misunderstanding?"

"I would rather not see him at the moment, that's all."

"I would be most surprised if Griff had behaved improperly. He really doesn't strike me as the type." She was pushing for an explanation. I couldn't tell this kind, innocent soul, who came from a generation who were chaperoned everywhere before they were married, that I almost wished Griff would behave "improperly."

"No, Granny, his manners are perfect." And I thought how horrified she would be to know that the police would certainly want to ask him a few questions about his being out and about when all the Americans were confined to their base on one of the nights before Ivy Wantage was murdered.

She nodded, her eyes thoughtful. "One hears such distressing things these days about our young women and some of these American GIs. But Griff is a gentleman, even if he is sometimes perhaps a little too informal. Was it Oscar Wilde who said, 'The English and the Americans are two peoples divided by a common language'?"

"I think it was George Bernard Shaw."

"Who? No, it wasn't him—it was probably Winston Churchill. Whoever it was, it is an apt observation. If there has been a misunderstanding, the best thing to do would be to sort things out and not let them fester."

As I might have said before, Granny firmly believes that a woman alone is a sad woman, and her generation loves to pair people off. I could see where she was headed with Griff and me.

"I think I want time to think it all through." I needed to have a conversation about Griff's more puzzling behavior with a worldlier woman. Someone like Ilona. Not the Ilona who lived in my head but a real-life woman of the world. Someone who most certainly did not exist in our little backwater.

I spent a wretched morning helping Granny in the garden, storing the last of the root vegetables for winter, and weeding around the Brussels sprouts. For all her matchmaking tendencies, she is an understanding woman and she kept any further advice about Griff and me to herself. We were washing our hands in the scullery when Grandad put his head around the kitchen door and told us that Inspector Hargreaves wanted to speak to me in the living room.

Hargreaves was standing in the window in deep thought, watched by an alert Bess. He asked me to sit down and then produced his battered old notebook.

"Can you tell me where you were the night before last?" He waded in without any preliminary explanations.

I must have looked witless because he went on to say, "Not last night, but the one before that."

"That would have been Sunday—my night off. I was here with my grandparents."

"You are quite sure?"

"Yes, quite."

"You did not leave the house at any time?"

Now I was alarmed. "Will you tell me what this is about, Inspector?"

"At half past midnight, last Sunday, a young woman in ARP uniform arrived at the house of Mr. and Mrs. Arthur Anstruther and announced that there was an air raid expected in the area. She told them to take a blanket and a torch to their air-raid shelter, which happened to be in the cellar of their house. They are an elderly couple." His eyes as he watched me were expressionless, his voice quite neutral. "They stayed in their damp and very cold cellar for nearly an hour, and then, having heard neither the air-raid siren announcing a raid nor the all clear, they judged that it was safe to come back upstairs." He paused, because even a man as stoic as the inspector is entitled to enjoy his moment of drama. "Where ... they found ... that they had been robbed." He opened his notebook, thumbed through some pages, and read, "All Mrs. Anstruther's jewelry, Mr. Anstruther's antique gun collection, and a valuable painting which was hanging in their drawing room had been taken, as well as a few other household items of no particular value." He gave me a long, appraising stare as he finished his list of stolen articles. "The ARP warden they described was a young woman, about twenty years of age and quite tall. She was well-spoken, and Mr. Anstruther, despite his years, said he could clearly see that she had red hair. Now, Miss Redfern, I would have said that this was an accurate description of yourself. What time did you and your grandparents retire for the night?"

I just sat there staring at him. I couldn't for the life of me remember anything about Sunday night. And I was so taken aback by the description of me, as a robber, that my mind refused to co-operate.

"I can't remember what time we all went to bed," was all I could come up with, and then gathering my wits: "But I most certainly never left this house, so it wasn't me who went to the Anstruthers' house. I don't even know them, so I have no idea where they live."

"They live in the area." He looked down at his notes again. "Does your grandfather drive a Humber?"

"Yes, he does, along with about a dozen people that we know of."

"This would be an old Humber Tourer, very like the make and year of the car at the bottom of your drive. A 1928 model, I believe it is."

"I'm at a loss, Inspector. It wasn't me who went to the Anstruth-ers' house and robbed it." I was feeling quite panicky now. This was like a bad dream. I would wake up in a moment and have breakfast with Granny.

"You didn't leave the house after your grandparents had gone to bed and drive over to the Anstruthers' house in your grand-father's car? I only ask because someone saw what looked like a Humber Tourer leave the village on the night in question."

"Who saw it?" I asked in desperation. "No one in Little Buffen-den is up and about after closing time at the pub."

"I think for the moment I would rather you told me about your movements after you and your grandparents retired for the night."

"I went upstairs to my room. Read for about an hour or so, and then drifted off to sleep. I did not go anywhere."

The inspector sighed. Returned to his notes and stared at them regretfully. "I need a little more than that, I'm afraid."

Golly, darling, you are in a pickle. I suggest you ask him to take you over to these Anstruther people—and make sure you wear your ARP regalia so that they see for themselves that it couldn't possibly have been you. Only way to clear up this silly confusion. I was so grateful for Ilona's cool, stay-calm-and-carry-on observation that I nearly thanked her out loud. Instead I reiterated her logical suggestion to Hargreaves, leaving out, of course, her asides to me.

"Would you be willing to go to their house and say only what I tell you to say?" he asked, quite clearly relieved that I was willing to clear my name. "I want you to replay what they said happened. Will you do that and abide by their reaction?"

I thought of two elderly people alone and scared at the thought of an air raid and wondered how keen or acute their observations might be. They could be a geriatric old pair for all I knew, with no ability to remember anything accurately.

"When would you like to do this?" I asked, wondering if I should talk to Grandad first. I might be getting myself into a frightful mess.

"Tomorrow night at eight o'clock. Can you make yourself available then, Miss Redfern? I would like to believe that this is just some sort of bizarre coincidence. With your help, I am quite sure that they will say that the person who came to their house bears no resemblance to you whatsoever."

I hesitated. I had made this suggestion and now I felt that I had impetuously involved myself in what could be a very complicated situation. "Yes, I think I might be prepared to cooperate," I said, "but I think it would be wise to ask my grandfather what he thinks."

When Grandad came into the room, his bushy old brows were down, and Granny, standing at his right shoulder, was clearly determined not to be excluded. Inspector Hargreaves went through his statement again. "Your granddaughter suggested that she accompany me over to the Anstruthers' house in her uniform . . . to see if they can identify . . ."

My grandfather looked alarmed. "Arthur Anstruther has to be almost ninety. I can't imagine that either his eyesight, or his hearing, is particularly keen. Gertrude Anstruther is perhaps the more reliable of the two, but she is getting on in years, too. What about their housekeeper?"

"There was no housekeeper at the house. It was her night off."

"I don't want my granddaughter to involve herself," said Granny. "It sounds like the worst sort of a muddle. Two elderly, frightened people—how reliable can their memories be after one hour in a cold, damp cellar? Suppose they say that Miss Redfern looks exactly like the woman who came into their house? What then? Will she be arrested on the say-so of two people who might not be quite compos mentis?"

"I am investigating a robbery, Mrs. Redfern. Your granddaughter fits their description and is the only female ARP warden in the area. Also, a Humber identical to the one owned by your family was seen leaving the village after midnight on the night in question." He laboriously read out the details of my grandfather's car.

Grandad grunted. "Mm, well, yes, that does sound like my car. But I know my granddaughter was not driving it. She was here with us all evening and then we all went to bed."

"I think it would be a good idea for us to go over to the Anstruthers' and clear this up," Hargreaves said with finality, and he flipped his notebook shut. "I think it would be better to do this tomorrow evening, which will give them an opportunity to prepare themselves. I will pick you up at half past seven if you will be ready," he said to me.

I nodded as my grandfather chimed in, "And I will accompany my granddaughter."

"I wouldn't have it any other way, Major Redfern."

"ARE YOU KIDDING me?" Griff was sitting in our living room at the green baize card table, opposite the Reverend Fothergill, with my grandparents on either side of him. I looked at my watch. It was nearly half past eleven; surely they weren't still sitting here playing bridge at this time of night? I stayed in the doorway, holding my ARP helmet in my hands, trying not to look resentful. It seemed that my possible arrest for robbery had been discussed among the four of them very thoroughly while I was patrolling the village. There is no privacy in this wretched house, I fumed.

Mr. Fothergill put his hand of cards facedown on the table. "This is far more fascinating than bridge," he said as he stood up to escort me to the sofa and then sat down on it with me. "Poppy must have a double somewhere. And who on earth said they saw her drive off that night in your old Humber?" He laughed, a rather patronizing laugh, I thought. "Has anyone told the inspector how hard you are on the clutch, Poppy? I mean, just the sound of crashing gears in the dead of night would be a complete giveaway." I managed to curb a cold reply that I was no longer sixteen, which was when he had taught me to drive.

"The inspector wouldn't say who saw my car being driven out of the village. I walked out with him and asked him, and he refused to tell me." Grandad was still irate. "It's preposterous that Poppy has been pulled into this!"

"Of course it wasn't Poppy," said Granny. "It could have been anyone—most people in the village know that Jasper leaves the keys in his car."

"Do you, Jasper?" the vicar asked, and Grandad pursed his lips and frowned.

"I always manage to mislay them if I leave them in the house," he explained. "It is easier to keep them in the ignition. You should know, Cedric; you borrow the ruddy Humber often enough." I could tell Grandad was worried; he rarely barked at the vicar.

"I think Poppy was framed," Griff said, and his fellow bridge players looked puzzled. "Someone wanted to incriminate her for a crime they committed." Griff had finally stopped trying to catch my eye. "But why? It's the most incredible thing I ever heard." He came over to the sofa and sat down on my other side. "Who would have thought that someone in this village could possibly be capable of such dubious activities? It all looks so peaceful and re-spectable on the outside." I almost laughed: who was Griff to talk about dubious activities?

"Yes, I see your point. But why would someone impersonate Poppy?" The vicar was clearly enjoying this conundrum. "I am try-ing to think of who covers ARP in the Ponsford area. Where exactly do the Anstruthers live?" he asked Grandad, who was star-ing into his whiskey glass as if looking for answers there.

"What? Oh, about a mile and a half outside of Ponsford village to the west. You know how small Ponsford is: couple of farms, a village shop, and that tiny little church. Who is the vicar there, Cedric?"

"Nigel Fosdick. His parish extends to include Middle Ponsford, about two miles away, and Upper Ponsford, which is on the other side of Ponsford. Together the three villages have a population of about thirty families. I remember the Anstruthers' house now. It's an old Georgian farmhouse, quite isolated."

Grandad poured everyone another round: whiskey and soda for the men and sherry for Granny and me. "I could find out who their Air Raid Precautions people are from my roster. In those small areas they sort of survive on an honor system for blackout: outlying areas are rarely the target of an air raid. We only have Poppy and now Sid because of the airfield."

A hand touched my elbow and I half turned to Griff. "Did you leave the house at all that night?" he asked.

I shook my head.

"How often do you drive the Humber?"

"Occasional trips into Wickham, so, rarely."

"But you can drive it, can't you?"

"Yes, of course I can." I slued my eyes over to the vicar and his disparaging description of my changing gears. "Mr. Fothergill taught me."

"I think the best thing to do would be to go over to the Anstruthers' and let them identify you as the woman who didn't come to their house."

"But they might be confused; they could say anything." I sighed because I had wanted to avoid any conversation with him at all. I felt myself being drawn back into our old relationship.

"Just because they are getting on in years doesn't make them fools."

"Grandad knows them. He said that they are very elderly: he's nearly ninety and in bad health, and she's in her late eighties. They might take one look at me and say, 'Yes, that's the one,' simply because of the uniform, and I would be arrested and charged with robbery."

A derisive snort. "It's fantastic: what could *you* possibly gain by stealing jewelry, antiques, and a valuable painting? I mean, where would you keep the stuff, and how would you sell it? Surely anyone who knows you at all would find the whole thing a complete joke."

Really? I wanted to say. Do you think of me as such a lame duck that I wouldn't know what to do with stolen artwork? When of course I wouldn't have a clue.

"If it is a joke, it's a pretty spiteful one," I said, and then because I was fed up with what I felt was their rather lofty attitude—another male club had formed right there in our drawing room—I appealed to my grandmother. "What do you think I should do, Granny?"

She shrugged her shoulders. "Darling, it's a joke as you said, and a spiteful one. There is a reason you have been impersonated." Her shrewd eyes caught mine. "Why would someone want to incriminate you?"

To get you out of the bloody way, that's why, Ilona put in her tuppence worth.

Of course, that's it, I realized. The same thing had obviously occurred to Granny, though she was puzzled as to why anyone would want to incriminate me.

"I think I should do it," I said.

"I'm going to come with you." Griff rose to his feet as if he were ready now.

"Thank you, but there is no need. Grandfather is coming with me." I stood up too. "I'm awfully tired. So, if you will all excuse me, I'll say good night."

I was halfway to the door when Griff caught up with me and opened it, his face serious. "You are still mad at me, aren't you?" When he said "mad," I supposed he meant angry. Americans have this way of using words we use in a different context.

"Not at all. I have never been saner."

TWENTY-FIVE

S SOON AS I HAD FINISHED BREAKFAST, I LEFT MRS. WAN-
tage banging about in the kitchen and hiked over to Sid's
house to remind him that he was on patrol tonight. Like everyone
in the village, Sid is nosy, so I was subjected to an in-depth inter-
rogation.

"The police can't suspect you of robbing those old people,
Poppy," he said as soon as he was satisfied that all I had told him
was accurately represented. "And don't worry, I hadn't forgotten
I'm on patrol tonight. The forecast says light showers, but I'll wrap
up warmly and take a brolly."

"Better put on some of your Foster's rub," I said quickly, just to
see what he would say.

"Don't use that stuff anymore," he told me. "Dr. Oliver says it
doesn't do any good at all. Just keep warm and dry, he told me.
Exercise is good for lung conditions, he says."

"What about your bronchitis?"

"Poppy, there is a war on, you know. We all have to make sacri-
fices."

A thought occurred to me. "How does everyone know about the robbery?" I was embarrassed that the entire village knew that I was Hargreaves's favorite suspect.

"Mrs. Glossop's niece married the curate over in Upper Ponsford. You know these small hamlets just live on gossip," he added smugly, as if cosmopolitan Little Buffenden was exempt. "Anyway, the minute they meet you they will know it wasn't you." His gentle brown eyes as they gazed into mine were clouded with concern.

"Fingers crossed, then." I lifted the pedal of my bike and caught, out of the tail of my eye, the lace curtain of Mrs. Ritchie's front parlor window twitch back into place. I lifted my hand to wave hullo. But there was no further movement in the window.

"I have to go in now and give Mum a hand with washing up," Sid said. "Then I'm going to start on my new model: it's an Avro Lanc."

"Super," I said, knowing there was more to come, and there was.

"You might not know this, Poppy, but the Avro Lanc—"

"Good heavens, is that the time? I must run."

And before he could say another word, I pushed down on the pedal and sped off on my way down Water Lane and turned a sharp left into Streams Lane.

AUDREY WAS HELPING her mother in the kitchen when I knocked on their door later that morning.

"You're up and about early," Audrey said. "Cuppa tea?"

"No, thank you, but I was wondering if you could spare a moment?"

She carried a tray of china over to the Welsh dresser in the corner of the kitchen, and Mrs. Wilkes picked up a broom and started to sweep the floor. I helped Audrey to put away the dishes.

"You didn't happen to see Grandad's old Humber go past your house last Sunday night, did you, Audrey?"

She shook her head, but Mrs. Wilkes looked up from her sweeping. "Would it have been very late in the evening? I mean more like half eleven or twelve?" she asked.

I couldn't believe my luck. "Yes, that would be about right."

"I can't put my hand on my heart and say it was your grandad's car, though, Poppy. A car did go past our drive at about that time. There was a bright moon and the size and shape would be about right. Mrs. Glossop said that the police were asking about it too. They can't honestly think that it was you who robbed that old couple in Ponsford." She laughed and shook her head. "That's the trouble these days. Too much crime and not enough coppers. No wonder they're having so much trouble about who killed those poor girls and attacked our Audrey."

If Mrs. Wilkes was right, then whoever took the Humber had driven over to Ponsford the back way, via Streams Lane. But why would they take the long way around, instead of leaving directly from our lodge and driving south in the direction of Wickham, cutting at least two miles off the journey? Audrey moved closer to me to hang up the last cup on its hook.

"Seems like whoever 'borrowed' your grandfather's car to go over to Ponsford wanted to be seen driving it. I think someone's playing a little game with you, Poppy, don't you?" She raised her eyebrows and, moving closer to me, said under her breath, "Ever thought that it might be because you are doing your own investigation into you know what?"

If she was right, and she might very well be, then the Little Buffenden Strangler was aware that I was investigating and was trying to either discredit me or get me out of the way. The thought was unnerving. I thanked them for their time and left them to chew over the details of the Ponsford robbery, and who, if it was not me, it could have been.

OUR TRIP TO the Anstruthers' came at the end of a day that felt as if it would go on forever. Grandad insisted on driving me over in the Humber, but Detective Hargreaves overruled him and we all piled into his battered Ford. It was already dark as we pulled up into a weedy patch of sparsely graveled drive in front of a very dark Georgian house sitting in the middle of a scruffy garden.

Hargreaves turned to Grandad and me, sitting silently in the back of his car.

"If you would wait here, Miss Redfern, I'll go in and tell them we are here, and then I will come out for you. I would prefer you to wait here in the car, Major Redfern. If you know the Anstruthes, I don't want to confuse them." He might as well have said that he didn't want my grandfather hailing them as friends and then introducing me as his granddaughter.

He was gone for only a few minutes. When he came back for me, Grandad gave my hand a squeeze. "Best foot forward," he whispered. "You have nothing to worry about."

Hargreaves stopped me outside the front door. "I will go in first. You wait in the hall; then when I wave you in I want you to enter the room and just say these words: 'There is an air raid warning for this area. You must go to your shelter at once. Take only a blanket and a torch.' That's all I want you to say, am I clear?"

I blushed to the roots of my hair and said it was. I already felt like a felon.

"Please repeat those words to me."

I repeated them, and pushed open the front door. He left me standing in a darkened hall, with a wide oak staircase going up to the upper floors of the house. I felt alone and scared, as if I was about to be convicted of shameful crimes I had not committed. I looked around me: there was an old leather-canopied butler's chair, a relic of the days when the gentry had scores of servants who waited at their beck and call. The only other piece of furniture in this ill-lit and drafty cavern was a low table for the daily post. A tall clock in a corner ponderously ticked minutes into hours. Far away in the distance toward the back of the house, I could hear the clash of plates and cutlery, a pleasant domestic sound that did nothing to quiet my fluttering nerves. Dinner was imminent. I imagined Mr. and Mrs. Anstruther sitting down to their potato-and-carrot pie after we had gone, tutting over the atrocious behavior of the younger generation. I can't believe that old Jasper Redfern's granddaughter has turned out so badly, can you, dear? What a terrible shame, I imagined them saying as they sipped a glass of wine and laced into their meager dinner.

What am I doing? I asked myself, skulking out here like a common criminal, already guilty of anything anyone wants to pin on me. My job was to help people—I took what I did seriously. I had trained in the dangerous East End of London. It was time to stop being so accommodating and speak up for myself—no matter how carefully I had been instructed by Hargreaves to say something that would possibly incriminate me. The man probably wanted this pathetic little felony put to bed so he could close his dossier.

Hargreaves appeared on the threshold of the drawing room door and beckoned me in.

"Just walk into the room and say what I told you to say—if you don't get the words exactly right I don't suppose it will matter that much."

I walked ahead of him into the room. Taking him at his word, I would say what any properly trained warden would say. I imagined that I was back in the dockland area of East London. I had been trained to be very specific in time of danger.

"There is no need for alarm," I said to the two elderly people sitting in their chairs like obedient children. I lowered my voice. "We believe that there will be an air raid in this area." I spoke clearly and slowly. "Do you know where your designated shelter is?"

To my surprise, a quiet, well-modulated voice answered me. "We have been instructed to go to our cellar." I turned my head to the elderly woman sitting in a high-backed wing chair. Her face was tranquil, her gaze steady. This old lady was as present and in command of her faculties as Hargreaves and me.

"Right then. I think it would be a good idea to take some blankets and a torch with you." She met my direct look and nodded.

A querulous old voice from the chair on the other side of the empty fireplace shouted, "Yes, that's the one, I'm quite sure of it, wicked girl." An old man—no, an ancient, wraith-like creature—with a plaid blanket across his knees lifted a shaky hand and pointed a long pale finger at me.

"No, my dear, it is not the young woman who came here the

other night. Inspector, there is no need to go any further. This is certainly not the young woman who came to our house. The other one was much more strident. I felt as if I was being harassed and bullied when she pounded on our front door. This young woman..." She paused and smiled. "This young woman has been trained to help people. Haven't you, my dear?"

Mrs. Anstruther rose from her chair and came to my side. Mild blue eyes gazed into mine. She was wearing a pair of pince-nez; her gray-white hair was piled on top of her head in a pouf. She nodded as she looked into my face, as if she recognized me from another time and place.

Her husband bent forward over a walking stick placed between his legs. "No, Gertrude, no!" His voice was petulant, and he pounded on the floor with his stick. "You should be ashamed of yourself, young woman. Utterly ashamed of yourself." His pale, soft face was puckered with anger.

"There, there, Arthur. Don't you see the difference? The other woman sounded like someone from a bad play. Overrehearsed and completely unbelievable. Surely you remember?"

He shook his head, his thin hands trembling on the rug over his knees. "I can't see her hair. The other one had red hair, long and curly." He rapped the floor with his stick again and frowned at his wife. "Gertrude, will you leave this to me? This woman told us to go down to the cellar. When we came back the house was stripped, practically empty."

"My dear, I am *quite* sure that this is not the same woman."

"Strapping young redhead, she was. Is this girl's hair red?"

"I have no idea; she is wearing a helmet."

"The young woman who came that night was not wearing a helmet?" asked Inspector Hargreaves, striving for more clarification from an elderly couple who were now arguing about helmets and hair.

Mrs. Anstruther walked over to her husband, stood behind his chair. She patted him into silence. "Yes, Inspector, she was wearing an ARP helmet just like the one this young lady is wearing. But her hair was down, loose around her shoulders. It was a rather strident shade of red."

Hargreaves turned to me. "Would you mind loosening your hair, miss?"

I wanted to say that I never wore my hair loose when I was in uniform, but I took off my helmet, unpinned my hair, and then put it back on.

"That's the one, all right," cried the old man. "Isn't it, Gertrude? That's the one, right enough. Wicked girl coming here and stealing people's things."

But Gertrude Anstruther didn't answer. She took off her pince-nez, polished them, and then put them back on. "I suppose . . . it might be." She peered at me: eyes narrowed, brow corrugated. She stepped closer to me. "Yes, it is the same length. But it's the voice. It just doesn't seem quite . . . No, I can't think it is the same woman." She smiled at me. "I am so sorry, my dear, that we have caused all this trouble for you." She shook her head and turned to include the inspector, her hands held apart as if asking him to forgive her, too. "It's her manner and her voice, Inspector. The other woman was loud instead of clear, and her voice was much deeper and harsher in tone." And then she turned her gentle face back to me. "My apologies to you, my dear. What an awful thing to have to go through."

I finally spoke. My hands were cold and wet with sweat. I carefully wiped them down the sides of my trouser legs. "Not as awful as your experience the other night. It must have been dreadful sitting down in your cellar wondering what on earth was going on."

"It was, rather, but no harm done. Eh, Arthur?"

The old man had lost interest in us. His faded blue eyes searched the room as if looking for someone who had probably not been there for years. "I'm hungry," he announced. "Isn't everyone here yet? Why hasn't Grant announced dinner?"

I exhaled a long, ragged breath. I couldn't imagine how this scenario would have gone if Gertrude Anstruther was not a woman of lucidity and command. I tried not to look over at her husband, who had apparently retreated into his own world.

"Any moment now." His wife's voice was soothing before she walked us out into the hall. "My husband's mind wanders, Inspector. He lives in a happier world these days, long before these terrible wars. Arthur is getting on in years and it is frustrating for him, sometimes, when he is lost in the past. But this young woman"—she turned to me and smiled—"couldn't possibly be the same one that came here the other night. Are you an air-raid warden in the county?" she asked me.

"Little Buffenden." And before Hargreaves could interrupt and bustle me out to the car: "I'm Jasper Redfern's granddaughter."

"Jasper and Alice Redfern? Of course, I can see the Redfern resemblance quite clearly now. No wonder I felt as if I knew you. Fancy the inspector involving you in this awful business. Anyone can tell that you are far from being a thief!"

She insisted on coming out to the car to say hullo to Grandad. And to the inspector's irritation they had a long chin-wag about the people they knew in the county fifty years ago, when they were young and life was a more straightforward affair. Hargreaves stood by his car, his hat in his hands, as he patiently waited for two old people who had much to share with each other to say good night.

As he walked around to the far side of the car to get in beside his driver, I asked Mrs. Anstruther, "How would you best describe the woman who came here the other night?"

"She was very much like a niece of my husband. I wouldn't like to say this in front of Arthur, because these things matter so much to him, but I thought his niece and the woman who came here were like the sort of actresses you see in bad repertory. Provincial repertory. She was stagey."

"Thank you, thank you so much."

"At any rate, she certainly wasn't what we refer to as a well-brought-up girl."

Hargreaves was glaring at us over the top of his car, and I gazed back at him. I had my answer now. If tonight had been grueling, it had also been fruitful.

"Will that be all, then, Inspector?" I asked as we slammed our car doors. "I am assuming that Mrs. Anstruther's testimony puts me in the clear." We watched Gertrude walk back to her house and close the door.

"Of course you're in the clear. Whatever next?" My grand-father's frown was deep, and his brows were beetling in a quite terrifying manner. "Now, if you don't mind, Inspector, we would like to go home now."

"I HAVE SPOKEN to Mr. Fothergill, and we both agree with you that someone was playing a very nasty joke. So, he is arranging for Sid to take over your patrols for a while. No, darling, please listen to me, this is very important." Granny looked tired and on edge. She had been cooped up in her drawing room with the Rev and Griff all evening, listening to endless advice.

I frowned at Mr. Fothergill. "Why?" I suspected I knew the reason, and it was such a worrying one, I could barely look him in the face. "It is important that I continue with my ARP patrol. I have made a commitment and I don't want to break it. What happened at the Anstruthers' was just a coincidence." But I knew it was nothing of the kind. It had been as Mrs. Anstruther had said, a well-staged performance. Someone wanted me out of the way.

But it wasn't Mr. Fothergill who answered me. It was my grandfather. "Your grandmother is extremely concerned, and I agree that you should stay home for a week, or at least until the police track down the Anstruthers' thief, who was malicious enough to try and incriminate you. And, if they are capable, they need to find the man who has been running around our village killing young women." He was using his and-that's-final voice. And, to make matters worse, Griff rose from the sofa to agree with Grandad so whole-heartedly I had difficulty in keeping my temper.

I know, darling. Of course Ilona was on my side. *It's awful the way they rush in to protect and preserve, isn't it? I have often wondered if deep down inside they doubt themselves in some small way.* I gritted my teeth, kissed Granny good night, and, ignoring Griff completely, took my little dog and went upstairs to bed.

TWENTY-SIX

OVER THE NEXT FEW DAYS, I CONCENTRATED ON MY WRITing, helped Granny around the house, and made Sunday lunch, once more without Griff's help, which turned out to be delicious.

If I wasn't being a paragon of domesticity, I took Bess for long afternoon walks, and at night I wrote. It was reassuring and refreshing to spend time with Ilona and her very complicated life, and by the end of the week I had only a few chapters to complete.

What are you doing about the Little Buffenden Strangler? she chivied me one morning as I finished a chapter. *You don't want the trail to get cold, d'you?*

I told her I was thinking.

That isn't going to get you anywhere. You have three good suspects, don't you?

I had drilled it down to two good suspects.

All right, then, time to lure them out into the open. Set a little trap. See what happens.

So, I set off to the village. Inspector Hargreaves had paid me a visit the day before yesterday and I hoped his arrival at our front door had been conspicuous.

"Strange sort of robbery, to be sure," he announced as I opened the door. "With Mrs. Anstruther's corroboration, Miss Redfern, you are in the clear. And since their property has been retrieved, we will probably let the matter drop." However thorough Hargreaves was, simple curiosity evidently did not play a large part in his investigations.

"Retrieved?"

He coughed and put on his hat. "In a barn in Ponsford. Every bit of it, and none the worse for wear."

"Common knowledge, is it, that you have found the stolen property?" I no longer felt it necessary to be placatory to the inspector.

"Well, gossip being what it is, I am sure all will be made known in due course. But for now, I think it would be best if you kept this information under your hat, if you would be so kind, Miss Redfern."

It had been then that I decided to make use of the malicious joke that had been played on me. All I had to do was wait for one of my suspects to make the right move, as soon as he heard on the village grapevine that I had information about the night of the robbery that would enable the police to make an arrest. It didn't take me five seconds to decide whom I should use to disseminate my information to the world of Little Buffenden.

I arrived to find the garrulous Mrs. Glossop polishing her countertop as if her life depended on it. She looked up as I came into her shop. "I was wondering when we were going to see you. We heard about the robbery, and Sid told me that you were no longer our

ARP warden. And a good thing, too. It's no job for a young woman out on her own every night!"

"Ten stamps, please, Mrs. Glossop, and I might as well take Grandad's newspaper with me."

"That will be one and sixpence for the stamps. Awful business, that, over at Ponsford. Constable Jones told me that you were their number one suspect for a moment or two." A sour little smile. "What is the world coming to, when thieves pretend to be officials and then go and rob two elderly people?"

I put a shilling and a sixpenny piece down on her counter. Goodness knows what inaccuracies were flying around the village about my part in the Ponsford robbery, and that was what I was relying on.

"Do you think someone was actually trying to lay the blame on you?"

Here was my opportunity. "Oh, I don't know about that," I said. "But if they were, it was a silly thing to do, because in the process the real thief left behind a very clear clue as to their identity. There are just a few odds and ends I have to tie up, and then Inspector Hargreaves will make an arrest. He came over to see me this morning." It's amazing what writing fiction will do to stimulate imaginative thinking.

"What sort of a clue?"

I took a leaf out of Sid's book. "Police business, I'm afraid. Now, I must push on. Good afternoon, Mrs. Glossop." And I left her with my nicely baited trap.

THERE IS SOMETHING altogether disorienting about waking up in the dead of night and hearing your name being called. I reached over and turned on my bedside light and looked at my alarm clock. It wasn't that late, a few minutes before eleven o'clock, but I had gone to sleep with images of Ilona being stalked through London's nightclubs by a killer who had become the master of surprise. I turned off the light, punched my pillow, flipped it over to the cooler side, and laid my head down to go back to sleep.

A rattle of pebbles against the window, and Bess sat up. Her hackles rose in a prelude to a bark, and Bess's barks are loud and shrill. "Hush, Bessie." I didn't want her waking the house. Once she gets going, it's hard to restrain her. "Quiet, Bess." But she continued to mutter, her ears pricked forward. I put out my hand and stroked her ears down the back of her neck, which she finds soothing.

Another rattle of pebbles. Someone *was* out there. Someone who clearly wanted to talk to me. I got up out of bed and opened the window a few more inches.

A familiar voice hissed up to me. "It's me."

I folded my arms—and smiled to myself.

"It's me," said the voice again. "Griff."

Had he already heard the rumor I had put about via Mrs. Glossop? He was obviously here to join me in the last leg of our inquiry. But I wasn't going to welcome him back into my investigation that easily. I yawned. "I was asleep," I hissed back. "What is it?"

"Developments," came the mysterious reply.

"About?"

"I have to talk to you. Can you come down?"

"*You* are one of my developments, Griff," I told him.

There was a long silence. And then he said, "Yeah, I know what you mean. And I'm sorry, really, I am. But come on down and let's talk about—you know, everything?" How much of my trap to catch the Little Buffenden Strangler had Griff's agile mind guessed at?

The trouble with American men—no, all men—is their conviction that if they ask you to do something, you probably will. "Of course, I *can*," I hissed. "But I am not sure that I *will*." I sounded just like Mrs. Ritchie giving a slow-witted pupil a lesson in grammar.

"No, don't be like that, Poppy. I promise it will be worth it. It's important. Meet me up at Bart's Field in the usual place—say, in fifteen?"

"In the morning." I started to close the window.

"For Pete's sake, Poppy. Come on, it's important. I have something to show you."

I closed the window and sat down on my bed and thought it over. I didn't like the idea of going out alone this late at night, especially since I had baited my trap. I would take Bess, and then no one could surprise me. I opened the window again. "I'll be there in twenty minutes."

I put on warm slacks, a sweater, walking shoes, and my old tweed hacking jacket. And then for some daft reason I found my ARP helmet and my torch. I put Bess on a leash and went down to the scullery door.

Bess loves outings at night. She had missed our patrols so much, she didn't seem to mind being put on a leash. We crept silently down the path to the gate; I opened it and we hurried down the lane to the High Street. Keeping close to the shadow of the buildings, we made our way toward the green, where we took a shortcut to Streams Lane through the back way.

The night was full of stars, and as my eyes became accustomed to the pale light, it was easy for me to recognize familiar landmarks.

As we padded along, I wondered what on earth Griff had to tell me that meant meeting him up by the badgers' sett. As I neared the stile that led to the wood, I decided against the dark shadows of its heavy trees. My nerve simply wasn't strong enough. I continued down the lane, and then, scrambling across a ditch, I pushed myself through a gap in the hedge to come out on the other side of the wood and at the bottom of Bart's Field. I would cut across the top of the wood at the airfield's perimeter fence to the sett.

Bess was thoroughly enjoying herself. She stopped and looked up at me several times until I understood what she wanted. I unclipped her leash and she was off across the field until all I could see was the white flash of her fluffy tailless bottom as she made short work of the slope toward the wire fence of the American airfield.

Although there was no need to be furtive, I bent low as I ran level with the fence until I came to the beech tree that stood sentinel over the entrance to the sett. I was almost there when a strong arm pulled me backward.

"For God's sake, Griff, would you please . . . stop!" I yelled as I was spun round. I couldn't see him clearly. He had stepped back as he turned me and was standing in the shadow of the beech tree. He held a mollifying hand toward me, and I breathed easier. And then he spoke, and when he did, my heart, which was already hammering, picked up the pace to a mad gallop of fear.

"It's me, Poppy," said Sid. "What are *you* doing here?"

"Sid?" I said, as if it couldn't possibly be.

"Shush. I don't think we're alone." He lowered his voice to a whisper. "In the trees over there. He's hiding in the spinney." He jerked his head toward the group of trees behind him. "I know who it is, Poppy. I know who killed Doreen and Ivy and attacked Audrey."

It took me a moment to adjust to this new Sid: composed, calm, and authoritative. So, Sid knew who the Little Buffenden Strangler was. But where was Griff?

"Listen, Poppy, just turn around and walk with me away from the spinney. I don't think he'll do anything now, but it's best to be safe. All right?" I nodded, and we turned and walked back toward the wood, and the hut on the other side of it, where Audrey had waited for Bill Peterson.

"How do you know he's in there?" I asked. "Anyway, who is it?"

"Poppy, you know who it is, don't you? You know who killed them. You've known it for a long time. You read his note to Doreen, didn't you? You just couldn't bring yourself to believe it. I am so sorry." His voice was quiet with sympathy as we reached the door of the hut and stood in its entrance.

His note to Doreen? He must have meant the note I had found in her dress, the one that had disappeared the next day. Why on earth would Griff write a love letter to Doreen? Nothing about this bizarre evening was making any sense. And what on earth was Sid doing here in Bart's Field?

"I am not sure you have it right, Sid," I said, wondering where on earth Bess had got to. I whispered into the night, "Bessie, here, girl, come on, Bess."

"She won't come," Sid said, and the faint note of derision in his voice sent fear crawling across my scalp. "She's back there by the badgers' sett. Tied to the beech tree. Luckily I brought some rope with me." He drew closer to take me by the arm, and in that moment the last piece of the puzzle fell neatly—and belatedly—into place, and I knew exactly why Sid was here. The Little Buffenden Strangler was standing right in front of me in the middle of a dark field, and not sitting in his vicarage study planning how to silence a woman who knew his identity.

I had watched Sid emotionally unraveling over the past weeks and had made him the lesser of my two suspects. His Home Guard training in Wickham on the night of Doreen's murder had given him a strong alibi. But there were only two men who were capable of masquerading as a woman: our actor-vicar and Sid, whose ability to mimic was faultless. Either of them could have driven over to the Anstruthers' house and posed as a female ARP warden, and both of them were more than partial to Mrs. Glossop's throat lozenges.

Well, my trap had certainly worked, but I had underestimated my suspect's cunning. I realized that I was in incredible danger. What was Sid waiting for, standing beside me so quietly in the dark of night? I breathed slowly to calm my thoughts. Griff would be here at any moment, because he certainly wasn't hiding in that spinney watching us. He would find Bess tied to the beech tree and know exactly where to look for me.

I willed myself to relax and wait for Sid's first move. If I was ready for him, I could take him by surprise. I would hopefully wind him when I threw him to the ground, and then I could reach for one of the rocks that littered the area around the hut, because there was no doubt that I would need a weapon. His grip on my arm when he had waylaid me by the badgers' sett told me that he was much stronger than I could have possibly imagined.

We stood there motionless in the starlight. And in the silence, I heard Bess's shrill, insistent bark on the other side of the wood. Had Griff found her? Her bark grew frantic, and Sid cursed.

He moved so fast as he whirled me into the hut that I was completely taken off guard. I was thrown back against the uneven stone wall. Its sharp edges cut into my back. Two hands encircled my throat. A tight, strong squeeze, and then a merciful release as I fought for breath.

"How many times, Poppy, how many times?"

I tried to shake my head. He released his grip so I could answer him.

"Answer me, how many times?"

It was heaven just to breathe.

"Didn't I beg you? Beg you! Crikey, I must have warned you off a dozen times. And all you could say was, 'They are here to help us, Sid. They are not all bad!'" He imitated my voice so perfectly, it confirmed what I already knew.

His hands were around my neck again, but this time he caressed the length of my throat. "I would *never* have hurt you, Poppy. Never do what that Yank did to you: telling you he loved you when he was really interested in that cheap tart Fenella." I was about to speak when I felt the terrible press of his hands again. "I *never* wanted to hurt you."

My skin began to crawl. Here it was. My end, my death. Here in this cold stone hut with the reek of Fisherman's Friend in my face.

I managed to say, "Sid, you don't want to do this. I don't care a bit for O'Neal." I had to play for time. Griff would be here soon.

"You *are* a liar, Poppy, aren't you? All of you bitches are." Biggles didn't use this kind of language.

"Sid, we're friends. I wasn't lying when I told you I wasn't dating Griff."

"Too late now, you treacherous bitch. And if you think help is on the way, just forget it." He laughed and then said so easily, so smoothly, that if he hadn't had such a strong grip on my neck I would have fallen to the ground in sheer shock, "Meet me up at Bart's Field. By the badgers' sett—say, in fifteen?" It was Griff's voice.

All reason, all thought, disappeared, and I started to struggle for all I was worth.

"I won't have you girls dating those filthy Yanks," Sid said. "You will stop it now; do you hear me? Say you will stop."

"I will . . . stop . . ." It was hard to get the words out. My throat was on fire.

He relaxed his hands, and I wondered if I could knee him in the groin. "Say you're sorry, you were so stupid."

"I am sorry. I . . . really . . . am." Even if I was going to die, I would never say that I was stupid. The pressure on my throat increased. I couldn't move, not even my legs. He was leaning into me with his full weight. I could only hear my pulse beating out a rhythm that was strong and full of life. I knew my eyes were open, but I couldn't even see his shadow against the stars shining in through the open door of the hut. The world grew darker. Pitch-dark. A singing sound, loud and strong . . . wailing. I was wailing for my life. And then, as all sound started to recede into a thick, heavy, black silence, the entire world was lifted and thrown sideways.

Up we went into the air: up, up . . . we were on a Ferris wheel of brilliant red, ochre, and yellow light. The colors were gloriously vivid. I hung for the briefest moment on the edge of the light. And then it was down, down, and down. There was a loud crack of fireworks and the unforgiving hardness of the earth as I landed heavily on it in a hail of dirt and pebbles.

But I could breathe! I could breathe, and was that my head I was lifting off the stony ground? A gentle patter of earth showered down on my helmet lying next to me in the grass. I lay still, too exhausted to move.

Silence. I smiled up at the night and started to thank her for saving me, and she answered in a long, maddened shriek.

There was an almighty percussive *whoomph*, and the earth shook underneath me. I opened my eyes and stared dreamily up into the sky above. It was lit with arc lights from the airfield, raking across the dark void above me. There was a familiar, deep staccato *ack-ack-ack* of antiaircraft fire. The thud and crash were as familiar as old friends. The smell of fire and burning petrol a blessing. It was an air raid! I was safe!

As the world lit up in fire and smoke around me, I sat up among the wreckage of the lambing hut. On my right, underneath a small hill of earth and rock, was Sid Ritchie, or what was left of him. I could see his boots sticking out at an almost ludicrous angle, one raised coyly above the other as if he'd been pinned while skipping.

The only thing that made me want to move was the thought of Bess. Tied to a tree, trapped, to be killed by a bomb. I must get to her. I had to overcome the desire to just lie here and watch the orange and red sky, and the pain that was shooting up my right leg. I sat up and started to push the boards of what had been the lambing hut door off my legs. It felt like an eternity as I pushed down with my feet to raise myself off the ground. But at last I was upright.

I steadied myself on legs that felt uselessly light. The airfield was bright with fire; the American ground artillery was firing sharp red bolts of light into the night. On the other side of the wood, an aircraft spiraled down to earth in a curling plume of black, oily smoke. There was a deafening explosion as it hit the ground.

The percussion, as the earth shook, brought me to my senses enough to propel me forward. I put the last of my energy into a stumbling shamble up toward the fence.

Now the sky was full of fighter planes. I looked up and saw Messerschmitts coming down fast on the airfield. A plane overhead banked above me, so close that for a moment I could see the swastika on its tail and the round head of its pilot in the cockpit. As I stood, half-upright, I watched it explode in a riot of flame. I started to run, up to the fence and toward the sett. I didn't stop as bits of burning metal thumped around me into the pasture.

The beech tree that stood sentinel over the badgers' sett was in flames, a huge crackling brand of fire; the sound of its branches exploding was almost as loud as artillery. The intensity of its heat made me lift my hands to my face. "Bessie," I shrieked like a demented creature. "Bessie." There was no sign of her. In a frenzy of anguish, I started to search the field: every clump of grass, every patch of weed, was distinct and clear in the orange glare from a plane burning on the runway of the airfield.

"Bessie," I called, though no one could possibly hear me. There was a terrible smell of burning. Oh God, how could he have tied her to a tree? I realized with horror that it was me that was on fire; the sleeve of my tweed jacket was smoldering. I ripped buttons apart, peeled off the smoking jacket, its sleeve blossoming into orange flames as I threw it to the ground.

I looked up as American Mustangs circled in the sky above me, sending Messerschmitts banking to the left and right on either side of them. The air was thick with the stench of oily smoke, and petrol fumes clogged the air. Above me the planes dove and climbed in a sky full of their sound. A fighter plane spiraled downward and smashed into the airfield. How many minutes, hours, I searched frantically, oblivious to the danger I was in, I don't know. My only real concern now was for Bess.

It's all right, I told myself over and over, she must be safe. Bess was adroit at slipping through her collar. Surely she was far away from the smoke and fire, cowering in a ditch full of cool rainwater.

My legs gave way and I tripped and fell. As I sat there, the sky emptied of planes as quickly as it had been filled with them, and I heard another sound, a blessed one. It was the all clear. The sound that Londoners waited in the Underground to hear, the sound that told them that they were safe for now, that they could come out and start putting their lives back together again, until the next time.

TWENTY-SEVEN

GOT TO MY FEET AND WALKED TOWARD THE PERIMETER WIRE. The Messerschmitt that had crashed through it had hauled the fence out of its posts, dragging a large section almost to the runway. I have no idea why I was walking toward the airfield; there was a huge crater in its concrete surface, and planes that had not had the time to take off before the air raid were a mass of fire and twisted black metal. I turned and looked around me. The beech tree was still burning, and in its diminishing light I started to search the area for Bess. My throat hurt so badly that when I tried to call her name all I heard was a faint croaking bleat.

"She's dead, I'm afraid." I turned to the man standing in front of me. His face was covered in blood and dirt. His clothes, torn from his body, hung in tatters. He looked as if he had clawed his way out of his grave. I turned to run, but my legs felt like lead.

"Get away . . . from me." My voice was hoarse, and he laughed as he took me by the arm.

"Not this time, Poppy. I can't let you go, you know that. Your body will be found among the ruins of the stone hut, but at least we can all say you died in the line of duty." Sid lifted his hand into the air. He had a rock; the bastard was going to brain me with a rock and my helmet was lying outside the lambing hut. Too weak to do anything at all, I closed my eyes.

He shrieked my name and I opened them. Sid was whirling in a frenzy in front of me. "You bloody, bloody bitch," he screamed as he turned, bent double, his arms ineffectually clawing behind him. It was Bess, covered in black ash, hanging from the back of his trousers with all her might. He was swaying on his feet, desperately trying to shake free of canine teeth deeply buried in the back of his thigh. I summoned all my energy as I dove sideways into him, caught him by his belt, and tossed him over my hip to land on his back in the grass.

"Bessie?" Was she pinned underneath him? A long, compact body bounded up from behind me, yodeling with delight as she leapt into my arms. I can't tell you how glorious it was to hold her to me and submit to her lavish dog kisses. I was still holding her in my arms—me laughing, Bess warbling—when we were interrupted by Bill Peterson's slow drawl.

"*Achtung*. Hands up." Then a stream of American German.

"It's me," I croaked. "Poppy."

"What the hell? Hey, Griff, over here. No, it's not Luftwaffe. It's your girlfriend." A barking Bess bounded out of my arms toward him. It was heaven to finally sag. To let all limbs go slack in the knowledge that I was safe. I buried my face in Griff's jacket and inhaled.

"Don't tell me, just let me guess. It was this little creep all along."

"Sid," was all I could say as I turned my head to look at the prone body of Sid Ritchie, lying in rags at our feet.

Griff gathered me to him again and smoothed sweaty, tangled

hair back from my sooty face. "Do you always arrest your murder suspects in the middle of an air raid?"

"I HAVE TOLD the inspector that he will have to wait until tomorrow for his report." Granny was standing over my bed, holding a cup. "No, darling, absolutely no talking. Dr. Oliver says if you talk, he will have to take you off to hospital. Now, if you promise to be quiet, you can stay here in your own bed, until you are quite recovered."

Her arm slipped behind my shoulders as she helped me to sit up. Banking pillows to support my throbbing back, she settled me comfortably upright before she handed me the cup. "Chicken soup, darling. No, I'll hold it for you." My burned right arm was swathed in thick bandages. "Now, tiny sips. That's the way." I don't think I have ever tasted anything quite so delicious as that chicken soup in my entire life.

When I had finished, I looked up at Granny, widened my eyes, and lifting my left hand, held up one finger, then the second one.

"Two days, you slept for two days."

I shook my head and held my hand out flat, palm upward, eyebrows raised—and?

"Yes, of course, you want to know about that wicked Ritchie boy, don't you?" I nodded. "He was arrested for trying to kill you, my dearest girl. Thank goodness you are safe." She helped me to finish the soup and then eased me flat, folded the top sheet back over the blanket, and tucked me in nice and tightly, the way she had when I was nine and had scarlet fever. It felt wonderful to be looked after so thoroughly. "Sleep, darling. Sleep and rest are the great healers." She bent down and lifted Bess onto my bed. A singed little animal crawled up close and licked my hand, and I felt the tears slide down my cheeks. I wouldn't be here without you, I silently told her.

"She's a gallant little dog, isn't she?" Granny put her hand on Bess's head. "She has stayed outside your room ever since Griff O'Neal brought you both back. She wouldn't leave even to eat. Grandad carries her out to the garden, and then she climbs back upstairs. Dr. Oliver says her thick coat protected her. Now, please rest."

She left me with a host of disjointed memories and half-answered questions. I couldn't for the life of me remember how, or when, Griff had arrived on the scene after the air attack. I had been incapable of speech. All I could remember was Sid Ritchie unconscious and flat on his back and me, blackened, fire scorched, and crooning over my little dog, but there had been no voice left to speak with.

"Sweetheart, I can't hear you, why are you whispering? You are trying to tell me that Sid is the Buffenden Strangler, aren't you?" Griff had drawn back, still holding on to me, so he could look into my upturned face.

I nodded, trying desperately to articulate, pointing at my throat. Gentle hands pulled my sweater and blouse collar to one side. "Would you look at her throat, Bill? The little tick tried to strangle you, didn't he, Poppy?" I nodded. "No, don't talk, I know what happened. Yeah, Audrey was right. Smell him, Bill, he reeks of liniment."

I shook my head. "Fi . . . fish . . . fre . . ."

"What's she trying to say? Fish fry? Fresh fish? I never know what they are talking about half the time." Bill Peterson had jerked Sid to his feet and held him drooping in his massive right hand.

"Fisherman's Friend," I finally managed, and Sid lifted his head and said, "You are such a bitch, Poppy."

I realized as I pieced this last together that Sid was not dead. I had not killed him. Sid was the Little Buffenden Strangler, and I had survived!

IT WAS A patient, a penitently patient, Hargreaves who took my full statement a couple of days later. Now that I was fully in my right mind, he wanted the details from me. In between sips of beef consommé, made by Griff, I croaked out my story. It took more than an hour, and when he had almost finished, I asked him, "Did Sid actually strangle Doreen with stockings and Ivy with a tie?"

He looked down his nose a bit, as if nice girls shouldn't ask this sort of question. "He tried to kill me and Audrey with his bare hands," I reminded him.

"The autopsy for both Miss Newcombe and Miss Wantage was that they were strangled. Miss Newcombe with a pair of stockings and Miss Wantage with an American officer's tie."

"With the intention to incriminate an American, any American?"

"Yes, that is what we know now."

"Why did you arrest Joe Perrone?"

"Because Sergeant Perrone was seen with Miss Wantage the night after Miss Newcombe was killed, when the Americans were confined to their base, and then days later she was found strangled. You were not the only one who reported seeing them together that night. Mr. Ritchie did too."

"I know it was Sid who went over to the Anstruthers' in Ponsford that night—pretending to be me," I said in what would have been a complacent voice if I didn't sound as if I gargled with gravel. I didn't mention that my other suspect had been our Fisherman's Friend—

loving, tweed-jacket-wearing actor of a vicar who believed that Shakespeare preferred his fair Rosalinds and gentle Juliets to be played by Rogers and Henrys. Griff O'Neal had been crossed off my list of suspects simply because his cockney accent was a pathetic embarrassment, and he would rather die than eat a throat lozenge.

"Yes, Sid Ritchie made a full confession."

It was all quite clear, I thought as I sat there. But then everything is, in hindsight. "I think Sid knew that the game was up. He knew I had been asking questions, so he tried to discredit me by implicating me in a crime. Of course, it meant that I got to the answer more quickly the minute I knew that it had been a man who had impersonated me at the Anstruthers'."

"You see, I wondered why Doreen had gone into her house and had then left it, on a night when her boyfriend, Bud Sandusky, couldn't see her because he was in the sick bay. She had been lured out of the safety of her house, the same way Sid lured me."

"He pretended to be an American?" Hargreaves looked up from his notes.

"That was how Sid enticed Doreen, Ivy, and me out at night. He is a talented mimic. He threw pebbles up at their bedroom windows and pretended to be Bud Sandusky to Doreen, and Joe Perrone to Ivy. And they went, believing they were going out to be with their boyfriends." The thought of Sid creeping around in the dark of night tricking us girls out of the safety of our homes made me feel weary and sad.

"Audrey, of course, was another matter. He knew she met her boyfriend, Bill Peterson, up by the lambing hut. He had been watching her, the way he had watched all of us. On the night of the air-raid drill he waited outside the farmhouse and then followed her.

"And another thing: Sid said something about my reading Doreen's love letter. You know, the one I found in the pocket of her dress? The one that had disappeared when I took you over to the village hall?" He nodded. "I remembered, unfortunately too late, that Sid's mother had a set of keys to the village hall. I don't know how he knew, but he must have taken it."

He was watching me closely, with a grudging sort of respect. Then he sighed and said, "I shouldn't tell you this, but Mrs. Ritchie knew her son was involved in the killings. She broke down when Mr. Ritchie made his confession."

"She knew and did nothing at all about it?"

I must have looked shattered, because he said, "It's not unusual for the parents of men and women who kill in this manic way to try desperately to protect them, or at least to pretend to themselves that their children are innocent. Mrs. Ritchie saw you with that note in your hand in the village hall storeroom. She had seen her son writing it and worried that it might connect him to Miss Newcombe's murder. She came back later and took it. She suspected that he was the killer because he had come home early from Wickham on the night Miss Newcombe had been killed: she heard him moving around in his room. When she awoke in the morning, he had already gone back to Wickham to finish his training. But she knew that he was capable of murder and tried to protect him."

I took a sip of warm consommé. My throat felt like cardboard and my eyes were so heavy I could barely keep them open, but I had one more question.

"How did Sid get here from Wickham and back again? Did he steal a car?"

His look of absolute surprise was so gratifying that it woke me up.

"Yes, he did. He stole a car by bypassing the ignition system."

"It's called hot-wiring," I informed him. "The Americans call it that."

"I expect they do. After he had murdered Miss Newcombe, he drove back to Wickham to finish his Home Guard training."

Was he really that cold, that calculating? I saw Sid's face again, his large eyes full of tears as he mourned the deaths of Doreen and Ivy. But I was simply too exhausted to make sense of Sid's complex and terrifying nature. "Between his mother's overprotective coddling, the cruelty of Doreen and her classmates, and then being rejected because of poor health when he wanted to join up, perhaps Sid deserves some sympathy," I told Hargreaves, because it seemed the easiest way to make sense of it all. "He was so proud of being in the Home Guard, until the Americans came and made him feel second-rate. You know the village children used to joke that he was dressed entirely from jumble-sale clothes? They used to call him Secondhand Sid."

Hargreaves wasn't having any of this sentimentality. "There is no such thing as a perfect childhood," he said. "Most of us have to deal with all sorts of disappointments and hurts in our lives. No excuse to murder half a bloomin' village."

THE LIVING ROOM was full of roses again; the scent of their soft petals combined deliciously with the wood fire burning brightly in the grate. Bessie was sitting on my lap and I was gently drowsing in the luxury of having nothing whatsoever to do.

The door opened, and a head came around it. "Sorry I haven't been here for a couple of days—we've been a bit busy." Bess got down from the sofa and walked over to him. Her greeting was enthusiastic but careful: we were both still aching from our exertions of the other night. Griff picked her up and put her back on my lap, then sat down on the floor next to us and leaned his back up against the side of my sofa.

"The airfield must be a mess," I said, and he smiled.

"Nothing that can't be fixed, but we have moved two squadrons down to the home counties until we are operational again." He looked me over. "Poppy, you look so much better than when I last saw you. Does it hurt to talk?" I shook my head. It did still hurt, but not as much as the bruises all over my back and legs, and I wanted to talk to Griff. Desperately wanted to talk to him.

"Can I ask you just one thing?" His face was unusually grave. "Why did you go out that night?"

"Sid was a brilliant mimic. He called up to my window. I couldn't see him, and I thought it was you. He imitated you very well. He even used the word 'developments'—an expression you're fond of. He asked me to meet him up at the badgers' sett, so I went." He thought this one over for a while.

"What a cowardly little worm. Did he really sound like *me*? How could he possibly do that?"

"I can only assume he followed you. I think he did that with all of us. He watched and listened and waited in the dark. He had you down perfectly, Griff. It was uncanny. It was how he trapped Doreen and Ivy—he imitated Bud Sandusky and Joe Perrone." Despite the warmth of the fire, I shivered. It was almost impossible for me to reconcile the Sid I thought I had known most of my life with the pitiless killer I had gone out to meet that night.

Griff took my hand. "He would have killed you if there hadn't been an air raid."

I shivered again, and his hand closed around mine. His touch made my heart rate race. I turned my palm upward in his hand and curled my fingers around his. When I woke in the night, again bathed in sweat with that stifled feeling that I couldn't take another breath, as the world was thrown up in the air, I would imagine that Griff was holding my hand.

"One last question, and then that's it, okay?" he asked, and I nodded. "What were you trying to tell us about fish? There was such a racket and you could barely speak, but was it something about friendly fish?"

For a moment I couldn't understand what he was on about. Fish? I started to shake my head, and then I remembered and had to stifle a laugh.

"Fisherman's Friend."

He stared at me as if I was what the Americans call crazy.

"A Fisherman's Friend is a throat lozenge. Wait, I have one here. Look in the pocket of my cardigan." He pulled out the twist of paper that Mrs. Glossop had given to me. "That's it," I said. "Try it." He popped it in his mouth as I explained. "That lozenge is what Audrey smelled on Sid's breath when he attacked her. He presumably ate Fisherman's Friends because he likes the flavor."

He nodded, and then, as the Friend took hold, he turned his head to spit it into the paper and threw it in the fire. "That's quite disgusting. You English really love to eat things that taste vile. Why is that, do you think?"

"I am not even going to try and answer that, Griff, because it is absolute rubbish and you know it. Now it's my turn, and I only have one question. Ponsonby was a German spy, wasn't he?"

He shook his head slowly from side to side. "That again? Poppy, you're relentless. *Yes*, he was a British citizen of German descent, and *yes*, he was spying for the Germans. We had kind of been on to him for a while. It was your badgers' sett that cinched it."

"Cinched it?"

"Settled it. Confirmed our suspicions."

"We?" I had half guessed this bit and I crossed my fingers.

"Yes, me and my opposite number in British Intelligence."

"Fenella Bradley," I said quickly. Now I had him. His eyes widened before his poker face blanked all expression.

"Aw, Poppy." He threw back his head against my sofa and laughed. He was so close I could see the blue flecks in his hazel eyes as he looked up at me. "You are so darn quick. Too quick for your own good, some would say."

I tried not to laugh because it hurt like the devil. "Well, however much you tried to deny it, you were seen giving a lift to Fenella Bradley. Just in case you thought all your meetings with her were clandestine. It was Sid, of course. He tried to make it sound like it could have been Ivy. He wanted to incriminate you in her murder; that, or convince me that Fenella was your girlfriend." To my relief, he looked unhappy at the idea.

"Absolutely not. Miss Bradley and I share a professional relationship and nothing more."

I nodded as if this made complete sense, even though I wasn't wholly convinced.

"Now, one *more* last question." He was at his most teasing.

"Trying to change the subject?"

"Nope. How did Sid Ritchie manage to get his hands on nylon stockings and an American Air Force tie? Do you happen to have the answer to that one?"

I believed I had half the answer.

"I am sure Doreen was wearing her stockings when she went out to meet the man she thought was Sandusky. She was always very particular about her appearance. But the American tie? I am not too sure about that. My feeling is that Ivy had Joe Perrone's tie and Sid asked her to bring it with her when he threw pebbles at her window and persuaded her to come for a walk in the moonlight. That would be the simplest solution. He definitely wanted to lay blame for the murders on an American."

"That's odd, because I talked to Joe and he told me that he never gave Ivy his tie. He still has it. It was proof, he said, that he didn't kill her with it."

A flaw—where had Sid managed to get an American Air Force tie? "Now, that *is* interesting."

"Isn't it just?"

"Perhaps he sneaked up onto the base and stole one," I suggested, wondering if Hargreaves had this information from Sid's confession.

"Here is a better idea."

I could tell by his face he was almost helpless with inner laughter. He looked up at me, his eyes shining with pure pleasure. "He put on his ARP uniform, and that lovely red wig he likes to wear, and then he pretended to be you. Some lonely airman, missing his girlfriend, took him out to dinner . . . and . . . that is where he got his tie."

I laughed, even though it hurt, and then felt guilty. "Poor Sid, we mustn't make fun: he is so desperately unhappy."

"Don't feel sorry for him, he's a psycho. A psychopath. Come on, Poppy, you use that word over here, I know you do. Psychos aren't right in the head: they display violent social behavior, like strangling young women. I can't bear to think that he hurt you, so I have no pity for him. None." He let go of my hand and ran his fingers through his hair.

"We caught the Little Buffenden Strangler, though, didn't we?" I said in an attempt to lighten the mood. "Whoever would have thought it possible?"

"You caught him, Poppy. I did very little other than prod you along." He was right; he had prodded me along, probably because he wanted to know what was going on in our little village. Because, by his own admission, one of his jobs was counterintelligence.

A log collapsed in the grate and he turned his face to look up into mine, his expression so serious that my breath caught in my throat. He picked up my hand again, turned it palm up, and stroked it with his thumb. "I can't imagine anything more awful than not helping you solve desperate murders, Poppy."

Oh, how I wanted to believe him.

"What other adventures do you have cooked up for us? I hope you have something in mind."

"We'll just have to see," I said in as level a voice as I could manage.

He lowered his head and I felt his lips brush my palm. "Just give me the all clear, sweetheart!" he said in his best Humphrey Bogart.

"HERE YOU ARE, Poppy darling, a letter just came for you." Granny has no compunction about examining letters to young unwed women: they must be alluded to, never opened or read—that would be unforgiveable—but remarked upon and if possible their writer's identity and intentions revealed. "Looks like it's from London." With some reluctance she handed it over.

It was from London. I turned the envelope and saw the blue embossed script on the back: "The Bodley Head, Penguin Ltd."

"Thank you, Granny. Do you need help with tea?"

"No, thank you, dear, you just stay here and read your letter. What's the Bodley Head, something to do with Oxford?"

No, I silently answered, something to do with my book. When she left, I tried to open the envelope with a finger that shook so terribly I had to resort to using the butter knife, which is why, to this day, there is a greasy smear on the first few lines of a letter that changed the direction of my life, once again.

Dear Miss Redfern,

Thank you for your manuscript of "The East End Murders."

Unfortunately, our publication list is small, at present, due to the restrictions of a wartime paper shortage. But we would be pleased to talk to you again, at a later date, when we anticipate resuming full publication.

With your permission, we would like to forward your manuscript to the Ministry of Information, Crown Film Unit, who are looking for talented scriptwriters. Please let us know, posthaste, if this would be acceptable to you.

Respectfully yours,
A. N. Owen

I managed to stop myself from bounding around our living room, whooping with delight. I had written and completed a book and now it had been commended by the company that published Agatha Christie.

I sat myself down and wrote to A. N. Owen, thanking him, or her, and saying: "Yes, please."

"THIS IS REMARKABLY good." Grandad took an appreciative bite of lunch. "Delicious, so very tasty, and so . . ." He closed his eyes as he chewed. "And so tender. That bird must have been an ancient old crock and you turned it into a spring chicken."

"Tender and succulent." Granny smiled at me.

"I *was* going to say chickeny," my grandfather said. "It's just like prewar chicken."

"It is good, isn't it?" Griff is rarely modest about the food he cooks. "There is nothing more flavorful than a rooster that is allowed to roam, and this one enjoyed a particularly free existence behind our mess unit with his wives. The French always reserve their old birds for coq au vin, which is the name of this dish. Poppy peeled the vegetables."

"Not to mention doing most of the washing up," I said, feeling a little stab of relief that when I moved to London I wouldn't have any time to spend in the kitchen.

Griff was at his most cock-a-hoop as he lifted his glass. "Congratulations to Poppy and a toast to her new job at the Ministry of Information." We all waved our glasses and drank some particularly delicious wine that had somehow managed to survive the air raid, despite a huge crater in the lane between the lodge and our old farmhouse. Fortunately, the village had not suffered more damage than broken windows and a group of terrified people racing up and down the High Street who were saved at the last minute by the carrying voice and efficient direction of Mrs. Glossop. At least they had left their golf clubs and cuckoo clocks at home, or so the vicar had informed me, when I suggested he make Mrs. G. Little Buffenden's next air-raid warden.

"Very luckily, I will be able to visit you often in London when I'm up there on duty," Griff said.

"What sort of duty?" I asked, wondering if it involved Fenella Bradley.

He laughed at me over the rim of his glass. "What is your job at the Ministry of Information about again?"

"I will be an assistant scriptwriter to the Crown Film Unit. The department writes and produces short films about the lives of ordinary people who do remarkable things in wartime."

"She means propaganda," said Griff, who knew all about manipulating the public. "Just wait and see: she will be churning out films like *Mrs. Miniver* before you know it."

Blimey, dahling, Ilona chipped in, in her best society-girl cockney. *I think he's actually right for once. Well done, such a talent!*

Why, thank you, Ilona, I replied, but thankfully not out loud. I could never have done it without you.

HISTORICAL NOTES ON BRITAIN'S HOME FRONT 1939–1945

THE BLACKOUT AND THE DARK OF NIGHT

To make it difficult for the German Luftwaffe (air force) to locate built-up areas, the British government imposed a complete blackout during the years of World War II. The occupants of all buildings had to ensure they did not leak light that would give clues to German pilots that they were flying over inhabited areas. Even the flare of a lit match or the glow of a cigarette could be spotted from above.

Thick black curtains or blackout paint were used to keep windows dark at night. Shopkeepers, hoteliers, restaurant owners, and publicans had to black out their windows and provide a means for customers to leave and enter their premises without letting light escape—they risked a formidable fine and even the loss of their license if they were not in compliance. Britain's streets were not lit at night and motor vehicle headlights, bicycle lamps, and flashlights were fitted with blinkers so that their light was cast downward.

AIR RAID PRECAUTIONS

The Air Raid Precautions (ARP) was run entirely with the aid of civilian volunteers. Their primary task was to protect civilians from the very possible danger of air raids.

ARP wardens patrolled the streets during the blackout to make sure that no light was visible. They also helped firemen and ambulance workers search for people buried in the rubble of bombed buildings, reported on the extent of bomb damage to their local authority, and issued gas masks and prefabricated air-raid "Anderson" shelters from their command post. When the air raid warning siren sounded, ARP wardens were responsible for helping civilians to the nearest shelter—in London the Underground was often the nearest and safest place to spend the night during the Blitz. During the war years, there were 1.4 million Air Raid Precautions warden volunteers working part-time in Britain.

RATIONING

With a civilian population of 50 million, the tiny island of Britain imported most of its food before the war. It became the principal strategy of the German war department to attack shipping bound for Britain, restricting British industry and potentially starving the nation into submission.

Petrol use was restricted as soon as Britain went to war. A few months later, bacon, butter, and sugar were rationed, and by August 1942 almost all foods were rationed except for vegetables and bread. By the time the war ended in Europe, there were children who had never eaten a banana and who thought of an orange as a rare treat.

Ration books were issued for each member of the population, and shopkeepers canceled food tokens with a rubber stamp. It was impossible to buy any controlled foods without producing a ration book, so if you went to stay with your friends or family you took your ration book with you.

The Dig for Victory campaign encouraged people with gardens to turn them over to growing their own fruit and vegetables, and people who lived in the country could shoot game for the dining room table, and fish for trout. As the war progressed even wild caught rabbit grew scarce.

Restaurants were prevented from serving more than three courses for dinner, which was considered restrictive when a celebratory evening out in a restaurant before the war consisted of at least five courses: hors d'oeuvre, soup, fish, game or meat, and pudding. Restaurants could only charge a maximum price of five-shillings for the meal itself, except for luxury hotels and clubs who were quick to add on all sorts of extras, especially if they offered a cabaret, or a band for dancing, not to mention a hefty price tag for a bottle of wine.

Coupons were required for even the simplest needs: clothing, fuel, and soap were in short supply even if people saved their coupons. The paper shortage referred to in *Poppy Redfern and the Midnight Murders*, when Poppy's book is accepted by a publisher but could not be printed due to the restrictions on paper use is a perfect example of how scarce paper had become! Radio broadcast news became popular with the drop in newspaper production and continues on to this day.

As for beer, it was considered essential to the morale of both troops and civilians, so it was never rationed—and the government actively encouraged women to drink beer to help them cope with life on the Home Front and its many deprivations.

For more on how Britain managed their food resources during World War II, I recommend visiting cooksinfo.com/british-wartime-food/.

THE FRIENDLY INVASION

In the late spring of 1942, when America joined in the war against Germany, the press called the arrival of the American armed forces, in Britain, the Friendly Invasion. British farmlands were requisitioned to build new airfields, and over 2 million American Army Air Force servicemen were stationed at aerodromes all over the United Kingdom. The arrival of US servicemen had considerable cultural impact on a population deprived by three years of war. Jitterbugging to the music of Glen Miller and, at the time, exotic and unknown foods such as peanut butter, Coca Cola, hot dogs, and chewing gum were gratefully welcomed by a country that had struggled for years on strict food rationing. Everything American became popular: the slang they used, the food they ate, the music they enjoyed, and the way they danced, especially for young British women whose boyfriends were fighting overseas.

The Americans had heard about "jolly old England," but none of them were prepared for the shortage, or lack, of life's basic necessities such as hot water, electricity, gasoline, and coal. They were surprised at how scruffy England's country towns looked and by the equally shabby population of "Old Blighty" who had suffered the rigors of "mend and make do" until there was little left to mend. The Brits knew American culture, through movies, as the land of cowboys and Hollywood, which hardly prepared them for young men of Italian, Polish, German, and Irish descent from America's large commercial and industrial cities.

The different expressions used by both cultures for what the British knew as car bonnets—car hoods; car trunks—car boots; jam—jelly; biscuits—cookies were many and confusing, but most Brits accepted the arrival of their allies with open arms. So much so in fact that by the end of the war in Europe forty-thousand women from the East Anglian counties of Britain alone followed their boyfriends and husbands back to the US in two cruise liners requisitioned for their journey.

The most confusing cultural habit that America introduced to wartime Britain was segregation, which in a country with a population of only ten thousand African and Caribbean people, was both puzzling and unacceptable. Nevertheless, the American Army Air Force designated some British market towns for white servicemen only, while others had alternate days for black and white serviceman.

CRIME

From blackouts to blitzed homes, the war years represented a new opportunity for the criminally inclined. The blackout and the bombs were the most obvious factors, and murder, rape, robbery, burglary, and theft all flourished in the dark and the chaos. But there were other reasons for this leap in criminal activity. The war brought new restrictions and regulations, which many people chose to break or circumvent for gain. Rationing offered huge opportunities to fraudsters, forgers, and thieves and created a vibrant black market while law enforcement lost one third of its officers and manpower to the armed services.

With cities and towns plunged into darkness every night, killers had a field day. A young airman, Gordon Cummins, was nicknamed "the Blackout Ripper" and roamed the bomb-ravaged streets of London in search of young women to murder and mutilate. He killed at least four between 1941 and 1942 before he was caught and became an early victim of the infamous British hangman Albert Pierrepoint.

TESSA ARLEN was born in Singapore, the daughter of a British diplomat; she has lived in Egypt, Germany, the Persian Gulf, China, and India. An Englishwoman married to an American, Tessa lives on the West Coast with her family and two corgis.

CONNECT ONLINE

TessaArlen.com
🐦 TessaArlen
📘 TessaArlen